Clown of Bombay

Clown of Bombay

a novel

AARON JUDAH

THE DIAL PRESS, INC. 1968 NEW YORK

"Daddy's in the court-house,
Mummy's at her club,
Gladys has a new boy friend,
And Dottie's at the grub.
Daddy's in the court-house,
Mummy's with her chums,
Dot and Glad are quarrelling,
So, Joey, suck your thumbs."

LULLABY OF
A GOANESE AYAH

PART ONE

If my father had not happened to be at breakfast I would not have answered Gladys. Dorothy I sometimes did, as she sometimes answered me; but if Queen Victoria were sitting here at our table with her pink pimple lotion on she wouldn't have got a grunt out of me. Not unless Dad were present. At the same time, as was so often the case, he might not be listening, and would to all intents and purposes, not be here. Softly I pushed my chair back.

"Well, aren't you going to eat that, Joe? You've buttered and jammed it thick enough for ten slices."

Out of the corner of my eye I saw the sun rise over the top edge of the *Times of India*. Dad's dome and half the circles of his glasses stared at me.

"Look, my pretty sister, as opposed to my clever one, when I took that toast I wanted to eat it; when I buttered it I wanted to eat it; when I jammed it I wanted to eat it; now I don't want to eat it. Here endeth the lesson. Or shall I repeat?"

She wouldn't have heard if I'd hammered it out in morse on her curlers with choir accompaniment. "It's a crime against all the millions starving on our doorstep."

"Well, go and give it to them with my compliments of the season."

"It's not a crime against society," came the Polish voice from her bedroom. "It's a sin against God. You must not spurn what God provides."

"Did God provide that?" interrupted Dot. "Dad did. Does God go to the High Court every day to work his fingers to the bone for us? Does——?"

"All right, Dorothy," my father said in the voice he reserved for his eldest daughter. "Let me decide what provisions I make. Whether I was the ultimate provider is not the question. The point is that Joe makes a habit of wasting food and the exact nature of his crime is strictly between him and his conscience."

"The point is it's a quarter to nine," I said, "so I'll thank you to decide on the ex-act na-ture of my crime in a hurry." I got up, scraping my chair loudly enough for the absent party to miss as little of these vital proceedings as was humanly possible.

"That's up to you, Joe," came the Polish voice. "You heard your father."

"But, Mum, you just said I sinned against God, and Glad said society, and Dot said——"

"I said nothing. We are all in agreement with Dad. It's entirely up to you."

"I'm going to get my topee of burning gold," I said, "and my satchel of desire. Then I'm coming back. If you haven't decided between you what wrong I've done I'm going to school. You can hang me from the nearest tree, with pleasure, but I'm blowed if I'm hanging myself."

I came back with my sola topee tilted at no more rakish an angle than usual and found them staring woodenly at me with the one-eyed blob of red jam and toast glittering evilly on the plate. "What's the verdict, jury?"

"Go to school, please," my father said pointing warningly to the bedroom.

"Good," I nodded loudly. "I'm relieved to hear I've done nothing wrong for a change."

"But you have——"

"Enough, Gladys," my father said, a telltale flush suffus-

8

ing his scalp. "It's not for you to tell him, it's for him to tell us. And in his own sweet time, from his own sweet lips I can promise you such a wealth of retribution——"

"Look Dad, this is my last will and testament on——"

"God!" burst out the Polish voice, "I can't bear this! Wills, testaments, retributions, society, crime! All over a miserable bit of bread and butter! Throw it in the dustbin and have done with it."

"No," Dot insisted, clenching her fist with the thumb inside. "This scamp's been getting away with murder lately. He——"

"Murder!" burst out Gladys, who took her cues from Mum. "Do you remember what Charles the Palmist said about the miscarriage that Mum——?"

"Oh, shut up about Charles the Palmist," hissed Dottie. "Superstitious barbarian. Look for the sake of peace *I'll* eat that toast."

"Oh, no you won't, that's *my* toast." I snatched it up, stuffed it into my mouth and strode out triumphantly.

On the way to the tram I crossed Wodehouse Road by the Catholic church, and in stepping up on to the pavement I had to bend my thigh rather higher than usual as at this point was a gutter set deep to accommodate monsoon waters, which when it rained converged here from both directions, and the pavement had a tendency to flood even at its present height. This hazard overcome, I was at first puzzled as to why the lifting of my leg had caused a crinkling sound in my pocket, and then remembered the letter.

I extracted and uncrumpled it. The name and address on the envelope was certainly Mr. Titmus's handwriting. I pulled my Latin exercise book out of my satchel and compared the red script with the blue. A bullock cart laden with empty milk-urns was jolting along toward the tram terminus so I walked beside it as I knew the nearer I got to the sacred

9

animal the less chance there was of motorists and horse gharries running over me. At the same time it did not escape my notice that the chances of being run over by the bullock grew greater. There was danger in avoiding danger, so much I knew. I looked at some of the red underlined remarks under my translations of Pax Romana. "Slovenly, vague, not funny, you must not guess at random, use your dictionary." "Mr. Abraham D. Hosea, The Pipals, Wodehouse Road, Fort Bombay." It was the same clear rounded hand. On the terminus platform I tore open the envelope and chucked it into the ticket bin.

Craig Thomas Episcopalian
High School,
Bori Bunder
26–8–39

Dear Mr. Hosea,

I am your son Joseph's new class master and am choosing to risk the fear of your displeasure by writing in disregard of the ethics imposed by my profession. The occasional conflict between profession and vocation a man of your judicial experience will agree need not lead to tragic consequences——

Clang! Clang! Clang! Clang! Tragic consequences! I saw a blind beggar walking straight into the path of a slowly moving tram and shuddered. Tragic consequences. How a word could make one quake. There were eight pages of his neat lucid handwriting, every syllable of which was addressed to my father. What was I doing reading my father's letters? At this stage I realized there was only one way of maintaining my innocence, and that was to yield it up without reading it. And this I did. Page after page I tore into tiny pieces and tossed them into the ticket bin. As one by one they went, indeed, wave upon wave of relief swept through me, then I felt a neat hole being drilled into the small of my back.

As this was a common occurrence when I happened to be

10

on time for school, I scarcely had to look to see Aaron the mugger standing there in his protective coverings: his mac over his shoulders, his waterproof hood over his topee, his satchel in his waterproof bag, his goloshes over his shoes. If there were portable lightning conductors on the market he'd have had the rust-proof model. I always had the uneasy feeling when I was with him that if one of us was to perish in an accident it would be me. He himself would be struck with nothing more than amazement. Everything that happened to me, or that I did, seemed to amaze him.

"Why didn't you take that tram, Joe? I saw it leave from Waterloo Mansions and you were standing right here. Doing homework? Why are you biting your nails?"

"Mugger boy," I sighed, "this morning the soothsayer arrived. There's doom about."

"Again? What happened?"

"This morning at breakfast," I explained, trying to keep a steady voice, "everything was going according to plan. I suspected nothing. I took a piece of toast from the rack and buttered it. I laid it on good and thick. Are you with me?" He had his ear to my lips, and moved in closer.

"You buttered it, you buttered it."

"I inserted my spoon into the strawberry jampot, scooped it up and dropped a crimson blob on to the yellow buttered toast. And another, and another. Gradually this single blob, made up of three lesser blobs spread and spread. It spread more slowly as time went by, until a moment came when I realized it would spread no more. In my innocence I accepted this as a signal to take a bite, but something warned me, and I put it down. I did this as well as I could as my hand was veritably trembling, you understand?" He nodded unable to reply, while I myself scarcely less incapacitated, screwed up my courage and went on. "Refusing to commit myself to any decision, I gripped my chair and watched. Flies approached, but none dared settle. The flies knew. And then I was to know

11

too. The moment the clock struck a quarter to nine, flickering straight out of that narrow margin of buttered toast, a tentacle appeared and wrapped itself around my throat. I grappled with it, tearing it away. But a second appeared, then a third, a fourth, a fifth. By now the family, always quick to respond in emergency, became aware that something unusual was going on and began to scream. Last wills! Testaments! Retributions! Crimes! Sins! Murder! God! Famine! What a time I had before it was over."

"How did it end, Joe?"

"Oh, I thought I'd better eat the thing and have done with it. But don't think it's over," I assured him. "Any morning that begins with a bit of bread and butter turning into an octopus is a sign we're going to miss this tram if we don't look sharp."

It hissed and we hopped on to it. I always made for the top deck as it was seldom crowded and there was less chance of being accused of pinching women's bottoms. It was getting to be a nuisance. For this and other reasons we took seats as far leeward of a school of screeching fisher-women as possible. Nothing passive about these. United in odour they were the only Indian women who really caught my fancy. Fighters every one of them, even their femininity bristled. Lean, high-bosomed, tight-wrapped saris over whipcord buttocks, if they didn't have rings in their noses I could have married any one of them, if I'd been colour-blind, deaf and had no sense of smell. In trams we could by tacking into the wind beat their odour, but the noise they emitted had to be accepted as Kismet.

Click click click. "Tickut tickut." He could hardly be heard, and it was only in the nick of time I slipped two pice into the mugger's hand. I then took out my now threadbare copy of *Bubbles Comic*, shrank smaller in my seat and put my thumb in my mouth.

12

"Ake aur arda, Bori Bunder," the mugger said, handing over the money.

"Yeh baba kitna burus hai?" the conductor asked looking at me suspiciously.

"Bara," replied the mugger, going red. I shrank further into my seat humming 'Animal Crackers' in my wettest Shirley Temple manner. The conductor hesitated. I drooled.

"Atcha," he nodded somewhat reluctantly. He clipped an adult and a half-fare ticket and went on. I waited for the usual little outburst and it came.

"I don't know how much longer you're expecting to pass for twelve, Joe. You may be short enough but what about your muscles? How can you expect a chap to give you a child's ticket when you look strong enough to strangle him? Where's your logic, your algebra? The trouble with you, Joe, is that you just don't care. You don't respect anyone or anything." A thought seemed to strike him then and he asked, "What hero did you pick?"

"For what?"

"Titmus's homework."

"Cyclops' hammers, it never rains but pours." I dived into my satchel. "Where are we now?"

"Khala Ghora. You've ten minutes, chapook maro."

I got out my English composition book and unscrewed my fountain-pen. I drew a neat tram-trembling line under, "Erratic, you must not write just whatever comes into your head."

"What do I do now?"

"You've got to pick your hero and write something about him."

"Whom did you pick?"

"Lord Nelson."

"Let's have a dekko."

"Don't be daft, this isn't maths. Your hero is your hero and my hero——"

13

"OK, OK," I told him. "Don't rub it in." I had a bright idea and dived for my Scripture book. Rapidly I began to write. "The Wisdim of Slomon the Wise."

Realizing that I needed an interval of absolute silence to complete the work, he discreetly turned to occupy himself by watching the passing scenery. Nearing Flora Fountain I heard him exclaim, whether in appreciation or horror it was hard to say, as almost simultaneously the tram then going full speed, braked.

Everyone of us, regardless of caste, colour or creed, fisherwomen, coolies, schoolboys and girls, Gandhi-capped Hindus, fez-hatted Moslems, and Parsees in high Greek tragedy hats, pitched forward. No accident occurred however and, as far as I could see, of the two or three hundred people involved, the only casualty was a blot on my composition book. When we resumed our journey I said, "Mugger, if one of us had to die in an accident, who would it be?"

"You," he said.

"What about between Wilfred and me?"

"Wilfred."

I went on to conclude my essay and as we were approaching Bori Bunder I heard him mutter somewhat grudgingly, "But if it were between Wilfred and me, I'd be the one to die."

"It's not good algebra," I commented, blowing on the ink, "X beats Y, and Y beats Z, but Z beats X. D'you know that? Life is bad algebra, come on let's go."

He was however transfixed staring in amazement from my essay book to the still open Scripture exercise book on the satchel. "What in Heaven's name have you done, Joe? Have you copied Mr. Latto's Scripture homework for your English homework?"

"Yes."

"That's cheating. It's highly immoral, Joe."

"Don't worry," I consoled him, replacing both books in the satchel, "on Judgement Day I'll level up. I'll copy my English homework for my Scripture." The tram jerked to a halt and we went clattering down the steps.

"Jese, you crib from me, you crib from Wilfred, and now you've gone and cribbed from yourself."

The pavement which we approached was rather high at this point, and during particularly stormy weather its tendency to flood usually made me get off the tram at the next stop. I raised my foot to mount it and heard a crinkling sound. It wasn't half as loud as before, but there it was all the same. Sometimes I really baffled myself.

I sat down and making myself as comfortable as the height of the seat permitted, began to read:

... such indignities. Your son I have had it from persons who should know is ineducible. We perceive an original mind behind his captious inconsistencies, even behind his one great ambition in the scholastic field: to stand last. He is currently, through no virtue of his own, second-last. The fact is (from whatever obscure cause it is sprung) young Joseph responds badly to competition. "I hate losing," he recently said to me, "and winning makes me sick." How can I phrase it myself? He competes with competition.

He is an odd boy, premature in certain ways, and retarded in others; and if I know anything about schools I must say that your son is ineducible—in this one. Indeed, I can think of no better institution, charged as it is with thrice the competitive spirit than most English Grammar schools, to impede Joseph's scholastic advancement. There are however several English boarding schools that run on entirely different lines to which I have no doubt whatsoever your son would make a wonderful response. If you are interested to pursue this correspondence, sir, I would be pleased. If not you may rest

15

assured I shall move Heaven and earth to add to Joseph's present store of English Literature, Latin and History.

Yours very sincerely,
Oliver J. Titmus.

I dropped the scraps in and booted the lever. Whoosh. I buttoned up and thought, whoosh indeed, what a coincidence. Only a few months ago when it was discovered that Mum was pregnant, Dad was set on sending me to some new-fangled English boarding school, but Mum had talked him out of it. Dot and Glad, in agreement for once, had voted for me to be packed off, little realizing at this moment a man named Oliver had joined their side. It was really a useful point to note, apart from this rather special case, how often I'd come to sort out my friends in the relative peace of the privy.

Before roll call Mr. Titmus who had only recently come from England, showed concern to find every single Parsee absent. These solid citizens took up the whole front row of the class, which was the reason why he noticed their absence before actually calling the roll. He had a chorus of answers to his queries. "It's a Parsee holiday, sir, Parsee holiday." "No, there's no school holiday for a Hindu holiday either, nor a Moslem holiday, nor a Jewish holiday, only Christian holidays."

"Not fair on the Christians, sir," I called out from the back. "There should be a special Christian holiday when school's open for Moslems, Parsees, Hindus and Jews to level up, sir."

"You may rest assured, Hosea, that God is already attending to this injustice."

We guffawed a bit too loud on his quips and he was just beginning to cotton on the fact we did not enjoy his humour so much as the opportunity to create a rumpus. He'd never lost his temper though, or thumped anyone, or kept us in

16

after class; and so far we couldn't make up our minds if he was a softie, or just didn't give a damn. He began to run through the roll, but stopped when he called Prior's name. He looked up and saw Wilfred's desk vacant. "Who answered?"

I put up my hand. "He's just down the road, sir," I protested, "I passed him in the tram."

"He could be run over a hundred times before he got here. Hosea, you will not answer any other name but your own. I regard this as a very serious offence."

"Sorry, sir, I just wanted to save time, they're filing out for prayers."

He went on without answering, and did not pause again till he got to the Rs. This was on behalf of a fat little Madrasee boy named Now Now. He had at last returned to school and was answering Mr. Titmus for the first time. "Rao Rao."

"Yeher."

This poor little rich boy, the nephew of a reigning prince, was sometimes off absent to take his allotted place in ceremonial functions, but mainly on account of throat and nose ailments. He had adenoids the size of which had to be heard to be believed, and we called him Now Now because that's what he called himself. He couldn't pronounce his consonants, converting them mostly to Ms and Ns, depending on the state of his adenoids at the time, not to mention his mood. He was highly excitable. I had a comprehensive guide to his speech in my total book, which included the alarming complications of a machine-gunning Madrasee accent; and when a master was completely baffled by his retorts I interpreted, though only with the greatest reluctance. The things Now Now said were always so much better than those he meant, and his masterpiece, which would be remembered in our school as long as Pythagoras, was a rendering of the latter's famous proposition.

17

"In any wry angered tangle the swear of the hippopotamus is equal to the sum of the swears of the other sides."

Naturally my interpretations of his were not always a 100 per cent right, as Now Now was quick to point out, and it was a general policy amongst the masters to confine the royal infant to written tests. Mr. Titmus however was not to know all this, and Now Now's answer to the roll, "Yeher," had him groping for a second.

"So you're Rao Rao."

"Yeher."

"What was wrong with you all this time?"

"Her, I was hick and hound win anna noise."

"You were that?"

DONG, went the bell. Mr. Titmus rushed through the rest of the roll, during which time Wilfred fortunately turned up, almost falling over those awkward feet of his. He couldn't afford the tram fare even when late and his brown concerned face with its two dark brown scars was wet with perspiration. We filed out for prayers.

Although Mr. Titmus took us in three subjects it happened we did not get him till after the tiffin break. The morning was taken up with double periods of Maths and Lab work for Physics and Chem. There were no unusual occurrences. My Lab partner L. S. D. Levy, overshot the mark sucking in a pipette full of HC1, and not knowing what to do with it drank it down. I urged him to take an equal concentration of H_2SO_4 to neutralize the stuff, but in answer to my warnings he assured me he wouldn't die. He might suffer, but he wouldn't die. "And even if I do, for God's sake, Joe," he implored, "don't tell anyone I swallowed that. I don't want to be laughed at."

After all these years I was beginning to understand how he felt. His one great ambition in life was not to be laughed at. On April 1st this year I gave him one of my Sharp's toffees wrapped in cellophane paper and he, overjoyed by this token of friendship, put it into his mouth and ate it. I, and several other boys who happened to be present, were witnesses to this heroic act. Only for the briefest moment after the second bite did he falter, then he munched bravely on, his little brown eyes twinkling with relish to the bitter end. A lesser man would have panicked and spat it out the instant he'd discovered what it was, but not L. S. D. Levy; he just didn't want to be laughed at. His brain was as dense as the matted thatch that surmounted it. He stood last in class, even after me, but he taught me a lesson not all the M.A.'s, M.Sc.'s, Ph.D.'s, and F.R.C.S.'s from England could. And this was simply that there was no bravery in the world. Hercules, Perseus, Samson, Horatius and the whole of that big over-sung brigade, did not have one dram of courage between them. They did what they did because they didn't want to be laughed at.

It was a good lesson. I was grateful to him for it. But it was his only one, and after four years it did begin to sound repetitious. On top of that I had in me a special dread of people who trusted me, and L.S.D. trusted me to Hell's gates. After two periods of just that and further in, two periods of close collaboration in Physics and Chem. I was relieved when the last morning bell went. That is not however to say I was annoyed to find him dogging me all the way back to class, as certain academic points of my titration had escaped his understanding, and I was only too pleased to clarify them. "What actually is the difference between blue litmus and red litmus, Joe?"

I pondered the matter, and as his father ran a hosiery store I replied, "Blue litmus is superior quality."

"Aha, I see! SUPERIOR QUALITY."

The oracle at Delphi could not have satisfied him better; and indeed such, in a nutshell, was the secret of my popularity. I could not then trace back to the source of this particular

19

lesson but it was no less the learned for all that. It was fatal to give a questioner right answers or wrong ones. The wrong answers caused arguments, and the right caused jealousies. I always found if I replied according to their station I kept everyone happy. In fact my reputation as a peacemaker was well known, for I never failed in my missions when my view of the questioner's station and his tallied. Some people, I learned, had exaggerated views.

With regard to station disputes St. Paul, my Goanese servant, and I had no trouble, although on paper a 100-years war was on. I had an inferior view of his station, and he had an inferior view of mine. Added to that he religiously walked the two miles from home to save his anna fare, so my food was invariably cold. Yet in the world of practical reality all was peace with St. Paul and me. The reason was that he always got my favourite place in the gym shed where the non-boarders took their tiffin, and in return for this he could have maimed and committed *mayhem* with my full approval. The cherished place was directly by the foot of the stairs which led to the teachers' and boarders' dining-rooms. Miss Entwhistle the teacher for Std. 3 usually was one of the last to go up, and I was unabashedly in love with her. When she arrived I naturally wished to look my best, which was not to have my mouth bulging with mutton curry and rice. So I used to nibble even at times when I was ravenous enough to eat the china, and only start stuffing after she'd passed. She was a *petite* fair-haired woman with the faint smile that always plays around the lips of beautiful women in public, and what happened to it in private I felt destined to find out. Indeed, so extraordinary were my feelings toward Miss Entwhistle that what I did not see of her interested me more than what I did! And Heaven knew that itself was enough. Miss Entwhistle was my vision of earthly perfection. A vision, it is true, that was—as it was now—occasionally late, yet in a certain respect the later she came, the better; for my sense of anticipation increased with time, and the almost unbearable weight of accumulating agony was on her eventual appearance touched as it were with a magic wand to leave me with an equal quantity of delight, tinged with but one regret: that she did not come later.

"Joe, baba, khana nai khata?" St. Paul's favourite question, inquiring whether I was going to eat or not, was purely rhetorical, so it did not involve a station dispute, as I did not have to answer. The trouble was that he thought I did. He was not very bright and could never connect my rate of eating with Miss Entwhistle's rate of arrival. There was no algebra in him, yet it was plainer than Maths. Every day at this time as she reached the foot of the stairs I'd catch her eye and she'd smile. That was all; Pythagoras was out of it; I saw to that. The data were: she, me and her smile. And even when she did not smile, she *almost* smiled. Godstruth, if she left the torment of waiting long enough, a frown from her would still have put me in Heaven. Right now it would have put me up there; but now, as I had vaguely realized all along, the crisis would come, when the resources of my nature would be extended further still.

It appalled me even to consider it. What strategy could I employ to console myself for this woman not coming at all? If she had the decency to send me a brief note of apology, even a couple of words, I could have milked the life out of them. But with nothing I could do nothing. And indeed a moment in that turbulent gym shed was reached when I realized human nature had its limits, and this was it: if Miss Entwhistle were to come now and smile at me I'd have picked up my plate and pitched it into her smirking, pudgy, pock-marked face.

"Joe, baba, khana nai khata?"

I speared a grain of rice with my fork, put it in my mouth and swallowed. My appetite had left me completely. I saw

21

Mr. de Lima go trotting up and noticed him absently strike the rope in passing. Our nimble little sports master had a habit of striking things as he went along. This rope which now hung quivering under his blow, was a massive piece of work spliced to an iron link at the ceiling of the shed. It was used for climbing exercises and was long enough to hang down to waist level. This end which was used to stand on during certain exercises, expanded to a bulbous shape the size of a football, but from its weight seemed stuffed with lead rather than air. When not in use the contraption had to be secured out of the way, and as now it was tied with a bit of cord (rather carelessly, I thought) right across the other side of the gym to one of the rails of the stairs in a slip knot.

It had, as a matter of fact, before now crossed my mind that if this knot *did* slip, for example during the most crowded part of tiffin time it would lead to results that were entirely unknown—unless of course it actually happened. If no harm accrued then it would disprove my fears and set my anguished mind at rest. If on the other hand the results were fatal, then the people concerned would take better precautions to see it did not occur again. In short, every cloud had its silver lining, but unless that knot slipped there would be no cloud and no lining.

The clatter of cutlery and voices shouting above other voices which refused to be shouted down, was now at its height in the confines of the shed, and as I sat there listlessly trying to throw off the black mood that had settled on me, I began to tinker about with the strategy involved. How could I in broad daylight unnoticed pull that cord? A smokescreen? A formula to make me invisible? I was working out alternatives in the realm of pure fantasy when I noticed six boys approaching the stairs with library books.

The library, which contained no *Adventures* or *Hotspurs*, was a place I did not normally visit, but it lay on the top of the stairs on the other side of the dining-rooms, and there was nothing actually to stop me using it. It was in fact encouraged. I put my knife and fork down, and got up.

"Joe baba, kalas?"

"Ha, kalas." I swung my leg over the bench and tacked on to the crowd of blokes just as they reached the stairs. I hugged the banister, cautioning myself to do nothing rash. If the worst came to the worst I would get a library book. But I was soon to learn my star was on the rise. Just as we drew abreast of the rope-end the Principal's voice boomed above the racket from his veranda on the first floor.

"Send those confounded beggars away!"

This was a weekly or bi-weekly event. The beggars used to collect outside the high iron gates at this hour, about fifty of them of all ages, their faces ranged outside the bars from knee-level up; their scavenging pots thrusting out like an orchestra of trombones every time a servant approached the refuse-bin. Our servants had strict instructions not to serve the beggars, who were nevertheless pretty persuasive in their lamentations whenever the refuse-bin lid was clanked open. The Principal from time to time used to appear like Caesar at his balcony to fortify his decrees, and on these occasions entertainments on the scale of Grand Opera were enacted by a cast of several hundreds. One afternoon a month ago the Principal had come down and hit a beggar who had the nerve to actually enter the gates; and only last week he'd hit a servant just to level up.

On this particular occasion the background of clinking and festive laughter was going on as usual to the tromboning wails of the beggars, who as a group pleaded their cause against the refuse-bin clankings of one servant, and at the same time pleaded their own personal causes against one another to a second non-refuse-bin clanker, when the bass solo of the Principal came in with arresting suddenness, and completely unnoticed, I pulled the cord.

23

As I expected the rope did not fall at once. I in fact took the precaution to check it. It was a rough surface on another, and the next loop had still to give. For all I knew of Mr. Pierce's lessons in Limiting Friction, it would *never* give; but I had done my share, I reckoned, and during the aria of the Principal crept away from the spellbound group on the stairs, and went on the far side of the quad near the bogs.

During this stealthy journey I noticed that a complete silence had fallen. One could have heard a pin drop. The servants and boys deep inside the shed could not see that the Principal was still standing with his red hands braced on the rail before him, his pipe like a cannon in his bulldog mouth, his spectacles flashing sunlight. But those that could must have communicated what they saw by their awestruck attitudes. There was just one exception, and that was St. Paul. He was not a mightily observant animal at the best of times. Just now he had three-quarters of a plate of curry and rice to dispose of, and hearing that the *tamasha* had stopped must have jumped to the conclusion the Principal had gone off. He pushed his way in and out of the massed tables with my plate and approached the refuse-bin.

As he came on it started again. The trombones came thrusting out. Clank—and the wailing began. St. Paul hesitated, lid in one hand, plate in the other. The wailing to my ears was utterly irresistible. It was certainly too much for St. Paul. Clank, he put the lid down again, and turned to the beggars. It was every man for himself and God for all; and the uproar was unimaginable. He was actually approaching the beggar of his choice—my own in fact—a particularly gaunt and dejected-looking crone, when the Principal took his pipe out of his mouth.

Conceited man. He was seconds too late, and in went the curry and rice to the disparaging chorus of the majority. At that range St. Paul could not have heard him with a megaphone. All he could have learned, and did too, was that five seconds later this red, bulldog-faced man was striding across the quad straight at him, his pipe in one hand and a fistful of blows in the other. And he panicked. Instinctively he kicked off his slippers and ran. In and out of the tables in the crowded shed he wove, while the Principal, on the track of his pound of flesh, followed roaring at him in a language he did not understand.

"Who in the devil's servant are you? Have you not been told——?" At this moment the knot gave.

Thanks to the rust caused by the monsoon, the rope turned with a squeak at the metallic junction of the links, and fell, thumping the Principal, fortunately before reaching the full force of its swing. He got off lightly. The sturdy frame of his spectacles took the brunt of the blow and went spinning off his head. He staggered, more surprised than hurt; dropped his pipe more by accident than intent, and stood on it. Then he went away clutching the side of his face. He stumbled on a cricket bat lying in the quad and almost fell. This way and that he floundered like a man smitten blind, and no one had the nerve to offer him a hand.

Fully five seconds no one moved. Everyone was staring at the boys on the stairs. They looked back. Then they looked at one another. Suddenly without further consultations they hurried down and at the foot of the stairs went off in six different directions like the fragments of a bomb.

I began to get hungry now. As I saw my food had without a shadow of doubt been disposed of, I went out to the Irani shop to buy a packet of Cadbury's Nut Chocolate. I also had a a hope of finding Wilfred there, as he had no servant to bring him food, neither cook nor hamal, and at tiffin could be eating anywhere outside, if he ate at all. I saw him one afternoon looking at the beggars waving their outstretched pots with a grimace of pity in his twice-scarred eyes, and said, "Poor wretched creatures, eh?"

25

He replied, "They're richer than you or me, dear boy. They can beg."

He wasn't in the Irani. I bought two packets of Cadbury's Nut Milk and went back, watching out for him all the way. I was fully aware I had by now forgotten what I wanted to speak to him about, but that was usual. I always remembered the moment I saw him. With the mugger it was the other way around. One look and I forgot.

I returned to class expecting to find the two Tenses hard at work. One was L. S. D. Levy, and the team he made with the mugger was much more harmonious than with me, as they were equally tone deaf. On paper their collaboration bore the promise of a life-long partnership, but in fact their concert was only performed during the tiffin break. L.S.D. would be frantically copying the mugger's homework done yesterday, and the mugger would be doing tomorrow's, and even next week's. I called them the two Tenses meaning past and future.

This afternoon however I found them to be very much in the present. Together with numerous other members of the class also there, they were looking concernedly at the blackboard upon which some cad, some filthy-minded bounder from another class no doubt, had written in large capitals:

MISS TITS

We were having Titmus first period for Eng. lit. and aghast, I cried out, "Good Lord! Who did that?"

"Don't know!" rang out the chorus. But loud as it was I noticed they were only composed of Anglo-Indians and Armenians. The Hindu chaps said nothing, as it would never occur to any of them either to do such a thing, or protest innocence if accused. The Moslems frowned darkly, implying they were answerable to Allah. The Jews were speechless with guilt, because that was how they generally looked at the best of times. The Parsees of course were silent because they weren't there; though their presence was felt. I for one felt it.

26

They'd had an oracle from the Temple of Zarathustra warning them of a disaster fated to fall upon us today, and was not this it?

"Miss Tits," I echoed, shuddering visibly. "A joke's a joke, chaps, but this is going a bit far."

"That's just what I was telling them, Joe," said the mugger earnestly. "I think I'll go and rub it out."

"I should hope so," I nodded. "You should never have done it in the first place."

"*I* didn't do it."

"OK, don't shout, I'm not accusing you. All I'm saying is this is entirely between you and your conscience. If you go and do this kind of thing——"

"I DIDN'T do it!"

"I'm telling Wilfred about this," I said, as he was also very fond of Mr. Titmus. He was sometimes in Std. 7 talking to a bloke called Skillet, but neither of them were there. Std. 7 was as empty as a tomb, and the moment I entered I had a strange premonition that something terrible was going to happen. I picked up a chalk and quickly wrote in block capitals:

CAVE! HERE COMES MR. LATTO!

HIS HEAD IS AS FLAT AS A PLATEAU,

WHERE HE STANDS AND DELIVERS

SUCH SERMONS YOU SHIVERS,

THOUGH NOT WHEN HE'S GOT ON HIS HATTO.

Then full of foreboding I dropped the chalk and ran. At the foot of the stairs in the front hall I found two small boys locked in a struggle to the death. I hauled them apart and led them contritely up to the top of the stairs where, next to the entrance of the Principal's office I lectured them soundly. "You," I said to the tinier one, "you should not bully your friend just because you're stronger." Before I could add another word the bigger one had flung himself on the other, and

27

once again they fell to kicking and punching one another mercilessly. Terrified lest I should see them topple headlong down the whole flight of stairs, I fled.

I couldn't find Wilfred anywhere. In the bogs I found Now Now. I was his best friend and the way his eyes lighted up I guessed he'd been looking high and low for me.

"Hunno Noe!"

"Hello Now Now, glad to see you back, we thought you were dead. Sticking around for a while?"

"Yeh, mud unvodunadny my ungelder may wince is vying vom New Yorg nuday and I god demean him."

"Lucky devil. Say, what d'you think of our new class-master?"

"Oh knees mawvenous."

"Yes we awning knees mawvenous. So nong, Now Now."

"So nong, Noe, see you naner."

He'd liked to have chatted longer as I was one of the few who could match his brilliantly fortuitous repartee, but unvodunadly I had a vull day ahead of me. Thinking I might find him in the library I was about to cross through Std. 5 to get there, when I noticed how extraordinarily perfect was the arrangement of desks and chairs here. Std. 5 had Mr. Hughes the librarian for class-master and he was a model teacher. He had monitors for everything. A monitor for the notice-board, a monitor for library fines, a monitor for the blackboard, a monitor for sports, a monitor for general order and tidiness, and I must say I was smitten by the very chess-board arrangement of those desks. I couldn't have done better with a slide rule, compass and spirit level.

There were about ten fellows standing around quietly talking, not taking any notice of chaps from other classes passing in and out. I was myself going to pass through when it occurred to me that by way of courtesy I should first ask permission to do so. "Attention! Boys of Std. 5! Oyez! Who's the monitor?"

"Monitor for what?"

"For giving permission to chaps to pass through your glorious classroom of course. You're a bit slow-witted today, aren't you? Who's the monitor for quickening your wits?"

"Keep him out!"

"That's Hosea!"

"Beat it, Hosea!"

They dropped whatever they were doing to close ranks threateningly in front of the class, and I retreated. "Peace, peace," I implored, backing. As I reached the top corner desk I for the life of me could not see why I should not leap on to it. At the same time I saw no reason why I should. It was exactly fifty-fifty and should have constituted a major problem, but in basic principle it was an old one I had often solved before; thus already knowing that the tortures of not doing what I should have done were much more unbearable than doing what I should not have done, I did not take a second to be half-way across the class, leaping from desk to desk diagonally in a white bishop's run to the far corner.

My move took them completely by surprise, and I would without a doubt have succeeded in shooting right off the board and into the corridor, had not a black knight been sitting at that corner. I made a gallant bid to leap right over him but he rather foolishly grabbed my calf and I crashed down on top of him. He lay quite inert on the floor, poor fellow, but before I could find out if he was still alive, the mob collared me. And what a perverse lot they were too. Instead of simply and effectively throwing me out of the doorway we were struggling in, they elected to drag me back the way I'd come. I was disgusted. I hung on to the desk I'd been caught at, but for an anchor I'd have been as well served by a fishing-net. They hauled me desk and all through to the opposite corner, finally wrested it from me together with two other tables and an assortment of chairs I collected *en route*, and booted me out into the corridor.

I looked at the state of their classroom as I slunk off nursing my wounds, and I thought, this is what comes of being polite. It's going to be a bad day obviously.

I heard joyous hurrays at this moment. Back-slapping and congratulatory cries were coming from the entrance hall, and I went down. E. E. Braithwaite had been made hockey captain. The hockey notice-board was over the cycle rack and there was a crowd there with Mr. de Lima the sports master and E. E. Braithwaite who was obviously a popular choice. He was a big tremendously muscular chap, a born centre half. He had a new cycle, a splendid Raleigh racer, in the rack, and regarding it thus I wondered how I could pluck up the courage to do such a thing. Apart from the strategy involved, the question more simply was Why?

I began to get worried. I felt a hole being drilled in the small of my back, and he said, "I've been looking for you. That thing's still on the board, I'm a bit worried——"

"Worry's a wonderful thing, Mugger," I said. "But what exactly is it?"

"Worry is worry. Just imagine Mr. Titmus coming with——"

"Take it easy, don't get excited, Mr. Titmus is not going to die. What's the good of worrying about a bloke who's going to LIVE? You want to worry about someone who needs your worry most, otherwise BOOM!" I really had to yell to let it sound like an explosion, as the hall was crammed now with E.E. admirers, and I thumbed to him not without significance. "This is your worry, Mugger."

"Him? He's hockey captain now."

"Precisely. Yesterday he was nobody. He was contented, as happy a bloke as I've ever seen. Now everyone's coming around patting his back and licking his toes, the poor chap's going to get ideas beyond his station. Isn't this just how the frog died?"

"What frog?"

30

"The frog in Aesop."

"You mean the one that thought he could be bigger than an ox and blew himself to pieces filling up with air?"

"I mean just that, Mugger, and if someone, some nice chap with a heart of gold, doesn't ease the pressure on Braithwaite he'll never do it himself. Look at him, he's already full, his eyes are bulging out of his head. A bloody tragedy is taking place and everyone's standing around singing hallelujah, pumping him up and up and up!"

"What can we do? We can't take air out of *him*."

"No, but we can take it out of his bike. Let's go, Mugger, I appeal to your better nature to join me in saving this unfortunate fellow. That's it, you're not alone, you take the rear wheel and I'll take the front." He hesitated. "Quick, here's the peon coming to ring the bell, what a chance! Just as he strikes!" We went and in the mêlée it was easily done.

On the way back to class he said rather proudly, "I unscrewed his valve. How did you do?"

I replied nothing, but patted him admiring on the back.

"You did do his front tyre, didn't you, Joe?"

"Mugger," I whispered, "that Braithwaite has fifteen-inch biceps. I'll carry your guilt with me to the grave."

We got back to class, and hopeful though I was to find that someone might in the interim have had the courage and the decency to have rubbed out the inscription, my faith in human nature proved unsound. Some fellows had been scribbling chem formulae on the other board, but that was wiped clean as a whistle. Mr. Titmus came in accompanied by a hush of expectance, with Wilfred just behind, as usual tripping over his own feet. Mr. Titmus sat down not noticing the writing on the board, but I could see Wilfred did.

"Get out your poetry anthologies. Just a minute, got to call the roll first. No Parsees back?" The front row gaped vacantly at him. "No. Rao Rao still here?"

31

"Yeher."

"Well we'll just copy out the morning's register," he said briefly scanning the rest of the classroom. He was ticking off the roll when Wilfred stood up.

"Please, sir, may I be excused?"

"But you've just come back from break."

"Yes, sir, I forgot."

Mr. Titmus's frown did not arise out of a desire to reprimand, as to do such a thing was in Wilfred's case unheard of. He was merely aroused by my friend's display of unconcealable nervousness. "All right and hurry."

Instead of passing in front of his desk Wilfred went behind. It was a tight squeeze between chair and blackboard, and Titmus looked around in time to see Wilfred's hand holding the duster sweep across.

He was not only too late, but way off the mark the first time. He was the cleverest boy in the class, but the clumsiest in the school. The mugger who was his Lab partner had to do every weighing in their experiments. He was excluded from bayonet drill, as twice in unfixing he'd jabbed his own face, on the forehead and the cheek, scars of which he'd bear to the grave. Six times he had to rub, while the class watched in dead silence, before the writing was completely erased. Then he returned to his desk as red as a beet. The book he fumbled for a child could have extracted sooner, yet here was a mystery that had not struck me before: why was his handwriting the very model of perfect form and clarity?

Still he groped, and still Mr. Titmus waited; and for some reason, perhaps on account of the way his head bowed as though in prayer with all those empty pews separating him from us, I felt a strange wish arise in me. I could not comprehend it. I wanted to please him. And when he spoke I strained forward on my desk in the back row to catch his words, they were pitched so low.

"In my five weeks here I have noticed that this particular

32

class, my class, has a range of two moods. You are either sitting in mute terror, or guffawing like apes. This is very boring to a teacher. Please make an effort to break out of the rut. I urge you to be a little more adventurous."

I put up my hand. "Yes?"

"Sir, I can't hear very well from here, may I sit at Moneywallah's desk?"

He nodded and said, "What's so funny about a request like that?" But some of the blokes carried on tittering as I came up and sat at the front desk facing him. "Prior," he began, "open your book to any page and read the first line of poetry you see."

"Yes, sir. ' 'Tis better to have loved and lost. . . .' "

"Who said that?"

I shot up my hand, "Touchstone in *Twelfth Night*."

"In the first place," he said smiling at my eagerness to answer, "Touchstone does not appear in *Twelfth Night*, but in *As You Like It*."

"That's the same play, sir, *Twelfth Night* or *As You Like It*."

"*Twelfth Night* or *What You Will*," he smiled.

"That's what I meant, sir, *As You Like It* or *What You Will*."

"Will you listen?" The smile began to fade, and that worried me enormously. "We'll proceed to the next point. Touchstone certainly did not say, ' 'Tis better to have loved and lost.' "

"That's odd, sir," I said disappointedly. "It sounded just like him. Is it from *Love's Labours Lost*?"

"Now look here, Hosea, I don't want to put a curb on your most welcome enthusiasm, but nor do I want any more random guesses from you this period. Keep quiet and listen. That will be just as much a change for you."

"Yes, sir."

"Can anyone except Prior here, tell us which poet wrote this?" There were blank stares from the Hindus, scowls from

33

the Moslems, guilty blinking from the Jews, mumbling from the Anglo-Indians, but no answer. "Well then can anyone complete the second line of this very famous quotation?"

I shot up my hand. Mr. Titmus looked elsewhere hopefully, almost despairingly, but as the Parsees were absent there were no other volunteers. "All right, Hosea, complete the quotation."

"Sir, ' 'Tis better to have loved and lost,
    Than to have loved and won.' "

"And who told you this?"

"It's logic, sir. When people get married and have kids——"

"That's enough, Hosea, I don't want another squeak out of you this period, understand?" I nodded dumbly. "For homework tonight you and the rest of the class will learn Tennyson's poem on page seventy-five by heart. Now you, Rao Rao, I want to hear you read, have you a favourite poem?"

"Yeher, I god dam moan carse pome inner hone mook."

"I beg your pardon?"

I put up my hand. "Put your hand down!"

"Sir——"

"Shut up!"

I shrugged. "Stop fidgeting!" I didn't even bat an eyelid in case he'd yell at me again. "Rao Rao, begin. And kindly make an effort to enunciate properly."

Now Now cleared his throat three times hard and let fly with the gusto that Kipling always demands. " 'Her Mallard Dove Eased and Wheezed, my Nadya Nibbling:

Oh, eased is eased and wheezed is wheezed,
And ne'er dew wane sale mean,
Nil erred and sigh sand pezzer knee,
And God's gun aid nudgemen need.' "

As all this came out in one breath he paused here for another.

"Just a minute, just a minute," interrupted Mr. Titmus faintly. "Bless me, boy, what are you saying?"

34

It was one of L.S.D.'s few chances of the term to put his hand up. "Do you know, Levy?"

"No, sir, the only chap who understands what Now Now says is Hosea."

Beep boop beep. Three honks from a familiar claxon rang out like a clarion call. It was the Prince's Terraplane. Now Now shot his fat excited little hand up. "Yes?" inquired Mr. Titmus cautiously.

"Her, my ungelder may wince is vieing vom New Yorg a name zubboz demean him win a gnarl and love us."

Somewhat brokenly Mr. Titmus replied, "Since Hosea appears to be the incarnation of Std. 6, would he mind translating?"

"Sir, he says his uncle the Prince is gravely injured in a plane flying from New York and requests his presence with a garland of flowers."

"I need nod nay any ding of a sod! I head——"

"You head may ungelder may wince in vieing vom New Yorg god gnarled——"

"Gnat is nod a naiad!"

"Gnat *is* a naiad!"

"Hosea! Rao Rao! I will not have——"

Beep boop beep boop beeeeeeeeeeeeeeeeeeeeeeeeeeeeeep.

It was unnecessary. On the second beep Now Now already had his satchel singing anoss his nolder. For all his fat he was a whippet when his ungelder may wince galled. Beeeeeeep! The frantic spurt with which he finally vanished made us all roar with mirth; yet at the same time I could not help envying him his place in those ceremonial functions; for it was nice to feel needed. Yes, it was nice to feel needed. Musing thus, idly attempting to recall when I last had my presence desired, where, and by whom, I became aware of our master. He was looking at me with such pain and despair I nearly got to my feet.

"Must I go back to my place now, sir?"

"You came forward of your own accord. You may go back. It is entirely up to you."

I heard suppressed laughter all around, and beginning to feel a little foolish sitting up there all alone, I got up and went back.

The last period was Scripture, and all the Christian boys had to come up to the front. It was strange how all the half a dozen religious denominations, which were pretty well strung out around the room, suddenly at Scripture became compact little fortified communities. Mr. Latto who also took us in Chemistry had remarked on this, pointing it out as an example of a mixture, as opposed to a combination. I was at the time of his first coming the exception and the proof of the rule, but by and by it had transpired that not all rules were in need of exceptions.

Mr. Latto devoted his time now to explaining the vital difference between the O.T. and the N.T., and I to mine. I always found Scripture to be an invaluable period for adding to my original store of limericks. Why? Should I not, like the more sensible Jews, Moslems, Hindus, Buddhists, *et alii*, be disposing of my homework? Precisely, why limericks? This was a question that really interested me and I'd made a list of sorts in my total book, which incidentally contained these limericks. It was a double list and very significant too. The Maths periods, for example, were better suited for the study of any other subject than Maths; but most suited for a particular one. In the case of Maths it was History. No other subject would do. During Maths I found myself craving body and soul for History. At History on the other hand I found myself ready for Gymnastics. At Gym I longed to be doing Scripture. And at Scripture I composed limericks.

It was a most tricky question, with each particular subject containing the kernel of its own answer; and I supposed that Scripture, as it should, provided the most deeply satisfying

36

one. And by Scripture I meant the N.T., since the other did not strike me as being Scripture at all. My interest in the New Testament dated back to the beginning of the year when Mr. Latto arrived fresh from England. He was very pleased with me at the time, and of course it was a feather in his cap to have so enthralled a non-Christian by the subject—despite the black looks and ominous mumblings from the Ghetto area. The Moslems thought it was a huge joke, and indeed the main reason for the laughter in Titmus's previous period was that in those days too I used to come up to the front for Mr. Latto. It was his practice then to narrate an episode from Jesus's life and get us to write a summary of the events on the spot. We then read out our efforts in turn and held open forum. There was no better way of conducting the study. I always used to throw myself heart and soul into these condensed action-packed versions, and received a lot of encouragement in return. This I realized was not thanks to Mr. Latto, but the man Jesus. The more I heard about him the more certain I became that here was the be-all and end-all of men—and women included. Once one really got to the mystery of Jesus one needed nothing more—no friend, no teacher, neither father, nor mother, brothers or sisters. I listened to Mr. Latto go through his life from start to finish; but here it was, at the very end, indeed, beyond the very end, alas, that disaster struck.

There was no precedence; no soothsayer's omen; no oracle; nothing. It came out of nothing; it was made up of nothing; but when it left, it left plenty behind. At this phase we had come to the events after his death, those immediately after the crucifixion, and Mr. Latto's narrative as I recalled it went as follows.

"The betrayal of Christ by Judas is a sad and moving theme. It constitutes one of the mysteries of our redemption. The character of Judas is very strange too. More has been written about him than any other disciple. That he did not

37

barter the Saviour's life merely for silver is obvious as soon after the betrayal he threw the money into a field, which thence was called the Field of Blood. But this was not enough to appease his conscience for the killing of any man, let alone the Saviour, so he then hung himself from a tree and was pecked at by crows, till (so alas we are told) his bowels gushed out. His death left a vacancy in the ranks of the disciples, and this they chose to fill from the next circle of devotees by the picking of lots. Hence it was found that the lot fell on Matthias.

"Now I want you to consult your texts and to write a précis of about a page on the events I have referred to. Not so much noise from that corner, please." That corner referred to the Ghetto, though a fat lot I cared whether it did or not, I was well and truly in the grip of things. As was usual with me, deed or word, they either came out in a rush or didn't come at all. On this occasion I finished first, and I let them know it too. It was short, even for a précis, but well packed. I didn't go over it with a fine comb, but that I knew: it was well packed. On the third raising of my hand Mr. Latto smiled benignly and nodded, "Yes, Hosea, read yours."

I got up and in a clear voice began: "Pontius Pilate, the Romans and the Jews crucified Jesus after he was vilely betrayed by Judas. When Judas saw what he'd done though he threw away his silver with a shriek of remorse, hung himself from a tree and died. The crows pecked him till his bowels gushed out, and the lot fell on Matthias."

Accustomed though I was to strong reactions to my work, the effect of this took me completely by surprise. And yet, I dared say, if Mr. Latto and I were alone together he would very soon have found that I was innocent of any kind of libel or slander. As it was, the censure of the Christians and the jeering of the Pharisees made a Roman of Mr. Latto, and so I just had to be nailed up. He had, to give the man his due, an effective way of dealing punishment. His was never as brief

38

as Mr. de Lima's knuckle-cracks and cane-cuts, since his slow and pontifical disposition gave him a natural preference for gradually twisting one's ears, pulling one's hair, and sinking his pencil through the gaps of one's ribs.

"Your interest in Scripture's unwanted," he said.

Your interest in Scripture's unwanted, I thought. Dee da da dee da da dee da da. And it was precisely at this point of my school career when I transferred my interest in Scripture to the composing of limericks. I could vaguely hear him all the way through, not the words so much as the rhythm. Dee da da dee da da dee da da, Dee da da dee da da dee da—— Every now and again he'd clear his throat and start on a fresh key. I'd find myself listening to the first couple of sentences, then back we'd go. Dee da da dee da da dee da da. Today he must have had a sore throat or something, as he broke off to clear it too often to be good even for the halting one-three beat of my lines, and much too largo. There was nothing anyone could do to quicken him up, I thought, but how wrong I was, and how soon was it proved.

"Before Jesus came the credo of the whole civilized world was based on—uhuh—Revenge. An eye for a—uhuh—eye, a tooth for a—uhuh—tooth. After Jesus came—uhuh—however——"

At this moment the fool Cranmer dropped a stink-bomb. I knew it was not for me to criticize. If Cranmer thought Scripture was best suited for dropping stink-bombs that was his pigeon. All I knew was what all of us knew, that H_2S+ Mr. Latto would combine to form a deadly explosive. And how right we were. Normally slow and ponderous of movement, he swept up his Scripture books, both O.T. and N.T., slammed the door in our faces and strode away.

"You can blooming well stew in your own juice!" came his parting blow.

Well some time after Jesus came and after Mr. Latto left,

39

the final bell rang. And the bell-ringer must have been the boy with the fifteen-inch biceps himself, as scarcely had the reverberations time to die away when he appeared. He hovered hesitantly in the doorway at first, apparently waiting for our teacher to depart. I took advantage of the brief lull before the storm to look at the mugger, and if ever I saw a frog who would never dream of being an ox, there he was. Poor fellow, if he had the resource to achieve the opposite: to diminish to something invisible, he'd have done it in a flash —and that's all the time he'd have had, for E. E. Braithwaite was well in now. And to my utter surprise, it was me he confronted, towered over, crouching—me, the innocent one.

"Hosea," he hissed, "did you fix that tyre?"

"Congratulations on your——"

"Did you bloody well push a penknife through that tyre?"

"What tyre, E.E.?"

"My front cycle tyre."

"You must be joking, E.E., your cycle's not down in the rack, is it?"

"Look here, Hosea, my Raleigh racer——"

"Have you a Raleigh racer? I thought you had an old sit-up-and-beg."

"Two days ago," he informed me, with much less enthusiasm now I thought, "I got a new Raleigh racer."

"Fancy that," I marvelled. "Did your dad give it to you as a present for being made captain of——?"

"Did you," he roared, coming to life again, "or did you not come into the front hall just before the bell rang after tiffin?"

"I was there a long time," I admitted, "I was trying to get through all those chaps to congratulate you on——"

"Right!" he roared, though not particularly to me, but to the world in general, as by now everyone was listening well enough. "Right!" Even louder. "RIGHT!" Realizing now that anything else he might add would never reach the same

40

heights of eloquence, he turned and strode off, covering the ground with those gargantuan muscles of his with astonishing speed. I managed to catch him within earshot though.

"Congratulations on your hockey captaincy, E.E.!"

So at last the day had ended, and we packed up in preparation for the next. But what made it clear that the mugger did not think it impossible for a catastrophe to fall on him even yet, was the rate at which he donned his protective coverings, the wide berth that he gave me, and the care with which he skirted the classrooms to avoid passing through the front hall. I dallied about and saw Wilfred leave too. "Wait for me outside!" I called, "I've something damn important to tell you. About that thing you rubbed out." One or two stray incidents occurred and I went down.

I saw the school-bus which took some of the chaps who lived on the mainland and the north end of the peninsula. It was standing with its engine idling by a telegraph post. It began to move, I heard crows and also the rhythmic drr-dutt drr-dutt of a mattress and pillow renovator working somewhere near by. Of such humdrum sights, sounds and smells, and the increasing roar of the huge bus, I was only vaguely aware. A boy from Std. 5, Nickie Sutherland, who lived—used to live in Bandra—was leaning looking backwards out of the window and caused a horrible accident.

I walked back home through the Esplanade Maidan and the Oval. On the road between the two maidans, right near the Sacred Well I was in time to see a squad of policemen armed with metal-bound lathis disperse a riot between Moslems and Hindus. It was pretty dangerous to be hanging around there all the same, but I saw a broken bottle left on the road, and I said to myself, "This thing could cause an accident. If a speeding motor-car punctured a tyre on it the whole vehicle could swerve out of control and mow its way

41

through a crowd of innocent bystanders." I went across and picked it up. "There, now," I said, "I've probably saved quite a few lives by this small but unselfish act." At the same time I was not the least bit afraid that someone might throw a stone and gash me deep enough to scar me for life. But the way things worked out, an English constable with a gun in his holster came and took me by the hand, and told me I was a very brave boy, but I had better go home now.

My sisters as usual were out when I got home. My father would be transacting justice at the courts till night. But my mother, whom I generally saw least of all, was at home due to her confinement. Although this was the third day I could hardly get over my annoyance at finding someone in the house when I returned from school. She was lying on the settee reading *True Confessions*, having first transferred the phone from its usual place by the piano to a table next to her. That is to say she will have seen to it the phone was transferred, as she liked to make full use of the servants. It wasn't that she was lazy—the contrary. The entire newspaper-reading public of Bombay knew that. She always said idleness bred discontent and made it common practice to walk a furlong to a servant to fetch him to move something a yard. My mother. Mother. How ill the expression sat. I'd often seen pregnant women before, and they looked very like women who were going to have babies. My mother looked as if during one of of her early fits of enthusiasm she'd bitten off too much and was now regretfully digesting it.

She complained all the time. She complained of pain to Gladys, and of loneliness to Dottie. Mum was an Einstein in her field; for if she'd complained to Gladys of loneliness and of pain to Dot, she'd have got wrong answers all the time, as Glad was her doting companion already, and one word of pain sent Dot flying to her favourite corner of the Sassoon library. Mum very seldom got wrong answers. I'd timed her

42

once in the sitting-room with a stranger just come in, and it took her just forty-five seconds to find out what complaint he'd respond to. On the other hand she'd had someone fourteen years and the battle was still on. The response to all stratagems so far was zero. She truly despaired of me—when we happened to meet. She'd so far only succeeded in complaining *about* me. She said I was inhuman, irreligious and, worst of all, ill-dressed. She said no one could teach me anything, not even she, my own mother. For once she was wrong. I learnt all my mathematics from her.

"Anything happened at school today, Joe?"

"Nothing."

I had a nibble of cake from the fridge and came back into the sitting-room to unpack my satchel. "You're lying on the settee where I usually do my homework, Mum."

"Don't talk nonsense, child, you can't write on a settee."

"I do all my reading homework there. I do my writing on this table, but you've put your telephone on it."

"Is there something gone wrong with this thing again?" she asked, more to herself though. She snatched off the ear-piece and listened. It uttered its usual contented purr, and she stuck it back on the cradle in disgust, as though the fact it was in good order annoyed her. She stared frowning absently at me, great dark circles under her purple eyes, as I unpacked my satchel piece by piece with scrupulous deliberation.

"Where did you pick *that* up from?" she demanded, her accent going very Polish, the way it did when she got excited. "And why did you bring it here? Can't you see how dangerous——?"

"I only want to put some earth in it, Mum, and flowers will grow."

"Don't be absurd. There's a whole garden full of——"

The phone rang. Her sinuous arm went like a striking snake. "Oh, it's you. You don't usually phone at this time, something happened? . . . Oh, I'm all right, only as bad as

43

yesterday, more vomiting though and headache and giddiness, but don't talk too long, I'm expecting a call from Lady Irving. . . . He's just come in as a matter of fact. . . . Why should he be suffering from shock? . . . No, he doesn't appear strange, he's just brought in a broken vinegar bottle, that's all. . . ."

I went into my room taking everything with me. She did not speak again for some time, but combined with the stomach noises of the ear-piece came the sounds of her laboured and irregular breathing, so I did not feel entirely alone in that interval. It was surprisingly silent all the same; for a thing had to be of extraordinary importance for her to listen for so long without interjecting helpful little remarks. I wondered what it could be, though not to the point of distraction as homework of unusual urgency remained to be done. I filled my fountain-pen which had run dry on account of the enormous amount of work I had done that day. I was in fact exceedingly fatigued, but rest being out of the question, I spread my books in an orderly row on the bed and prepared to write in a kneeling position. The stomach noises in the meantime had continued at their low steady rate, but her breathing had quickened.

History. "Explain the term SCORCHED EARTH POLICY, giving one example of its application." I soon got my facts clear on the matter, but before I could set down a single word, I heard her utter an indrawn cry, and she began to jabber in such a raucous Slavic accent that further study was out of the question. I kicked shut the door but it was paper to knives. "God! God! That such a thing should occur *now* of all times in my condition! But Abraham, this can't be true. I just ASKED him if anything had happened at school today, and he said, 'Nothing. Nothing,' he said. 'Nothing.' " She burst into a flood of helpless weeping.

I went and stood the broken bottle with its jagged ends up on the dresser, and thought, "It's a good thing I picked this

44

off the road, there's no knowing just how many lives a simple act like that could have saved."

"No Abraham, I won't. . . . All right, all right, I won't say a word to him till you come. . . . Yes, I'll wait, I'll wait. . . . Oh, I feel fine, too good for words. . . . Good-bye."

The phone cut off with a cling. It was funny about these clings. They were of scientific fact always the same sound; yet when a conversation ended happily it was a joyous, heart-warming little cling; when it ended wrathfully it was a vicious piercing noise that buzzed into one's ear like a hornet. Then there was the cling melancholic, the cling inconclusive——

"Joe!" She pounded the settee three times with a fist which I knew would be gripped with the thumb in. I entered still holding my ruler and pen, and there it was: that ineffectual fist. "Is it true?" She was drawn rigid, staring straight ahead at the picture hanging in the alcove. If she would only look at me, I thought, bravely, directly, I would go up to her and take her hands. I would talk to her and show her how to make a fist, a real fist with the short strong king of her fingers in its rightful place outside. She turned suddenly to look me straight in the eye. "Is it true that a boy from Std. 5, named Nickie Sutherland——? Come here!" she screamed. "Don't you dare run away!"

"I haven't moved a bloody step, darn you!" I screamed back; and not without effect. It quietened her at once, like a drug. It was the only thing that worked: when she started screaming, to scream louder. She'd started bolt upright, arms a-begging like the sphinx. And when she spoke it was in a husky voice much lower than normal. "I said, come here, Joey." I came. Physically I had nothing to fear, I was already stronger than her and the two girls put together. "Do you see the picture on the wall?"

"Yes, it's hanging crooked, it's been like that for days."

"So you admit it!" she flashed, as though she'd been ex-

45

pecting to catch me out in three moves and done it in one. "You confess you saw this picture of my mother and father hanging crooked for days and you did absolutely nothing about it."

"Yes, I confess."

"And you intended to do nothing about it EVER."

"That's true, I didn't."

"There!" She lay back smiling. "Are you sorry?"

"Yes, I'm sorry, Mum, very sorry. I honestly am." I put a hand out to her, but she was not looking.

"And when you go back to school tomorrow, you'll tell Nicholas Sutherland you're sorry too."

My flesh crept. I gaped at her, horror-struck. Was this some sort of joke? If it was, then would I sing, Hallelujah! and raise her enthroned in my arms. My mother has a sense of humour. "Won't you, Joe?" She leaned towards me, and I shrank back revolted. Leprosy was nothing, a scientific fact. "You will apologize," she entreated, "won't you, hmm?" Her voice was rising to insistence again. She was not joking; yet she was not serious—for God's sake then, what *was* she? Of all things, my mother, not right, not wrong, my station my goddamn stinking rotten luck. "After all," she reasoned— *reasoned*! "Nicholas Sutherland is——"

"Are you going mad, Mum? Didn't Dad just tell you that Nickie died in the school bus this afternoon?" Too late to realize how she'd struck it again, the answer, the right answer, I went on, "Everyone saw that, his brains were on the pavement, crack! like an eggshell."

I looked at her smiling. So that's what it was all about. Her genius. No, there was no bravery in the world, but there was genius: contemptible, cowardly genius. And in victory they shivered. "Joe, get me a glass of water. Don't call the servants, get it yourself." Yes, and one would have thought such a prize put to shame the Golden Fleece.

I opened the fridge door, and crammed into my mouth the

rest of the cream cake. I filled a glass of water to the brim so that she should spill it all over herself, but when I offered it to her she told me to put it on the table. "And sit down here by me—here by me, I want to talk to you before your father comes. You mustn't be nervous."

I was not nervous. That was a fact, the truth, the whole truth. But what good was truth—in her hands? "I am not nervous," I said.

"Exactly!" she stated, taking a drink, for her hand was perfectly steady. "You give the impression of being completely hardened to it all. The truth is——"

"The damn truth is I didn't do anything! Understand? I didn't *know* anything till it was all over. I was just——"

"I know you're innocent, Joe."

"I want to tell you what happened, Mum. I was just walking by the bus——"

"I know you're innocent, God bless you, my child. Tuck your shirt in, will you? It's just that other people don't understand. I know you, and you know me, but others may think simply because you don't *look* sorry, you *aren't* sorry."

"I'm *not* sorry. For what should I be sorry?"

"For poor Nickie Sutherland, child."

"But he's dead."

"Yes, yes, but his soul in Heaven?"

"It must be happy. Heaven is a pleasant place."

"Tuck your shirt in, Joe. And these soup-stains. You really must be more careful. Look here, Joey, I know exactly how you feel, I'm your flesh and blood after all. And I don't feel sorry for Nickie either, he was killed by God's sanction. It's his mother I'm sorry for."

"Has he got one? I don't know. And if he has, maybe she's glad. I don't know. Oh, let go my finger, Mum! I'm sick and tired of talking to you, you're hurting me."

"Now listen here, Joey, I know exactly how you feel. But your father won't. Understand? I only want to show you how

47

you can show your father how you feel. I know your father, and I know you; and I'm telling you once a misunderstanding springs up between you, no power on earth will stop it from dirtying the whole matter. There's going to be a trial, understand? And we've got to start off on the right foot. Do you know what right is? Look Joey, I want you to see." She let me go to fumble about in her handbag, and pulled out her mirror. "Do you see?"

"Yes, I see."

"Do you see how brutal, raw and callous an expression that is? Don't you see how important it is to give people the impression that you sympathize with the bereaved? Joe, please, I beg of you to do it for my sake. You won't put on your tough little James Cagney act, will you?"

"What shall I do, Mum? Shall I cry?"

"Yes, Joey, cry. Cry for Nickie's mother's sake."

"Godamn Nickie's mother!" I burst into tears, tore myself from her embrace, and went blindly into my room. I flung myself face down on my bed, and wept. Again and again I tried to stop. I could not. And for what cause I found, in the midst of my sobs, the beginnings of an answer. I had found my station. I had found my station. It was not laughter.

After some time I came to a dry-throated halt, and lay in the wetness of my pillow exhausted. Outside I heard the cooing of doves, and looked out into darkness that was not night. Thunder rumbled. The rain came pattering on the path outside, and soon after, my mother's voice, soft and anxious.

"Joey?"

I wiped my face on my sleeve and went sniffing into the sitting-room.

"That was very good, excellent. Here, blow your nose on my hanky. There's a good boy. But, please, not so much crying next time, hmm? Just a little to make them see you're sorry. If you cry too much they'll think you're guilty, understand, hmm? There's a precious boy. By and by I'm going to

48

give you a very pleasant surprise. Tuck your shirt in and ask the servants to serve tea, will you?"

The pinks and purples of a monsoon twilight were merging to darkness when we heard the wash of his car wheels in the gutter. Then the creak-creak of his handbrake. A few seconds silence followed during which he would be collecting his briefcase, his umbrella and any other article he would have considered essential to his well-being this evening. He would not employ a chauffeur; he said he was not going to put *his* life into anyone else's hands, and *he* ought to know since half of his prosecutions were directed against cases of criminal negligence, and of these half were motoring offences. Mum said he wouldn't have a chauffeur to stop *us* using the car. Glad agreed. Dot was not interested. I said the only thing that could logically be said about a poor beaten up old Ford like that. Bang! Bang! Bang! Three times he had to slam the door before it would shut.

The torrential downpour had stopped a minute ago, which in a way heralded my father's arrival with the bland surety of a red carpet for the new Viceroy. He had more luck than any potentate; that of the devil. He was small, bald and fox-faced, but if the elements were going to stop buffeting this Earth for a minute it would be to let my father get out of his car, lock it, and walk at a leisurely pace down the garden path into the warmth and security of his loving family. It was infuriating. Avalanches, floods, famines, massacres, plague—they all turned out to be aces up his sleeve. As far as I could tell from my fourteen years with Dad he had only one stroke of bad luck, and that was me. His only son, his heir, his trump, his last hand. Me.

He entered softly on his thick built-in crêpe soles, just missing classification with gnomes by a hairsbreadth. Just missing; only just; always only just. If my Dad entered a competition for the tallest man in Bombay he might not have

49

won, but he'd have emerged with a prize of a kind. Some ruffian, presumably a relative of a defendant for whom Dad had got life imprisonment, once seized him as he was getting out of his car in Kalbadevi, stabbed him in the chest and fled. The point embedded itself barely half-way through a wallet crammed with ten-rupee notes and turned out to be an interesting antique.

He never boasted about his luck, or gambled. He seldom raised his voice, even in court, and then only at the end of his summing up, to say how grieved he was, how deeply grieved to have to demand the full penalty of this wretchedly wicked and dangerous man. In my earlier days I used to go and see him at work with Dorothy (he would not permit Mum or Glad to show—as he put it—any one of their forty scarlet nails in court). And for a long time I supposed from his gentle, lulling, pleading manner that he was *defending* the crumbs. Only a few months ago did I learn from Dot that he'd never been a counsel for the defence in his entire career.

Dad was no threatening blustering prosecutor in the Hollywood manner. In the last trial I saw him a year ago (Dot had stopped going for some reason) I got the impression he was playing the role of no one in the court—neither defence, prosecution, nor judge—but the warder, kindly, gently and tactfully nudging the prisoner to the gallows. I remembered how strongly it crossed my mind, as I sat up there in the gallery, that the only person in the world who could have saved Ali Ikbal Kassem (matricide) was Mum. For while it was true that Dad had never lost a battle to Mum it was equally certain he had never fought one.

"I'm sorry I didn't come home earlier. I came as soon as I could. I couldn't come any earlier."

When the occasion arose, when it was serious enough, he talked to people as if they were precious citizens, members of the jury, monkeys on thrones. His statements then were structural masterpieces—for monkeys of course. His second

50

sentence was a précis of the first with a small new addition; the third was a précis of the first two plus a small addition; and then when everyone was craning forward on their chairs to hear it a fourth time he changed the subject. I'd once attempted to practise the technique myself on the mugger, but only got some very fishy stares. There was more to these repetitions than met the eye, perhaps a certain menacing change in tone, which compelled one to keep listening although one had already heard it three times over. "She's sitting on the toilet," for instance, after his third repeat sounded like esoteric poetry; and I must confess some of the most eerie experiences of my life were household conversations with Dad.

"Why don't you put on the light? It's getting dark. Is there something organically the matter with the lights?"

He could have reached the wall switch himself, but when his suggestion met with no response it would have been most unlike him to do anything to conclude the matter. He seemed to be regarding us as we crouched on the settee with her great distended belly between us; this belly like a table in the dying twilight, our heads nearly touching. It did occur to me then it was a very unusual position for us to be found in, but since the accident that had just occurred was itself something out of the usual, he made no comment and went into the bathroom.

When he came back we were still as we were, though much more in the dark now; and had he been listening from the bathroom he would not have got any information out of Mum's alternating gasps of dismay and exclamations of glee. The joy of all the gossip columnists in town, she could never do anything without accompanying it with some kind of verbal report. She didn't *mean* any harm, though; she was fundamentally a darn fine woman, a pillar of society, and the things they wrote regarding her social activities were very sound. When everyone was just sitting around complaining about some dreadful cataclysm, Mum went and formed a com-

51

mittee to *do* something. My father did not appreciate her, they should indeed never have married; he could never see what she did in the right light, the varying light, he was too inflexible; this light for instance, she was really very lovely now, what we were doing did not matter, it was she who taught me that, to catch the light, what light there was, the stray light, the lamp in the street illuminating her great gorgeous eyes. No, he just had to have *his* light.

"Now then I know what has happened has cast a shadow on our lives, but it surely cannot help us to crouch here in the darkness getting melancholic about it. Put on that table-lamp, Joe."

God, I thought, of course it couldn't last. We were just too happy, and how unnatural that was. What hope was there of happiness here, when the greater it was the greater grew the fear of its end?

"There, then." He snapped on the wall-switch, and the light hit me with almost physical violence. My initial impulse, although I was fully expecting this, was to pick up the board and smash his big smooth shining skull through it. But then I remembered the days for doing that kind of thing were over.

"Whose move is it?" she asked, blinking to accustom her eyes.

"Yours, Mum. I've crowned."

"Are we playing flying crowns?"

"Flying crowns, Mum."

"Oh, my, oh, dear. I'm in the soup then. No flying crowns, please, Joe."

"All right, then one-step crowns."

"Where's Dorothy? And Gladys? Have you two been alone all evening?"

"Oh, hello, my dear, now just do me a favour and forget about that unfortunate accident. We've had it all out, it's over."

"This is preposterous." The volume of his voice rose to a

point that was just right. It was archery, that exactness, not speech. "My son is involved in an accident resulting in the death of a classmate——"

"Sutherland is in Std. 5." I corrected him, "*Was* in Std. 5. Your move, Mum."

"Take that board away. Take that disgusting board away."

With an air of resignation that was intended to fool no one, she gave the board to me. "Careful, put it on the carpet here and we'll finish in a minute."

"I want you to come into my study."

I gripped her silk gown sash and sat tight. "Now," she warned me, "listen to your father—you won't run out of the house and hide in that Catholic church again, will you?"

"No, I promise I won't."

"You, see what a good boy he is, Abraham? He's promised; but whatever induced him to do such a thing? Mother of Moses, it makes me quail to this day every time I remember it. Have I smacked you yet for that? No, but never mind, everything is forgiven and forgotten. Why didn't you run to the synagogue?"

"The church is nearer."

"Nearer, indeed! To think that for the sake of mere yardage a son of the famous Hoseas should——"

"Nina, do you mind?" I was wondering when it was coming, but did not anticipate it half as well as she. "This matter of the Catholic church is closed. It is over and done with."

"Yes, Abraham, just as closed as the other, so don't start upsetting him all over again. I've just managed to calm him down. And what's the fuss about anyway? Nickie died by God's sanction and that's all there is to it."

"That's all, eh? That's all."

"Yes, turn around, Joe, let me tuck your shirt in."

He extracted his snuff-box, took two lightning pinches, then the snap of the lid went off like a pistol shot. "God's sanction, God's blessed sanction. Well, well, well. HE had

53

better tell Master Sutherland's parents that, and the Sunrise Insurance Company, and the Bombay Electric Supply and Transport Company. Mr. God is going to have a busy time fluttering about running messages in a red chuprasi's turban, but not Mrs. Hosea and Company Limited. Oh, no, they're going to sit around playing checkers, and then when things get really bad, Mah Jongg." During this speech he was moving. His movements and the sound of his voice flowed like two brands of the same oil. By simple variance of tone or gesture he could speak without drawing attention to his movements, or move so as to make it extraordinarily difficult to listen. It was only when he paused to polish his lenses that I really became aware he had drawn up a chair to form a triangle with us.

"Joe, go get your father a glass of water, he's frightfully hoarse."

"Sit still, and listen to me, young man."

"Listen to your father, Joe. Don't breathe through your mouth. And none of this James Cagney louring, you promised——"

"Nina——"

"Yes, yes, Abraham, do go on, we're listening. My goodness, d'you smell that heavenly Queen of the Night? The rain has certainly freshened things up a bit. Hand me my knitting, Joe, what a darling, keep your mouth closed, there's a dear. I wonder why Lady Irving hasn't phoned yet."

Looking at him now, I felt that the only reason why he would not physically clap her mouth shut was that he had not done it before. Perhaps it was because of her superb sense of timing. She knew exactly when to stop.

"On my way here I had some strange thoughts," he began, "odd thoughts, you'll see. I said a tragedy has occurred. A human being brought up with infinite care and patience, a man-child of our own son Joe's age, has died. How sad that is, how sad we shall never find out. Yet in the end it may do some good. Every cloud has its silver lining. Perhaps this one will be the achievement of a miracle, the hitherto impossible: to make our son understand that he's grown up now, that life is not one big circus, and to measure up to his responsibilities as a citizen, a member of the Hosea family. Yes, I will never let that slip into the darker recesses of my mind. I will keep it held like a torch before us; I will defend him tooth and claw; I will save his tender young mind from permanent scarring in the battles ahead of us, because I know this will be the cause of his turning over a new leaf. I come home. What do I find? Scarring!" He coldly and accurately side-kicked the board, sending the pieces spinning over the carpet and clattering on to the tiled floor.

This was the incident which might have warned Gladys that now was not quite the right time to introduce her new boy-friend. Poor Glad, she had nothing of Mum's timing, and the worst luck in the bargain. "Mum! Dad! I want you to meet Samuel "Geegee" Milhaily! He's just down from Bangalore! He trains racehorses! He's settling in Bombay! He's staying to dinner!"

My father, always very quick to respond to an introduction, moved forward firing a word of welcome at every step. "I— am — very — pleased — to — meet — you — Samuel — "Geegee"—Milhaily——" he took the eagerly proffered hand without breaking stride and swept on to the front entrance hall with it and its tall, suavely dressed, cream-sharkskin-suited possessor, "—delighted—so—do—drop—in—again— Goodbye." The door slammed, and Samuel "Geegee's" cantering footsteps died away before Gladys could move.

"Go to your room. Gladys, go to your room and shut the door. I'm sorry, I'll explain later. I said you are to stay in-doors, girl! We'll entertain him another time. We'll serve him best by appointment."

"Mother! What's happening? Why——?"

"Come here, my child, you've hurt her."

55

"GO TO YOUR ROOM! Not YOU, Master! You just sit where you are, and leave off sprawling over your mother. Better still, sit here." He gave me his chair. "Don't for a moment think you can escape responsibility by turning yourself into a thumb-sucking infant just as it suits you. Last week you claimed you were old enough to start driving the car— quite old enough. Right, then, somewhere in between your toddlers' shoes and your driving licence we're going to find that narrow strip of road where the going is straight and consistent—be it on the brink of Gehenna." He kept throwing glances to his left as if he were aware of some invisible jury, but as this was actually in the direction of Dorothy's room I eventually concluded he was remarking on her absence.

"I wonder where Dorothy's got to," said my mother, knitting rapidly.

"Yes, it's high time we had dinner," I added looking accusingly at him. "We can't keep the servants up all night; they start work at dawn, marketing, sweeping, cooking, washing, and their day never ends till midnight. Is it——?"

"Yes, Joe, you've often shown us the generous sweep of your social conscience, but tonight it's your individual one we're after. The spoor——"

"I forbid you to utter one more word about this accident, Abraham. We've had it all, it's over."

"All of it? Do you know the Sutherlands?"

"No, and I don't want to."

"Well, whether *I* want to or not: I do. Did you get a call from your son's Principal this evening?"

"Now, look——"

"Well, I did. And I made a few, quite apart from the one I made you. Now don't get me wrong; I'm not making any accusations. I just want the truth, the plain simple consecutive occurrence of facts; no distortions, no omissions, and no deft little switches in sequence. What happened, Joe?"

"I don't know. I told it all to Mum."

56

" 'I don't know. I told it all to Mum.' Young man, if you say such a thing in the witness-box, he'll split you down from crown to crutch and eviscerate you. What did you tell your mother?"

"He just said——"

"Your turn will come, Nina. I said what did you tell her?"

"Nothing."

"Then start telling me. Is Nicholas Sutherland dead?"

"Yes."

"When did you find that out?"

"Today after school. I was walking on the pavement towards the school-bus——" My mother was knitting slowly with her eyes shut now. "I was going to join my friend Wilfred Prior. It was stationary with its engine idling next to the telegraph-post. When I reached the tail end it started moving; it was still going very slowly, much slower than I. I reached a point about its middle when I heard a kind of snapping in front and just above me, and there he was against the telegraph-post. That's all."

"You felt nothing?"

"Honest to God, he didn't touch me."

"I didn't ask if he touched you. How was it that Sutherland who was inside the bus was killed with his head out?"

"He was reaching, as I overtook the bus, to tip my topee off."

"Why didn't he see the post?"

"Because he was looking backwards towards me. And I couldn't see him because I'm so short and had the brim of my topee down at the front, and slanted. You know how I wear my topee don't you, Dad?"

"Show me once more." I put it on, not exaggerating one bit. "So you definitely did not see him."

"Not a hope. If I had I'd have warned him. I'd have yelled out, 'Cave, Nickie! The telegraph-post!' I swear to God I'd have torn it out of the ground, with my bare hands."

"But you didn't see him, and so could not warn him, and so he was killed."

"Yes." For some reason, his saying this sent a wave of relief sweeping through me. At the same time my mother opened her eyes. "Well, thank God that's over."

"There's one small question," he remarked, idly taking out his snuff-box. "Did you speak to anyone after seeing the mangled effects of Sutherland's skull?"

"Oh, Abraham, you——"

"No! Dad, I didn't. Honest, I just took to my heels. I ran around to the maidan. It was empty. I walked in the centre, speaking to no one. I went on through the Oval. Look, Dad," I exclaimed, diving my hand into my pocket, "I've evidence. You know those ticker seeds that grow around the coconut trees during the monsoon? Well, here are some I collected on the way, that's evidence, see how fresh they are." I wet the end of one of the long torpedo-shaped seeds in my mouth and put it on my hand. After a second or two it split with a ticking sound and flew somersaulting into the air.

"Excellent." He pressed shut the lid and inhaled deeply. "The evidence that you spoke to no one after the accident is entertaining if not conclusive. How did you know Sutherland was going to tip off your topee?"

"I saw—I mean, I felt—I mean——"

"Well, you didn't see him, and he didn't touch you. Did you smell him?"

"Dad, he sort of half-brushed my hat."

"Yes, but what makes you so sure he was intending to tip it off?" I didn't answer. "Perhaps he wanted to pin a rose in it. God knows it needs a bit of decoration, you appear to have lost your third badge this year."

"They keep pinching it," I protested. "Dad, you don't know what a pack of hooligans those chaps are."

"And you? Do you never pinch other boys' badges?"

"Only those who pinch mine."

58

"Naturally," he nodded. "Is Nickie Sutherland a hooligan?"

"No, he's——" I swallowed. I began to feel a bead of perspiration flow into my eyebrow, and realized what he was up to. "Nickie was a good chap."

"Yet you say he was hooligan enough to tip off your topee."

"That's nothing, Dad. It's not a crime, everyone at school does it."

"You too?"

"Of course."

"Did you tip Sutherland's topee off? Now you just keep away from your mother. Did you tip his topee off?"

"Look, Dad, how in hell was I to know——?"

"When?"

"On the stairs coming down to go out."

"Did anyone else see you?"

"About a dozen chaps."

"Can you recall who they were?"

"Yes, you see there was a fellow called Braithwaite who had a new cycle that some cad had punctured with a knife, and he was repairing it."

"Did you speak to any of them?"

"Yes, I asked Braithwaite, who's a very good friend of mine, if I could help. He said he could manage, thanks. I told him that cads who did such things should be publicly whipped. I don't think anything else was said, and I left through the front gates, where this accident happened."

"A dozen witnesses. With his death so close."

I heard a sigh and looked at my mother. Her knitting had tumbled to the floor. She was staring into the blackness of the window, her eyes half-shut, as though the effort to close them completely was beyond her. "Can I go now, Dad?" I begged, "I've important homework to do."

"Briefly, do you know what this means? If the Sutherlands

59

bring an accusation of criminal negligence against the bus company, the latter's only defence will be that the contributing factor of the accident was horseplay amongst schoolboys. The Sutherlands will reply that Nickie was a well-behaved boy, unless provoked, and they'll have seven hundred witnesses to prove it. This will lead the insurance company to the provoking agent. In other words: you. And you? How many witnesses will you have to prove *your* well-behaved character? One? Two? Your mother? Your father?"

I saw her suddenly clap her hand to her mouth. Her stomach convulsed, and she rolled her great violet eyes in mute appeal. My father ran into the bathroom to fetch a basin. But when he offered it to her she pushed it aside. She attempted to rise and he helped her. She leaned heavily upon him on the way across to their room, and this she was able to do well on account of the great difference in their heights.

She did not appear at dinner, which was served half an hour later. Nor did Gladys, nor Dorothy. During the meal Gladys attempted to see Mum but he stopped and directed her to the table. She retired without a sound. She was on a diet anyway. The absence of Dorothy was more noticeable as she had never been known to miss a meal in her life. Her absence tonight was only less remarkable than the silence of the telephone. Mum and Glad between them had scores of callers, and only when the phone was out of order did meal-times pass without interruption. In fact at one point of the meal, no word yet having been spoken, my father got up and went to the phone. The flex that entered the ear-piece was loose. My mother had a habit of unconsciously twisting and pulling on it as she spoke. Tonight at least Dad seemed quite relieved about it. Towards the end of the meal he said, speaking in the kindest voice he'd ever used in addressing me, "You need not worry too much about this business. The Sutherlands are a poor Anglo-Indian family. He earns about Rs. 150 p.m. at the mills and couldn't possibly bring a case."

60

I thought it was very considerate of my father to relieve me of a problem that could easily have preyed on my mind all night. All through the meal in fact I'd been running around in circles trying to fathom how on earth the news had got abroad so fast. Had the Principal really phoned Dad? Perhaps. But in retrospect it sounded a bit too much like something that would fit neatly into his sort of sentence construction, his esoteric verse. And even if the Principal had phoned how could *he* have known all the piddling details of this topee tipping? Holy Moses! I nearly bit my tongue off. Had not the Principal in front of my own eyes left the school with his wife in their car the period before the last? And another thing, yes, several other things—how could my father have happened to have such intimate information about an Anglo-Indian family in Bandra?

It was, indeed, during such moments of harrowing doubts about my parent's intentions towards me, that he'd relieved me of the problem. I felt confident that he had my welfare at heart, by whatever methods he undertook to show it; and realizing at the same time the infinitely greater problems that would confront me if I were to question these methods, I relaxed. I stuffed my homework books back into my satchel and went to bed.

During the night I had a pleasant dream. I was driving a truck through a flat and limitless maidan fringed on the horizon by mountains. These turned out to be clouds, however, and the grass on which I was driving grew not out of earth but also of cloud. That explained the swerving plunging but altogether pleasing roller-coaster sensation; and also the music, the pipes of Pan. I soon deduced where I was: in Heaven. A divine policeman stood at a crossroads and gave me the signal to pass. I went and, noticing it was Wilfred, waved out to him. He saw me, but apparently afraid, very afraid indeed, that any chance motion of his hand might be misinterpreted by others and so cause an accident, he did not wave back. I went on accompanied by the same music, and lulled by my surroundings I grew careless. I surrendered the wheel the better to regard the divine countryside. Almost instantly some premonition compelled me to look to the front, and Nickie Sutherland's face appeared in the windscreen. I stamped down the foot-brake and missed it. There was a dreadful, hollow, snapping sound, and I awoke.

That is to say I proceeded to awake, for it was not instantaneous. The tentacles of the nightmare held on to me for a while, yielding me the struggle back to reality sucker by sucker, slowly. These moments, far from being accompanied by feelings of victory, had a special horror for me, a murderous, suicidal resentment that was not contained either in nightmare or the full awakening after. Why did I *have* to dream this? Why? Why?

I reached for my bedside light, as I always did after such occurrences, and crawled out from under the mosquito-net. The contact of my feet with the insides of my slippers comforted me, and when I walked to the pantry to get a glass of water it was not to quench my thirst so much as to get rid of the last traces of that random balderdash from my mind. At the fridge I heard a rustling that would have made me leap out of my very skin were it not that it was quite a familiar sound. This combined with gnawing, grating and the metallic clicking of the bait-hook being struck like a boxing-ball against the grill of the capacious trap only meant that the Hoseas had caught another rat. Simultaneously I realized it was the hollow snap of the trap that had awoken me.

As I poured out the water I could not help but feel a sneaking admiration for the authorities concerned in the fabrication of dreams. If they wanted to organize a motor accident they didn't fret themselves sick, but took what was going: the snap of a trap, a footstep on the gravel, or even a snore from the dreamer. This kind of cavalier resourcefulness really tickled me pink, and I fairly spluttered into the glass with uncontrollable laughter.

I shut the fridge and went and switched on the light in the pantry. It was a large female, brown with white fur on her underside. Sometimes when they were so big their pink hairless tails stuck outside the trap, but this one luckily was all inside, so she could at least have a peaceful night.

I switched off the light and went back to bed. The method of disposal depended on the kind of servant we had at the time. I tried to put the matter out of my mind and go back to sleep, but at once found I had a problem here. Whereas a few minutes ago I needed to awake to get rid of an unpleasant fiction, I now needed to go to sleep to be rid of an unpleasant fact—and indeed the latter was unquestionably more harrowing as I had freedom of thought. In my nightmare I was trapped. It just had to end the way it did. But did this? Did the rat?

The servant before St. Paul used to take the trap out into the garden and pour boiling water through the grill. The one previous used to pin it down with one poker and stab it with a second. Tomorrow morning St. Paul would open the trap an inch, let her head emerge, and smash it with a dandu, which he produced suddenly to the creature's complete surprise. He was the kindest of them all, and took much pains to conceal the instrument, claiming that during the few moments the trap was opening the victim lived in the increasing expectation of being freed, and so died happy.

It was a highly practical point of view which satisfied all parties, and I was positive that if he'd been our servant from my earliest childhood before I'd started reading Grimm, it would have been my point of view too. As it was, the early influence, that attractive and rather frightening influence, still remained, although it had never at any time been strong enough to actually put it to the test. I really shrugged to answer why now, when that childhood influence should have been at its lowest, it should suddenly burst the bounds of reason and demand instant satisfaction. But like my occasional lapses into thumbsucking, there it was, there it darned well was.

Now that I knew she was there I could hear the frantic clicking and gnawing through two doors. I crawled out from under my net again, and opened the door leading to the garden. It was a night worthy of any night scene from the hand of the Master. Low, brooding animal-shaped clouds drifting across the crescent moon, made life of it for a moment, a leering, peering half-shut eye dragging at the face. It was a real dream of a night when I felt that anything could happen.

Both my father and Dorothy were light sleepers, so I did not put on a switch till I got to the pantry. Yes, she really was a splendid-looking thing when one looked closely without prejudice. I took up the trap, which nearly overbalanced due to the added frenzy of the creature. I steadied it, taking damn good care not to bring my fingers into contact with the grill, for I was not so absurdly romantic as to believe she knew I was going to free her.

In the garden I put the trap down on the grass, and turned it so that a shaft of moonlight shone into the grill. As though this were some sort of cue for the magic to begin, the pipes of Pan, exactly as I'd heard them in my dream, recommenced—the same carefree lilting tune.

"What are the words?" I whispered.

Her teeth reflected lights as sharp as their points.

"Abracadabra, who is that jabberer?" I pressed open the trap and she bolted out. At the foot of the wall that separated us from the next house, she turned and looked directly at me. My heart missed a beat. The music cut off. Now, I thought, now. At the same time what should have occurred to me long before did so now. Should I not have changed into apparel more suitable for such an event? I bit my lip at the thought of

64

the ungallant figure I must cut in my floppy felt slippers and my pyjamas bagging almost to the ground. Was I worthy? Wasn't I now supposed to give a full account of myself? Produce my credentials? I straightened up to my tallest four feet nine, but before I could strike the pose I had in mind, that of the statue of the Prince of Wales by the Bandstand, she turned and flew with an effortless, a magical ease straight up the wall.

At the top she once again paused to regard me. This wall was heavily surmounted by barbed-wire, the final results of some misunderstandings I'd had with the previous tenants, and how subtly was their revenge exacted. That the worst did not happen was hardly the point. It was the fear that it might that gave me the screw. Would she now? Would she now? Surely she knew, to stand amidst barbed-wire was fine for a rat, but to change she could pick her position. The dilemma was settled by the shrilling of the pipes, at the sudden sound of which the rat disappeared over the other side of the wall.

The magic continued for a while, then gave way to coughing, a tremendous amount of phlegm-hoiking and spitting. The beggar who since the start of the monsoon had taken to sleeping in the shelter of our pipal which overhung the pavement like a canopy must have earned enough to get himself a flute. I stood around undecidedly for a few more moments, although the mosquitoes were at my ankles now. Then I shuffled back in and went to bed somewhat relieved. Holy smoke, what would I have done with a bewitched princess anyway?

I went back to bed thinking that Grimm had lost a fan. I could not sleep—not that I tried, no more than that rat would have. I felt like one, a trapped rat. Nickie Sutherland had a brother in Std. 1, and their resemblance was marked. He was one of those two small boys whom I had attempted during the tiffin break to pacify. I thought back on the events of yesterday, all of them, they came crowding to my mind uninvited; and I felt if I did not go to school tomorrow it would help me enormously. I used to get recurrent attacks of malaria which were not closely questioned. Mum would be keen to let me stay, Dot would say nothing. Glad would disagree, as I was the only subject on earth that she disagreed with Mum about, so she generally seized on these occasions to open up all her guns. What would settle the matter, though, was Dad. I had more than a sneaking suspicion that he would get me to school tomorrow if he had to deliver me in a hearse.

No, there was no escape in that direction. I could do better than bloody my fists on a locked door. That rat had kept on gnawing at the grill when it was evidently hopeless. What she'd needed to do was to effect her transformation—to change. TO CHANGE! I nearly shot through the top of my mosquito-net. The whole answer in a nutshell. I had to change. I had to stop looking for chinks in my prison-house, and simply change.

At this point I began to think of Mr. Titmus, of something he'd said about being brave—or was it adventurous? This had also occurred during my passage through the maidans. For some reason it was to him that I directed my explanation of the tragedy, but while his appearance in such a setting was new, the setting itself was almost as old as myself. These imaginary courts of inquiry and judgement were an infallible source of entertainment, but as I knew from bitter experience when measured up to the actual facts they crumbled at a touch to dust. The verdict, the unanimous one, that of Mr. Titmus, my father, and mine, was that I had to change, to be adventurous, to get out of the rut. That was the verdict in theory. The question, in practice, was how?

Till dawn I continued wrestling with it. There was no magic wand to do the trick. I felt lacking in implements. But at dawn it finally struck me I indeed possessed the instrument to effect the first stage of my transformation: a brake. The first step I had to take was, paradoxically, to come to a dead halt. And this brake was a word, a small simple three-lettered word used even by infants. Why? From today whenever I found myself about to do something I would stop and ask, why? Why would be my Theorem 1. In which case it would have a corollary: Why not? Without thinking a whit further on the subject, I fell asleep vaguely aware that the coming day was going to bear witness to events of historical importance.

I woke up to a sharp, almost pin-pointed blaze of light focused on my left eyelid. My bed didn't ever catch the sun, and I wondered what it was. Was it for instance someone, some presence, shining a torch into my eye? I had only to look to find out, and after some slight hesitation did so. It was one of the many broken edges of the bottle on the dresser reflecting sunlight into my eye. The angle at which the sunbeams were coming into the room showed it was early yet, and I was turning over to go back to sleep, as I was habitually a late riser, when Theorem 1 occurred to me. In future I would rise early and I got up.

The presence of the broken bottle annoyed me and before dressing I got rid of it in the manner I usually disposed of such things. I pitched it through my window into the next garden. That house could never keep its tenants long, and from the time when I was old enough to ponder upon such phenomena I had suspected it was haunted. It must indeed have become common knowledge to those who looked for homesteads in Wodehouse Road, as it had now remained unoccupied for several months, and my own association with it was strictly confined to observing the pile of junk gradually mount up on the lawn. There were, in my opinion, many articles which could have been of considerable value to the next tenants, depending of course on their profession. If for example they were——

I ducked under the window-sill—whether in the nick of time or not, I couldn't say. It was close whatever it was. A pink-faced man with a ginger moustache and a peaked army officer's hat was looking around suspiciously through the amply spaced gaps in the barbed wire on the top of the wall. It all came back to me now. I had been in such a dazed condition returning home last evening I hadn't paid due attention to the green Austin parked in that driveway. The other and much more important point I was reminded of, as I crouched there softly scolding myself, was Theorem 1. If I had stopped to ask why I had wanted to throw the bottle away before doing so, I would have been spared this trouble. And trouble I was going to have all right, for I could not think of a single article in the whole of that heap in which the British Army would rejoice. No, from my experience, my considerable experience of the fastidious demands of the previous tenants, this could only mean one thing: War.

I peered through a chink in the curtains. He was still there, and as I watched that altogether strange unsmiling visage, I began to perceive the germination of a problem. I was a reformed character. I knew it and pretty soon my family and all my acquaintances would realize it, and in due course we would be deriving the benefits thereof. They would point and say not without a certain pride, "There goes Joe, he used to be a feckless clown; now he's the soberest judge in town." And very nice too. But how was I to impress the marvels of my change on a fellow who'd come on the scene so late? He would think I was a good boy because I was like the mugger, a milksop, incapable of evil—and that I saw at once was a grave disadvantage to all concerned. Well, well, I shrugged, it was a hazard I'd have to overcome when I came to it, and that moment I saw was to be postponed when his face after a last blistering look around turned and vanished.

I was now not at all sorry that this near disastrous event

had taken place so early in the day, as I felt everything from now, being conducted with intimates better acquainted with the villainy I was capable of, would in comparison be smooth sailing. I bumped into my mother in the bathroom—she was getting easier and easier to bump into—and I said in the cheeriest voice I could muster, "Good morning!"

In need of spectacles at the best of times, she peered down anxiously at me and asked, "What warning?"

"May I borrow your comb, Mum?"

"You know the sound of that tissue-paper racket drives your father mad," she said.

"I want to comb my hair," I explained.

"You want to comb what?"

"My hair."

"Oh, you want to comb your hair! Yes, take one from our room. What a splendid idea, it will be nice if you go to school looking nice today of all days. I spoke to your father about letting you stay home until the whole thing blows over but he didn't think it would be a good idea and I fully agree, don't you? But never mind, let's have no more about this accident."

"Just whatever you say, Mum," I nodded, for I now began to realize that in the battle for my transformation I would need allies. Before I could leave, Gladys came sailing in. "Good morning!" I sang out.

"If you're not washing buzz off, this bathroom's getting crowded. And when you're at school," she shrilled in what she fondly imagined to be a threatening tone, "just you mind out how——"

"Oh, Glad, darling, I told you we're to have no more talk about this wretched accident."

I went out and knocked on Dot's door opposite.

"Who is it?"

"Joe."

"What d'you want?"

"To say, 'Good morning.' "

"Why?"

Why? This was Theorem 1. What had *she* been up to last night? I went and knocked on their bedroom door. "Come in."

"Good morning, Dad, I've come to borrow a comb, Mum said I could."

"Why?"

"To part my hair."

"You've never parted your hair in your life, have you?"

"No, but I've——"

"Look here, Joe, I understand perfectly why you want to start now, but don't. We need not have seven hundred people suddenly noticing you've parted your hair. Just you go to school as you usually do and when you're there, behave more or less as you usually behave."

"But, Dad, you told me yesterday I had to turn over a new leaf!"

"Yes, but not overnight."

"I thought among my best friends and relations how easy it would be——"

"Your father's quite right, Joey. Any sudden change in your behaviour will mean you're guilty. That's enough, no more talk about this accident, and do keep your lips closed when you're not speaking, and go and have your breakfast, he's brought your eggs, and don't let's have the same wicked scene we had yesterday."

I felt my blood rapidly coming to the boil. I felt my brow lower in the manner of a ram about to charge. Then I thought, why? I went and sat down to breakfast.

Dot was already there, and while we were used to seeing her eat heartily, a four-egg omelette was exceptional. "Good morning, Dorothy." She nodded, for the moment unable to reply.

"Where were you last night, Dorothy?" asked my father

from the bedroom. "And when did you come in? I was awake till midnight and didn't hear you."

"I wasn't out. I was in my room reading."

"Why didn't you come to dinner?"

"I wasn't hungry." She didn't often blush, and it could not have been because she'd had a lover in her room. She was a man-hater.

"Do you mean," said Glad flouncing up to the table, "that you didn't hear all that went on last night?"

"Why should I?"

"You don't know that yesterday afternoon a boy named——"

"I said why SHOULD I, Gladys?"

"Now then, girls," came the Polish voice, "not another word about the accident. Forget it, just forget it."

As I was a few minutes later sneaking out through the front door someone unseen called after me. "Good-bye and good luck, Joey, don't mention a word about this accident to anyone, just forget it." I wondered who it could have been.

I was in good time for school, and some way from the Convent of Jesus and Mary I began to brood over the "pleasant surprise" my mother had given me before Dad came in last night. Her parents—or as she preferred to call them, without any permission from me, my grandparents—were coming here from Poland in a couple of months. I'd been infected with her enthusiasm regarding the event at the time, but now in the harsh light of day it didn't look so rosy. Whose room would they have? Were they? Did they? Shouldn't they? And above all, why? In brief, I concluded: two more enemies in the house.

I was drawing near the Catholic church when a green Austin passed me. At the same instant I recognized it as the Army man's, his large pink muscular gold-flecked arm came

71

out to give the slowing-down signal. The car stopped at the kerb about thirty yards down. My first impulse was to bolt into the church, as they knew me there. Then I thought why? I kept slowly and calmly on. The low mean skunk, he had the valour to chase a child out of his house and belt him in the street, but at the threshold of a church he turned tail. He was plain yellow, that's what he was. The memory of that particularly painful encounter from the remote past startled me by its suddenness and I clean forgot about my present source of peril until he accosted me.

"Good morning."

Nothing could have sounded more ominous. But I kept doggedly on. "Any chance you going to Craig Thomas Episcopalian High School, laddie?" My first impulse was to say No, but I stopped myself; and as the only other alternative was Yes, I nodded. He said, "I'm going there myself. Hop in, I'll give you a lift and you can show me the way. I'm not long in Bombay."

As I got in, it occurred to me this was my first impulse. But it was too late, I was trapped. I just had to keep a sharper check on my impulses in future.

There was plenty of traffic around the Wellington Memorial at this hour, and the going was tedious. "What sort of school is Craig Thomas?" he asked chattily.

I just managed to stop myself, and then said, "It's an excellent school."

"The best in Bombay?"

"Better."

"Then my troubles are over." His bristling array of pips, embossings and military decorations glared threateningly into the corner of my eye and I felt thoroughly intimidated.

"What's your father?" I asked.

"A clergyman."

"*My* father is the most brilliant barrister in Bombay. He's utterly fearless and has never defended anyone in his life. If

72

my father set his mind to it he could send a chap to the gallows for littering."

"That's a comforting thought—for me particularly."

"If *my* father were in the army *he'd* be a General. What are you?"

"Only a major."

"Hmph. Well, we can't all be Generals."

"Christ!" He stamped his brake down in the nick of time. A small boy I happened to know had pulled away from his *ayah* and bolted across the street without looking. Another inch and he'd have caught it.

By and by I asked, "Major, have you ever killed anyone?" He laughed in surprise or embarrassment, and said, "Well, as a matter of fact I have. That is to say——"

"Oh, you needn't make any excuses to *me*, Major," I interrupted softly, "I know exactly what it is to have killed someone."

"You do, eh?"

"Yes, Major, I'm no child, you know." We were just managing to squeeze our way around Waterloo Mansions, and nudging him confidentially I said, "That's a dirty bookshop there. If you want any dirty books, just mention my name."

"Thanks."

"Are you coming to see our Principal?"

"That was sharp. What *is* your name?"

"Franklin—I mean, Joseph."

"Joseph Franklin?"

"Yes, why not?"

"Do you live next to me?"

I stopped myself. That was an old ruse. He wasn't going to catch a son of Abraham Hosea with a chestnut like that. "Why, where do you live?" I asked.

"Next to you, if I'm not mistaken."

"Which side, left or right?"

73

"The side with the pile of junk on the lawn."

"What a filthy lot of bounders these natives are, they've no civic sense." I whipped out my catapult. Then I stopped myself and put it back.

"Why did you do that?"

"D'you see that well-protected-looking chap tucking in his shirt which is already in as tight as a drum? There by the Cowasjee Jehangir Hall. That's Aaron the mugger; I was going to let him have a stinger but changed my mind."

"Why?"

"I'm turning over a new leaf. Yesterday a boy was killed just by my—" I stopped.

"Your what?"

I said nothing, but watched the mugger as we passed by, still desperately tucking in his shirt. "Do you know why some people are always neat and tidy, Major?"

"That is an explanation the Army would give a fortune to know. Why?"

"Because they're afraid of being laughed at."

"And aren't you?"

"No, I've never been afraid of being laughed at. My grandfather was a clown in a Russian circus, you know."

"And he was completely fearless too?"

"Yes."

"And you?"

"I think I've only one fear," I said, "I'm frightened of boring people. Am I boring you, Major?"

"Not a bit. How old are you?"

"That depends," I said cautiously. "Mathematically speaking I'm fourteen."

"Why, that's the very age of the boy for whom I'm inquiring about the schools here."

"Your son, Major?"

"No, I've a daughter, Penelope Ann. You'll meet her——"

74

he stopped himself, "—perhaps. This boy I spoke of is the son of a friend who's on his way over."

"I'll show him the ropes," I offered, at the same time pulling out my history exercise book.

"What are you doing?"

"Homework."

"What, now? Joseph, tell me, where do you stand in class?"

"First. I mean, it depends, yes, why not? First."

He seemed keen to question me further but as we were caught in a jam on the tramlines around Flora Fountain I seized the opportunity to dash the thing down. "Explain the term Scorched Earth policy, giving one example of its application." As I had already done my research on the subject I would have put it all down in a minute were it not that I noticed the Major looking on interestedly. This perturbed me as I knew that a long string of musty historical data would bore him stiff. God, I winced, better a blow on the nose, or ten years in jail. I reframed my answer.

"Scorched Earch policy is a way of winning a war without fighting. You pack up and take your goats and sheep and toothbrush and shaving tackle, and leave the enemy to starve along with your wife and children. Then when your enemy phone to say they've given in you come back. An example of this is when my mother goes berserk my father doesn't come home in the car but sleeps at his chambers. By and by Mum phones to say she's given in and he drives himself back. Concluded."

I saw him reading this with such fascination I could not help but feel a glow of triumph. He was really quite an engaging bloke when one got to the heart and soul of him, I thought. "Did you shoot him, or stab him to death, or strangle him with your bare hands, Major? Or was it a woman?"

We narrowly missed a victoria slowing for the kerb near

75

Cox and Kings, and it wasn't the victoria's fault. This army man seemed to have some personal problem on his mind. "What sort of a man is your Principal, Joseph?"

I stopped myself. "He's a most wonderful man, the best I have known. He hit a beggar at tiffin break, then he hit a servant. Yesterday he was going to knock down St. Paul, but was hit by a weighted rope that thick." I showed him.

"I see." He accelerated to make the most of a long break in the traffic, and seemed anxious to get there as quickly as possible. "What do they teach best at your school?"

"To level up." As I was now working on my map of the world showing ocean currents, he very politely said nothing more till we got to Bori Bunder. "Here's the school, Major, the big green building." I was keen to be seen walking in with a magnificent figure of a man like him, especially today of all days, as I calculated it would help me in some strange way in whatever was to come. And as luck would have it, Now Now turned up at the same time.

"Here's the prince's Terraplane coming in," I said, not a little proudly. "The prince's nephew attends our school too, and we also have a rajah's cousin."

"All the best people come to Craig Thomas then," he said, swinging the car around to stop nose to nose with the Terraplane right opposite the gates.

I was first on the pavement, and was greeted by Now Now, who was puffing his way out. I had nothing to fear from him at the moment as I had already recalled he had left early yesterday and would not know anything just yet.

"Hunno, Noe."

"Hunno, Now Now. How's nings gnawing we due?"

"Oh, Knees is! I'd a nerry bin dime nas nige. My ungelder may wince needle gum nil mid nige." He waddled through the gates slapping back his satchel disgruntledly.

"Nins um, Now Now," I consoled him. "Nings good me nurse."

76

I'd left the car door open for the Major to get out. He leaned forward. "Tell me, laddie, what language is that?"

"English."

He pulled the door shut, and restarted the engine.

"Aren't you coming into school, Major?"

He replied something which I couldn't hear for the noise of acceleration.

For a few more moments I stood there, gloomily watching the blue haze of his exhaust spread and disappear; and while I had no concrete evidence to back my pessimism, I had a pretty shrewd hunch that if I had not presented the Major with my transformation all in one lump, or done it in more gradual stages, our meeting would have ended in much the same way. Those Hindu chaps were dead right. Everything was predestined; effort, futile. I tried with all the power in me to avoid looking right in my walk across the pavement, but it was hopeless. I was destined to see. A semi-circular tract around the post on the kerb was scrubbed hideously clean.

Dear Miss Gilbert,
   I love you beyond all earthly delights,
                                    Yours faithfully,
                                    Joseph Franklin Hosea

I only saw Miss Gilbert when I was sent for by the Principal. She was his secretary, and we were old friends. Most times I merely wrote, "I love you." It was when the expected penalty was too terrible to comprehend that I added "deeply", "most dearly", or "more than I can express". Indeed on trifling occasions I'd written, "I am quite fond of you." Whatever their content, however, these letters had all to be very brief on account of the short time permitted me *en route* to his office; because even when I knew the day before he was going to send for me, nothing, no power on earth could have induced me to compose a more elaborate *billet doux* until I saw the axe actually rising. It was then, and only then, that I fell in love with Miss Gilbert; passionately, tenderly, or just *en passant* as it were—depending on the size of the axe.

Today was extraordinary in that it was not the Principal's peon who came for me. I found it profoundly upsetting that the whole ritual of the proceedings was altered. Mr. Titmus, before stepping into the class to call the roll, gestured me silently out into the corridor, and told me not to go to prayers, but to see the Principal instead.

"Instead of prayers, sir?"

"Yes. Immediately."

"Before the roll, sir?"

"Before the roll."

"But when you call my name, who shall answer for me?"

"I shall answer for you, Joseph. And another thing: after school I want you to stay in and see me."

The way he spoke and the fact he addressed me by my first name gave me much help in bearing up against the next blow that struck. Miss Gilbert's office was in the ante-room of the Principal's, and it was from her that I used to get the go-in signal. She wasn't there. Of course not. Miss Gilbert was devoutly religious, and always attended prayers. She in fact played the organ. I put the note on her desk anyway, and sat quietly down on the bench reserved for such occasions in the hope I would not be noticed; then I could always say I was there all the time.

"That you, Hosea?"

"Yes, sir!" I went in pushing the swing-door at the same mark I had reserved for myself. It was getting quite grimy.

"Is it very like you not to make your presence felt?"

"No, sir, yes."

He had on a pair of spectacles with different coloured rims, and this pipe was more curved and bulbous than the other. A snaky venomous sort of pipe; if ever there was a pipe the

78

opposite of the pipe of peace, that was it. He was reading a boy's exercise book laid exposed in front of him, and it was with a curious thrill of horror that I noticed it was one of mine. That Mr. Titmus should be reading it was in order, but seeing the Principal poking and peering at the pages I felt I was in a room naked with some vile-eyed reprobate at the keyhole.

He turned to the latest effort. " 'The Wisdim of Slomon the Wise.' " He read in a series of tuba-like grunting sounds. " 'So these 2 womin took the baby kicking and yelling to Slomon the Wise and said, 'Deside.' 'Get a chopper,' desided Slomon the Wise, 'and chop that brat and take half each.' 'I bags the head!' screeched womin 1. 'I bags the head!' squaked womin 2. 'Chop lengthwise,' ejacklated Slomin the Wise. So they chopped it up and thank the Lord it stopped and all was peace and quite in the world and they went off with a bit each chuckling. 'So who d'you think was the mother Slomon?' yawned Sheba raising herself perpendickularly. 'Eh?' 'There's somethings we needn't ever know,' smirked Slomon the Wise. Concluded.' "

As he was reading I could hear the seven hundred minus one boys filing into the main hall for prayers. He seemed unaware of the noise and was probably so accustomed to it as a background to his duties he did not hear it at all.

"It's not my intention, Hosea, to appraise this document for its literary merit. I leave that to Mr. Titmus. What perturbs me is its immorality. It is corrupt, and shows a mind that could be injurious in its influence on other boys. But this is not the reason why I sent for you this morning. Do you know why I sent for you?"

"Let us pray," came the Revd. Dewey's voice faintly from below.

"Well *do* you?"

"Yes, sir," I mumbled. "It's about Sutherland."

"What other land?"

"Nothing, sir."

"Tell me, Hosea, were you or were you not the author of that limerick about Mr. Latto in Std. 7?"

"—in the name of the Father, the Son and the Holy Ghost——"

"Yes, I was, sir."

"Amen."

He reached for his cane, but as was part of these rituals he gave me his usual talking to. The tone of voice he used mixed capitally well with the concerted mumble coming up from the hall, and I found my attention shuttling freely between the two.

"—not only Mr. Latto——"

"—which art in Heaven, hallowed be Thy Name, Thy Kingdom come, Thou wilt be done on earth as it is done in Heaven——"

"—and while I know no kind of punishment will make you atone for what you have done——"

"—give us this day our daily bread, and forgive us our trespasses, and we will forgive them their trespass against us——"

"Bend over, Hosea."

"—for Thine is the Kingdom——"

Whack! Whack!

"—of Power and Glory——"

Whack! Whack!

"—for ever and ever—"

Whack! Whack!

"—Amen."

"No, not finished yet, boy." Whack! "Right you are then."

"We will now turn to Hymns Ancient and Modern No. 347."

The warm, soft, comforting strains of the organ came ringing out. "Tuck your shirt in and go back to your classroom."

> *"Jerusalem the Golden,*
> *With milk and honey blest,*
> *Beneath thy contemplation,*
> *Sing heart and voice oppressed.*
> *I know not, oh, I know not,*
> *What social joys await us——"*

I picked up the note on Miss Gilbert's desk, and stowed it away in my pocket.

My fears of being openly and by insinuation accused of Sutherland's death were soon proved unfounded. How forcibly did my Jewishness strike me that morning. Only a dyed-in-the-wool Semite could have been capable of such guilt-ridden self-consciousness. A man was presently to die of thirst in the Sahara, and it was I who was withholding water from him. With what uncanny readiness had I presumed that the moment the school heard of the accident they would cry, "What's that scoundrel Hosea's part in it?" The general reaction in point of fact reflected off something entirely removed.

Early in the year when Sutherland had first come to our school he'd been struck down by a taxi on Hornby Road. It was a minor accident, and he'd returned to school a day or so later with a few bruises and a couple of stitches in his knee. Why had I not connected this with the second accident? Could I not have shaken my head regretfully, like they all did, and passed it on from tongue to tongue, Hindu to Parsee, to Moslem and so on? "That poor chap Sutherland, he was *always* being knocked down by motor-cars, he was fated."

No, I couldn't, for I was a Jew. I just had to rush off scattering sackcloth and ashes like Judas Iscariot, crying, "I did it! I did it!" and hang myself from a tree. Poor fellow, if the truth was he had done nothing of the sort in that year of A.D. 35 he will have been the butt of some sort of joke—not

81

the best joke in the world of course, though certainly the longest. It was in fact still going on, and I would there and then have laughed myself silly were it not that I was guffawing over my own little one. To think I could hardly come to school today in the dread of having to face some Court of Judgement.

That morning passed off with less incident than usual, no little thanks due to the return of those pillars, the solid citizens of Bombay, the Parsees. The only absentee was Wilfred. Mr. Titmus waited till his first period after prayers before marking him on the register, as he was often late, but never till now, absent. I did not give the matter any thought, as it had nothing to do with me, although Mr. Titmus did appear to look inquiringly in my direction. I looked back at him blankly, very blankly indeed. What was I? Wilfred Prior's keeper?

At tiffin I found that St. Paul was unable to secure my accustomed place, but I soon cut short his apologies. "Kooch nai ficker, roj roj dusra jugga lugao." I further made it clear that the once cherished spot by the stairs was the last place in the shed I wanted—though of course I did not explain how strongly I now felt that Miss Entwhistle, or her absence—I cared not what—had provoked me to commit a very dangerous piece of mischief yesterday.

All the same, however delighted I was by his failure to get that now distasteful position, it was my misfortune this afternoon to find the five bespectacled faces of the brothers Shalom confronting me. Furthermore, the mugger's servant stood on my left, and L. S. D. Levy's on my right. An all-Jewish Tribunal, to be sure. I wondered what else was going to contribute to an unrestful lunch, and instinctively looked upward. The rope was attached in the same place, but now chained to the railing with a padlock. To be spared the ordeal of Damocles was something I was grateful for, and as tiffin progressed I made the most of the opportunity to take that, alas, ever-diminishing comfort from the fact.

82

I did not anticipate any direct assault from the Shaloms, nor did I get it. They took eating seriously and were generally in the tiffin shed first, second, third, fourth and fifth out of five hundred. Completely silent all the way through— if gobbling vulture noises were to be discounted as conversational offerings—they were this afternoon having their favourite dish: curry, rice and meatballs—that is to say, one meatball in descending order of size apiece, no more no less. This crowning part of their dish surmounted the lava-like spread of the curry, which in turn overlay the white hill of rice completely, except at its very base. Now while I in my method of attack went for the meatball first, and then worked on the baser ingredients with as much enthusiasm as I could retain, the Shaloms did it the right way. They spun their plates in an anti-clockwise direction, the same preordained motion of the celestial heavens, eating the tasteless, untinctured rice around the periphery first. This done, they began to spiral into curryland, each spoonful going down with increasing relish, till at last, the *coup de grâce*: the meatball.

The precision of their attack, from oldest to young, was a scathing reminder of my feckless way of life, and in my occassionally serious conjectures of Judgement Day, my resourceless imagination could never overleap the fact that David, Ezra, Saul, Isaac and Benjamin would be there, silently and accusingly working their way up to their meatballs, exactly as they were doing now. But for the moment I had nothing to grumble about, I had to concede. They weren't eating *me*. All things considered, I was the luckiest boy in the school. Last night I had been under sentence. Now I was free.

"You and Wilfred," groused the mugger, suddenly turning up. He usually spent ten minutes washing his hands before eating for the sake of the germs. "What happened to you two yesterday? I looked around for you when the ambulance came, and you'd both disappeared."

"I wonder who keeps the key of the padlock," I said.

83

"Where were you when the accident occurred? I was on the pavement on the blind side of the bus, or I'd have seen the whole thing. Same as——" He frowned suddenly, his fork hovering in the vapour of an immense baked potato. His food was still piping hot, since *his* servant had the special model tiffin carrier with a compartment for live coals at the bottom; and as he gradually sank his fork into the heart of the potato it seemed to utter a sigh of lament. Out of the corner of my eye I saw him turn to look at me, while in front the machinery of rotation went inexorably on. Then L. S. D. Levy turned up, rocking the bench in squeezing in.

"How many whacks did the Prin give you, Joe?" I made as if I could not answer with my mouth full of food. "What did he haul you up for, Joe?" On and on the cogs turned. I saw Wilfred's face as I had seen it last, the drr-dutt drr-dutt, the snap of the trap, Dorothy's extraordinarily high-pitched scream, "Why *should* I, Gladys?" The mugger digging his indubitably clean fingernail into my thigh, the breath of his baked-potato whisper in my ear. "I just thought of something. Wilfred was on the same side of the pavement facing the bus when Sutherland got killed. I was looking at him. He saw the whole thing happen at point-plank range."

One by one the Shaloms had undercut their meatballs. With lumps of bread they wiped their plates clean. They drank large tumblers of water to clear their tongues of any interfering tastes. They cut their meatballs into halves, quarters, eighths; and then, and only then did they begin, slowly, maddeningly slowly, to think of eating them.

"Jaldi khana khow, Joe baba. Gurmi bhot kham hai."

"Go on, tell us, Joe. How many whacks and what did he haul you up for?"

"If Wilfred saw what was happening why didn't he call 'Cave!' or something? If it had been me, Sutherland——"

"Look here, Mugger!" I yelled. The noise around us instantly diminished. "You know my mother's on the Committee for the Bengal Famine Relief?" For the first time the vulture heads looked up. "Well she's got to sell a hundred raffle tickets, only four annas each."

"Is that so, now?"

"Yes, I knew you'd be interested. She's got to go into hospital and asked me to sell them for her. I said I would be only too delighted to aid in the saving of so many thousands of human lives. Gosh, you should see those photographs of those poor Bengalis, make your heart bleed; all skin and bone and dying off in the streets. Anyone like to buy a raffle ticket? The first prize is a four-seater Austin so if you chaps club together in groups of four and donate an anna each——"

"See you in class, Joe, got homework to do." He hoisted himself up by my shoulder. Those meatballs had vanished seconds ago, followed in quick succession by two Parsees and a Hindu. A son of Mahomet was on his way out now, and perhaps one day it would move the mountain too. Why not? It had worked wonders on that first occasion before the long-delayed commencement of the monsoon, when my mother, in one of her fey bursts of enthusiasm, had attempted to dispose of tickets in this way; and I saw no reason, no reason in the world, why it should not continue to do so to the end of my days. When I was gasping for a bit of solitude, when my love for humanity and Hitler's were one, I spoke of selling flags for good causes. There were no ugly bloodstains, no body-disposal squads. People just vanished. Occasionally in the spirit of sheer mischief I would corner them like rats and watch them squirm. It was incredible: the number and variety of loopholes in a perfectly air-tight trap. The Jews said they would like to give, but were starving themselves; the Moslems said that Allah would provide; the Hindus declared it was all predestined; the Parsees would give if I erected statues of them; and the Christians gave regularly to a much greater cause. It was just as well, I reflected, I had no tickets.

"I'll buy one, Joe. Here's the money. I know what it is to

starve. It's not nice, is it?" His soft, misty brown eyes moved easily to tears. He believed in me. He was my burden.

"Jaldi khana khao, Joe baba. Bhot tuklif hogia."

The shed was almost empty now. Rather needlessly I looked up. Yes, it had fallen, quite some time ago. But on whom? I felt his hand, his warm, moist, trusting hand on my shoulder, and I wanted to slam his big, dense face. "For God's sake keep your money, Levy; what happens in Bengal you didn't cause. Forget it, you're free."

Taking advantage of the fact that our servants had removed our feeding things, he crept in closer. "Joe, you're the most understanding chap I've ever met. If I tell you a secret, you won't let it out, will you?"

"Why tell me at all?"

"I've got to tell someone, Joey, I just have to."

"All right then, get it over with; I've got homework to do."

His voice dropped to such a whisper that even in the now empty confines of the shed I could hardly hear him. "Do you know who made that rope fall on the Principal yesterday? Me. It was because I tied it so sloppily."

"Did you really?"

"Yes, it's the truth. All night I was wondering how I could face coming to school today. I wanted to sham sick; I thought everyone would notice that our class had Gym the last period the day before, and I was the chap picked to tie the rope. But no one said a word, not a single word. Isn't it fantastic? D'you think the Prin might send for me yet?"

The tables were empty. The food had been removed. The trash-bin lid had clanked its last, and the sepoy stationed to move beggars on had taken the cue himself to depart. And then came the servants employed by the school. Working in pairs from the far end of the shed, they took up the boards and tripods that served as tables in readiness for the Gym in the afternoon. And soon they would come for the one we were at, but we still had a minute, so we sat and sat. And whispered like children.

"Shall I tell you another secret, Joe?"

"Yes, you do that, Lee."

"I saw who it was who wrote Tits on the board." The noise was approaching, they weren't far now. "I'll give you a clue. It was——" Bang! I started up as though shot, but it was only a fellow who'd let fall a board. "It was the same chap who——"

"Are you accusing me, Levy?" I threatened, suddenly turning on him.

"No, I'm not——"

"Then you're accusing someone else. Admit it, aren't you?"

"I suppose," he blinked, slowly wiping his face with his hand. "Well, I suppose I am. It was——"

"You don't *have* to accuse anyone, do you, Levy?"

"No, all I'm saying is the chap was—aiee! What's the big idea? Let go damnit!" I gripped tighter, but the confounded stuff was heavily oiled, and the harder I gripped the quicker it slipped, or I'd have torn out a handful by the roots. Both disappointed and disgusted I wiped the residue on his shirt, and said, "D'you get my meaning? You don't *have* to accuse anyone. You just keep your big trap shut or I'll go straight to the Prin and tell him who let fall the rope, see?"

He nodded. He was convinced. The table moved as strong brown hands laid hold of it, and he got up still dumbly nodding. He knew. There was no joy in suicidal resistance.

"You should not suppose for one moment that what you see going on around you are true representations of Christ's teachings. There are many unlabelled Christians like Mahatma Gandhi in the world, but only one true Church of Christ."

So that was what was at the bottom of him. A firebug— religious cracklings. He didn't know I had been singed before;

87

rumour had it he did not mix with the other masters. But in this particular case he did not need to; my expression must have been enough, if it was anything like Dorothy's on the same subject, and he branched off in another direction.

It was exactly a week later. I hadn't stayed in the afternoon he'd asked me to, as I'd forgotten. And he hadn't mentioned the matter the next day, or the next, though I had my excuse ready. He was a real softie. I did my best not to take advantage of him, and some of the chaps complained I was favouring him. "Why did you suddenly remember I'd asked you to stay in a week ago? Why didn't you come when called?"

"I forgot, sir."

"Why did you forget?"

"Because I'm not afraid of you, sir."

"Do you suppose I need to strike fear into you to make you obey?"

"Everyone does it, sir."

"Everyone in this school I can understand. What did the Principal say to you that morning?"

"Six or seven whacks, sir."

"He said six or seven whacks?"

"Oh, he spoke about things first, sir, like morality and stuff."

"You didn't believe him?"

"No, and neither did he."

"What makes you say that?"

"He caned me, sir."

"You've no idea, Hosea," he said for the first time raising his voice, "how difficult it is in a school of this kind, with boys of seven different religions and a dozen separate and intermixed races, not to resort to caning. With no common spiritual authority to appeal to, it is very easy to install the brute one."

I put my hands in my pockets and jingled the coins. It was not that I wished to take advantage of his meek nature, but simply that it was my most comfortable standing position. He appeared to notice, as a faint pink flush stole into his face. He said nothing however so I continued jingling the coins.

"The Principal told you that he thought your essay on Solomon immoral, didn't he?"

"He told you too, sir?"

"Yes, at grave length."

"And what did you reply?" I asked him curiously.

"I told him I did not think it could be either moral or immoral, since it was incomplete."

"But I did finish it, sir, I wrote Concluded."

"I wish you wouldn't, ever. No, Hosea, nothing you have ever done was completed. You are incomplete as a person. You dwarf, you are less than small, you are a piece of something abandoned in the making. You are less than junk, which had its use at some time in the past."

I gaped at him, stunned more by the unexpectedness than the fury of his attack; though fury there was, fury of a kind. "Would you like me to give you a sample?" I nodded. "Do you remember what the Queen of Sheba said as she raised herself perpendicularly? She asked who *was* the real mother of the baby they'd so accurately chopped in half. Do I quote you correctly?" I nodded. "Solomon never answered her. He said, 'There are some things we needn't ever know.' Concluded. But what *is* the answer?"

I licked my lips. "Sir, I suppose neither of them was the real mother."

"That's what I thought. Why were they fighting for it then?"

"Because neither of the greedy, dog-in-the-manger whores wanted the other to have it!" Of the two of us I thought I was the more surprised by my outburst, which for the life of me sprang out of nowhere. "Sorry, sir," I muttered.

"Concluded," he replied, with a wry sort of smile. "You know, Hosea, there's no such thing as immorality. An act is either concluded and moral, or else it is unconcluded and amoral. Do you know what amoral is?"

"No, sir."

"It is morality suspended through laziness, cowardice, lovelessness. It is unChristian——" He stopped and sighed. "I expect I am taxing your understanding."

"No, sir, go on, I understand every word."

"Never mind, another time. I wanted to ask you about your friend, Wilfred Prior. Why has he been absent all these days? Have you been to see him?"

"No, sir, I don't know anything about him."

"He's no father?"

"I don't know, sir." I paused and added, "Once I was complaining to him about my dad——"

"I notice you do."

"—and he said, 'It's better to have a bad dad than no dad.' So I suppose his old man died. He came with his mother from Lahore at the beginning of the year, and lives with his aunt."

"And his mother?"

"I've never seen her. I think she lives in a posh flat in Marine Drive."

"How's that?"

"Don't know, sir, none of my business."

"The Sutherlands are also from Lahore."

"Oh, are they?"

"Nickie Sutherland and Prior went to the same school."

"Well, fancy that."

"They were in the same class in fact."

"Well, fancy that."

"All right, Hosea, that will be all. If you do happen to be passing his house——"

"Sir, I wanted to ask you something. What shall I do with this pice?" I showed him one of the silver coins I had been fingering in my pocket.

90

"Isn't a pice bronze?"

"Yes, sir, a couple of weeks ago in the Lab Prior told me if I rubbed silver nitrate on it, it would turn silver. It worked, but the trouble is I can't spend it now. I tried to buy a pice worth a gram from the chunnawallah near the gates, and he gave me the chunna together with seven annas three pice change."

"He thought it was eight annas?"

"Yes, sir, I showed him it had no milled edge, and that nearly sent him off his head. He snatched back his chunna and the change and practically threw the pice in my face. It's a bit annoying, all this time jingling about in my pocket, and I daren't spend it, because even if someone does take it as a pice *he* might pass it off for silver."

"I see you have a problem here to tax Solomon the Wise. This is not a coincidence, you know. When you have a major problem that remains unsolved, everything you encounter automatically becomes a facet of it. And this coin is just that: one of the facets of your problem; your dealings with the counterfeit. When this story ends we'll have a morality, so keep me informed, will you? In the meantime I'm sure you want to be off, so——"

"Sir," I implored, "there's just one more thing. Could you set me two or three hundred lines?"

He gaped at me dumbfounded. The sun had now sunk low enough to flood the classroom, and checker the floor and desks with patterns of light and shade. Motes swam in front of his china-blue eyes enhancing his confused expression. He was really quite a nice-looking man. "But I don't understand. Apart from anything wrong you've done, it is not my policy to set lines. I am against punishment of any kind."

"Yes, sir, I know," I pleaded. "You're very strict about not punishing us, but from all what you said, and I want to tell you, sir, in all honesty, I believed you," a great lump rose in my throat, "I thought you wouldn't mind giving me a few

91

lines out of charity—you know——" I stifled back a sob, "Ch-Ch-Christian charity, sir."

"Hosea," he said, his eyes beginning to narrow suspiciously, "aren't you due to play for your House this evening? I do recall seeing on the Rugger notice-board——"

I burst into tears. "Th-th-that's right, sir. It's n-not that I m-mind or-ordinarily, sir, but in these H-House matches they put me scrum-half because I'm quick and s-s-small and all those big—uh-uh-uh-uh——" I wept, "h-h-hefty chaps from the upper c-c-classes—uh-uh-uh-uh——"

"Stop it at once! I said stop it!"

"A-A-And it h-hasn't rained for d-d-days and d-days the g-g-ground's as h-h-hard as r-r-rock—uh-uh-uh-uh-uh——"

"At once! This instant! Shame on you!"

"Uh-uh-uh-uh-uh——"

"So that's why you decided to be kept in today, you conscienceless vermin!"

"Uh-uh-uh-uh-uh-uh——"

"All right then, all right, confound you, boy! Take three hundred lines. Write, 'I must be complete' in your best hand, understand?"

"Y-Y-Yes, sir, th-thhank you, sir, s-s-s-s-sorry, sir." I blew my nose gratefully.

"You see why you resort to these miserable tawdry pieces of trickery, don't you? You hollow, abject, unfinished buffoon. There's nothing in your head, nothing in your soul. Nothing but what is counterfeit." He slapped a pile of books in front of him and began to correct them—or tried his best to. "You snatcher, you grab at any coloured whim that happens to be floating around, and in a second it's gone. You shiftless child, you prince of impermanence—oh don't nod and think you're unique. I've met a hundred like you; you know where? In an orphanage! They, poor creatures. had an excuse, but you? Have you a father?"

"Yes, sir."

"A mother?"

"Yes, sir. And two Grandmas and a Grandpa."

"You have no excuse!"

I let him rage on, as I knew he'd burn himself out like my mother always did. I used to hear such sounds emanating from my parents' bedroom, with my father's quiet interjections coming through too. "Yes, dear, yes. Quite so, precisely. I know perfectly how you feel." They were the only sort of replies one could make to another in that state, and as they were easily said I did not let them interrupt my work. I got on with my lines, looking up attentively whenever a fresh burst of indignation came out of him. I nodded appeasingly, and uttered indistinct noises of agreement. And eventually he calmed down.

The sounds of late departing boys died one by one away. The checkered patterns crept slowly up the wall. We worked on silently and as a team, I thought. And when next he spoke it was in his usual voice. "Who'll play scrum-half instead of you?"

"They always have a reserve for me, sir, as I'm never trusted to turn up."

"You're quite happy about it, aren't you?"

"I'm very happy, sir." I could not recall ever being quite as happy as this, though. I was not even worried that it would end, for I had a feeling deep inside of me that there would be many many more evenings just like this.

"What's that you're singing?"

"Who, me, sir?"

"Yes, you were singing."

"I didn't realize I was singing *aloud*, sir."

"It was loud enough. Sounded like a mixture of east and west."

"That's the Goanese style. My ayah used to sing that at bedtime, just a bit of childish nonsense."

" 'Daddy's in the court house?' "

93

"Yes, yes, sir, just nonsense."

"You're embarrassed. Are you actually capable of human feelings?" I did not answer, but carried on rather more quickly now. "That writing looks very good from here, I must say. How many lines have you done?"

"I don't know, sir, the sun's not gone anyway."

"You must have done well over three hundred. Hand them up and that will be enough." I passed them over, and carried on writing just as determinedly as ever.

I must be complet.
I must be complet.
I must be complet.
I must be complet.
I must be complet.
I must be complet.
I must be complet.
I must be complet.
I must be complet.
I must be complet.
I must be complet.
I must be complet.
I must be complet.
I must be complet.
I must be complet.
I must be complet.
I must be complet.
I must be complet.
I must be complet.
I must be complet.
I must be complet.
I must be complet.
I must be complet.
I must be complet.
I must be complet.

I must be complet.
I must be complet.
I must be complet.
I must be complet.
I must be complet.
I must be complet.
I must be complet.
I must be complet.
I must be complet.
I must be complet.
I must be complet.
I must be complet.
I must be complet.
I must be complet.
I must be complet.
I must be complet.
I must be complet.
I must be complet.
I must be complet.
I must be complet.
I must be complet.
I must be complet.
I must be complet.
I must be complet.
I must be complet.
I must be complet.
I must be complet.
I must be complet.
I must be complet.
I must be complet.
I must be complet.
"Go home, Hosea."
I must be complet.
I must be complet.

I must be——

"Did you hear what I said, boy?"

"Yes, sir."

"What?"

"You asked if I heard what you said, sir."

I set off from school about half an hour later with two errands to run for Mr. Titmus. The first was to go and see Wilfred; the second, to achieve greatness. The former was openly requested, but the latter, which I felt was even more insistent, was my logical interpretation of the demand he had made me copy out several hundred times. What could being complete mean but the achieving of greatness? And what could greatness mean? Not physical greatness (that was the folly of the frog), but the fulfilment of a single undivided ambition. I was grateful to Mr. Titmus, and that sense of gratitude, like some hymn of thanksgiving, seemed to achieve in practical terms the very proof of his teachings. Without realizing it he had shown me what a poor father I had. Abraham Hosea had told me to turn over a new leaf; but there were no leaves to turn. Nor could I change, like a bug into a butterfly, since I was not even a bug; I was nothing. I was a hard callous husk that needed to be filled—filled with a single burning resolve; and to this I was set on sacrificing all personal pleasures.

The evening which had started so clear was rapidly clouding up. It looked like we were going to continue with the monsoon at last, and I had no mac. I could have taken a tram but had already spent my fare on sesame-seed toffee. Such minor setbacks had to be taken in one's stride, however, and I walked on immersed in thoughts of glorious undertakings, scarcely noticing the people I bumped into.

At Flora Fountain, apart from the hazards of crossing through the traffic which was always particularly congested here, I came to a halt before the First Parsee Member of

Parliament. And the sight of the familiar, magnified figure made me realize with no little misgivings that I was standing here, not a whit different a person from the one who had stood here yesterday, immersed in daydreams of the vaguest kind: procrastinating. It was all very well to crowd one's empty little mind with visions of greatness, but were they in fact any better than air? Again I recalled that wretched frog and my depression deepened. I had to decide what exactly I was to achieve greatness in. Would I be a politician? I might be. Then again I might not. To be so specific on such a matter at a moment like this was acutely confusing; and that was the only honest decision I could come to. So here I stood by the pedestal, thus, little realizing whether in fifty years I would return to this historic spot, or not, to remember how as an unknown boy I stood thus, little realizing that in fifty years I would, or would not, return to stand thus: a tall—no, not tall, but none the less distinguished, silver-bearded man, top hat in hand, in full salute to the march past of the massed bands of the King's Own Scottish Borderers, the cheers of the millions, not unmingled with regret, as they remembered how they passed that unknown boy thus, little realizing that in fifty years he would be returning to revisit this historic spot, as Prime Minister of England. Yes, but what would I do in the meantime? Wait. And when I got hungry? Eat. And then? Wait. And when I get bored? Play. And then? Wait. And when I fell in love? Marry. And then? Wait. And when I got old? Get older yet. And then? Wait. Wait! Wait! Wait! What sort of a life was this? I would not enjoy eating, or playing, falling in love, marrying, growing older, because I would be waiting! waiting! waiting! as I was waiting now, with the precious minutes of my life slipping unsavoured down the drain.

"Lucky face, sir. Tell your fortune?"

I looked up. A Sikh fortune-teller was approaching and saw the danger in the nick of time. Thus, little realizing how,

97

as an unknown boy, I would be turning my back on that historic spot, never to remember, never to return, I bolted in the direction of the West End Watch Company where the crowds were thickest, and the secret of my ambition mercifully lost.

Was I down-hearted? Down-hearted for what, my hairsbreadth escape from a horror worse than life-imprisonment? Not terribly. My abrupt resignation from the above-mentioned post, although it would cause no stir in the Commons, I regarded as the greatest of my personal triumphs. And how elated I was to have discovered so early in my career, before the first wave of enthusiasm, this heritage of my woeful mother, could gather sufficient strength to dash me to my doom, that—my own greatness aside—there was an enormous fund of happiness to be derived from knowing what one is *not* suited to be. So far, so good. What next then? It was not enough to sow; one had to go and reap; and reap I did. Aye, and what a harvest was there at the entrance of Vallabhai Mahal, in the bounteous and ever-growing proliferation of signs that festooned it. These were the people; everyone of them blandly telling the world what they had achieved; people who'd discovered their stations in life. Ha! Ha! I, for one, knew better. Were not the greater part of them simply, and how pathetically, clinging to childhood ambitions that had long since withered and fallen away? Egyptians; worshippers of the dead.

The boards, flaked and faded, grimed with dust, looked very like entrance signs to tombs; and amongst the more mundane offerings of solicitors, dentists, horoscope readers, yogis and estate agents, were some I particularly rejoiced in.

PAINLESS LOVE TATTOO CO. INC.

TATTOOISTS TO H.M. KING OF DENMARK

RAPID REMOVALS

J. J. PINTO SARTORIAL RESORT   DR.RAMDAS M.D. MEHTA

SUITABLE SUITINGS   IMPOTENT SPECIALIST

GHERKINS MADE TO ORDER

PRIVATE TUITION
K. R. D. V. CHAUDRI B.A. (failed)

For one who saw the secret of happiness in discovering what one was *not* suited to be, he could not have spent a more pleasurable hour in the world than the entrance of Vallabhai Mahal. And my spirits soared, alighting from one musty cracked old board to the next, blithe as a bee in a bed of piquant flowers. I felt the wind catch me now, and rejoicing as I did in all things natural, let it sweep me on and on to the great black horse at Khala Ghora. I was so transported by my mafficking ride, I did not notice what was happening in the sky, and it was more by luck than planning that I arrived in the arcade of the Sassoon Library the minute the rain came lashing down.

We were life members, but the library had no attraction for me whatsoever. I gave it a wider berth than the one at school, as it was larger; and nothing so distressed me as to be in the centre of a vast accumulation of either people or books that had, and would have nothing to do with me, but to demand so much of what I had so little: SILENCE. The longest I had ever spent there at one stretch was a heart-breaking fifteen minutes at the shelves of the *Encyclopædia Britannica*. Although I was only ten years of age at the time, I had unassisted become aware how big a headache I would have been saved if I'd found my name and however sketchy an account of my doings there. But I proved myself on that occasion too, to be unduly optimistic. All I discovered to my profound annoyance, some other Hosea already there.

Today I found my point of interest in the shop window in the same building: LUND AND BLOCKLEY JEWELLERS WATCHMAKERS—especially in my present state. It was not the shop window itself that was the source of so much attraction (to an audience of other boys as well), but the two Hindu

99

gents squatting on their heels in close contact with one another. Above their heads the immense clock of all nations ticked variously away, a goldfish swam around a waterproof watch, while before them the gathering of no less than four different nations looked on agog.

The professional member of the couple was in a pale yellow turban, with a small shoulder-slung satchel of instruments, which in the squatting position lay open on the pavement. His client had his turban off, and his head attentively acock not so much by choice but thanks to the way the other grasped him, humming as he worked a tune meant to soothe. The operator, like most professionals, was impassive to it all, but not so his client, whose expression was a grimace, partly smiling, at the prospect of pain.

"Aaaah!" Sounds of anticipation went up from the audience as with the skill of a conjuror a probe appeared. His left hand which all this time had been gripping his customer's ear with thumb and forefinger, so that he could not run away now if he wished to, pulled up higher, and at the same time the thin spatula-tipped instrument dipped out of sight. Came a shuddering gasp, a round of applause, as out appeared an incredible accumulation of orange-hued wax, which he displayed with no little pride to his client, who nodded in the wondrously expressive manner of Hindus: admiring, encouraging, yet at the same time, cautioning. The orange matter now having ceased to serve any useful function both in and out of his client's ear, the professional wiped it off on a spot which could only have been located after centuries of practitioners before him. And then the action was repeated. So I supposed, for I did not have to savour the performance any longer to rejoice in the certainty that the profession of ear-cleaning was not for me.

I elected to suffer the briefest soaking in crossing the road to dash into the private garage between the library and Elphinstone College. It housed a brand-new Studebaker, which was partly the attraction; and I also wanted to find a secluded place in order to redress my experiences. I sat chin in hand on the front fender of the car. How did I feel? I had been happy before, that was certain; for if I had been so fortunate as to have been miserable then, I would not have been suffering such misery now. What had gone wrong? For sure I could see a black, slime-covered, naked man about to redescend into an opened drain flanking the Prince of Wales Museum, and other divers activities proceeding simultaneously in this teeming city of ours, all of which I could well delight in never dedicating my life to; but it was no good kidding myself. The old thrill was gone. The wonder, indeed, was that it had lasted so long. It was counterfeit. I had algebra homework to do, I recalled, and if there was any life in maths it was this: the sum total happiness one could derive from knowing what one was not suited to be was equal to the grief of not knowing what one *was* suited to be.

So I was back where I started. What was I to do to achieve greatness? The rage for action was quite undiminished, but into what should I cast myself? Was I indeed of a cast capable of greatness? The statue of King Edward VII in his plumed hat, astride his stalwart black horse, caught my eye through the flashing rain; at the same time I accidentally knocked the left mudguard of the car. TONG it went in the amplifying confines of the garage, and my heart leapt. The sound coming as it did at a moment when I had argued myself into a dead end pleased me out of all proportion to its musical quality. TONG, I struck it again; and the fact it emitted precisely the same note was strangely comforting. This TONG was permanent; no argument could disprove its existence. I could depend on it for all time, yet I had more than a sneaking suspicion if I struck it often enough it would bore me stiff. The pitfall I had to watch in my over-wrought condition was not to expect too much out of the front left mudguard of a car. If I feared boredom so frightfully then I

101

should make an effort to widen my horizons, be more adventurous. What about the front *right* mudguard? The mascot?

I looked cautiously at it. I didn't know why I should have felt like a thief. I opened my satchel and searched around for my rule as a safe-burglar might look for his jemmy. I struck the mascot. TING, it went. It was in its own way just as good as the TONG, though the feature of this business was that they weren't competing. The TONG was a good TONG and the TING a good TING, and that was an end to it. So I thought, but I was mistaken, and never in my life had I been so far off the mark. The fact they weren't competing did *not* mean the matter was ended. Indeed, if they *were* competing it would have ended sooner; for I had in the next moment struck them together, TONG TONG TING, and it sounded very like the start of GOD SAVE THE KING—more like than I could unblushingly deny, and I at once saw that the consequences of this lack of competition, this harmony, had presented me with a task I could less easily refuse than a boot in the ribs. Thus without further delay, for better or for worse, I rolled up my sleeves and set to.

What I needed now, if I had my tune right, was a note lower than TONG, to wit: TUNG. And this I found by the only method I had at my disposal, trial and error, on the *rear* left mudguard. I now had TONG TONG TING TUNG TONG TING, the whole of the first line, and as far as I could see there were only two things that could possibly have stopped me now: interruption by the owner of the car, or my own physical collapse through exhaustion. It was a large car, and since the rain continued unabated I felt in less danger of the first than the second. It was indeed no musical feat in the ordinary sense to play the first three lines, which after some time I found went: front left mudguard, front left mudguard, mascot, rear left mudguard, front left mudguard, mascot, rear bumper, petrol cap, mascot, front left mudguard, mascot, front left mudguard, rear left mudguard.

102

I was bathed in perspiration at the commencement of the fourth line and at once ran into trouble. Not only was, SEND HIM VICTORIOUS much too high for anything I had hitherto struck, but as I was reaching up to find what I could bang out of the roof, I saw a small Parsee boy in lace-frilled pants staring at me from the rear seat with stark horror in his eyes. My surprise over, I could not for the life of me see what he was frightened of. I hadn't laid a finger on him. He himself had sat there quietly watching me all this while, yet the moment he saw I'd seen him, he screamed. He was going to let out another, when I glowered at him, put my fist inside and shook it under his nose. That seemed to quieten him; and I set about SEND HIM VICTORIOUS, pausing every time I heard him draw a breath to shake my fist at him. The conditions for work were not entirely satisfactory and the best I could do in the circumstances was: front left small lamp, front left small lamp, front left small lamp, front right small lamp, front left headlamp. I was setting about HAPPY AND GLORIOUS, when the blighter started screaming again.

He wasn't looking at me this time, but at a fast approaching, sari-flapping Parsee lady who could well have been his mother. The kid must have been a nut case. He'd kept quiet when he saw me; he screamed when I saw him; he kept quiet when I threatened him; and then started screaming again at the sight of his mother. Much as I would have liked to, I had no opportunity to investigate this curious behaviour as the woman herself appeared no less demented, and seemed to take her offspring's screams as a perfectly valid excuse to start lashing at me with her umbrella. I held my ground thanks to my military training, and parried her blow for blow with my ruler. I myself did not attempt to hit her once, and what reason she had then to run out into the rain again, yelling, "Sorab, Sorab! Police koo bullow!" I hadn't the foggiest.

I calculated I had another minute to work on the National

103

Anthem, but I was tired. The kid's screams were going off like exploding shells in the garage, and the prospect of more trench fighting with the woman and the city police did not so much quell me as make me see reason. What was the row about anyway? It was a question that had brought to an abrupt end many of my battles in the past, and I withdrew. Collecting my things I walked slowly into the arcade of Elphinstone College. No one as dejected as I could have hurried. If the police caught me they were welcome. Perhaps they could have made something of me, for I myself had failed. What had I been doing? Memory was the key to progressive endeavour. Had I forgotten I'd given up hammering tunes on other people's cars when I was ten? Half an hour ago I was drawing the biggest breath of my life in order to take my first leap into manhood, and then had backslid into childhood. I wrenched my thumb out of my mouth. I'd have bitten it off, it offended me so; but the sight of a handless leper in the arcade with his begging bowl clutched in the air with his toes encouraged me to seek another solution.

There came a time in the life of a bloke when he needed advice. Even bad advice was all right—from the right person, someone who could fill one's head with the vision of greatness without having uttered one word about it. And in the end it was either that or nothing: a life in which the most trifling decision seemed beyond one's scope. For ten minutes I had been hanging around the Sir Cowasjee Jehangir Hall debating whether to cross, or turn right into Mayo Road. There was no apparent need for my indecision because I was homeward bound and either way would take me there with equal celerity. Certain questions occurred to me—very simple ones which a week ago I would have answered without hesitation if I'd troubled myself to do so. Now I found instead of going directly to the point I hung around it wondering what Mr. Titmus would have thought; for a bad answer from him would have been more attractive than any from myself, and none, most grievous of all.

What was happening to me? Apart from the excitement of this new and strangely arisen association, I felt simultaneously apprehensive of losing my independence in a field where I had hitherto never sought advice, neither my own nor anyone else's. I had run wild. No one was going to make me do anything I didn't want to, not even Mr. Titmus. Although I had said I would see Wilfred, deep down I had no intention of doing so. I had avoided speaking of him in general, as the past week I had been hoping more and more that Wilfred, like his former friend Sutherland, would for some reason or other cease coming to school altogether. I had come to loathe the very thought of him. He was a traitorous scab who deserved to be exterminated and hung up for the crows.

During the time of twilight yesterday I was on the wild reclamation land approximately between Churchgate and the sea. The virgin vegetation was just getting a grip on the rich soil, and while there were no trees yet, the entire area was a patchwork of bushes and clumps of towering elephant-grass: ideal ground for games like Cops and Robbers. I was making my way back home at the time, as it was hardly the place to be trapped in after dark, being associated with gruesome stories of goondas who murdered for less than the shoes on one's feet. From time to time I heard mysterious rustlings, but after years of exploring in such areas I could tell lizard from rat, let alone human. And in any case, what if it was human? I had an itch for one, goonda or not, as I was frankly bored to death with myself. I had all evening been regretful of the fact the mugger had not come with me, for I had yelled for him soon after tea in the hope of getting him to accompany me to see Wildred. He'd yelled back he'd homework to do, and during my attempts at persuasion which had to carry through the traffic on the Causeway and ascend two floors, his father had appeared at the adjoining window. And that was an end

105

to the matter, as I was not approved of by the tribe of Judah. So I had come here instead.

I knew exactly why I hadn't wanted to confront Wilfred alone. It was not because I was scared, but simply that I did not want to accuse. It was a position I was loath to find myself in, and I felt sure if we met in company all the events of the past would in the general hubbub lose their poignancy, and so go thankfully forgotten. The trouble was that the question of time was becoming a pressing factor in the case, as his non-appearance each day aroused fresh curiosity. More and more people were beginning to ask questions regarding the coincidence of his absence with Sutherland's death, and the whole matter of the accident, which to my relief had been written off so casually, threatened to erupt again.

Curiosity was a dangerous thing, and I myself felt no less snared by it with respect to my friend's behaviour. In spite of my efforts to lose myself in the general confidence I had from the beginning accorded him, it was becoming increasingly difficult to ignore each new piece of evidence that thrust itself uninvited into the scene of judgement, that Wilfred Prior had not only let Nickie die, but had evil intentions towards me. The reason why I had not been able to locate him during that tiffin break a week ago was simple. He had been following me. He had spied on every move I made and then attempted to destroy me by passing information through devious channels to the authorities concerned: Mr. Latto and the Principal for example. Yet at the same time I did not fail to remind myself that these charges were entirely undefended, and nothing could be settled until he was actually accused. And that I was unwilling to do. I intended to speak to him on matters removed, and slowly let time prove I was wildly off the mark. But time could not work for him in his absence; it could only go against. The slightest suspicion, however absurd, in his absence, grew and festered. The situation was getting intolerable. If only he would come. If only——

I heard a sound behind me and stopped. A row of lights twinkling where once there was nothing brought me to my senses. It was now quite dark. Not only had my mind been wandering, but my feet as well. The rustlings increased as the creatures of night began to grow active. I hurried on, not altogether lost. When the undergrowth completely obscured my vision, the boom of the waves against the reclamation wall gave me the bearings I required. In and out of the maze of clumps I wove. Behind me I now began to hear sounds I'd imagined I'd heard before; sounds like my own: soft squashy footsteps in the sand. It was all very brave to boast I had a yen to meet a goonda, but when it came to it—ah, when it came to it.

Forcing myself not to panic and bolt, lest I should fall straight into the arms of those lying in wait, I kept going steadily in the general direction of the lights, which reappeared from time to time through the grass. The footsteps got neither nearer nor farther, and I began to think it might have been some animal after all, when I got clear of the scrub. I walked more rapidly now, and was in fact about to burst into a run when, on throwing a last glance backward, I saw who my shadow was.

Immediately relieved at finding that my supposed assailant was someone I knew, I stopped and called to him. He stopped too, but did not answer. I went towards him, speaking. He at once retired into the foliage and vanished. Unwilling at this tardy phase to enter into his curious game, I continued my way across the more open ground towards Churchgate Railway Station. I looked back and saw him following. I slowed. He slowed, always keeping about twenty yards between us. The indignation which had been arrested by my initial relief at finding it was a friend who was following me, now began to simmer up with a vengeance, and at a point where we were well clear of the elephant-grass I turned and went for him. I had never struck him before, but had no doubt in my mind what I was going to do to him now; and he seemed to know it too, though this time he did not attempt to regain concealment, running in an arc on the open ground.

At this point I at once assumed I would catch him as there never had been any question of my superiority in either endurance or speed; but to my astonishment I could not for the life of me get anywhere near him. It was no good saying that the unevenness of the ground was the cause, as no one could have been at a greater disadvantage for that than my opponent. No, this was not the clumsy, tripping boy I knew. I found I had stopped, given up the chase, and could see him standing there waiting, his two longitudinal scars glistening with sweat. Oh, yes it was him, but some part of him I had never been permitted to see. And with this realization I turned and made rapidly for the lights.

He did not follow, though it was all I could do to stop myself breaking into a run again with the fear that he might. Fear, I always thought I knew what it was, I thought I knew it now; yet as soon as I said it it would be out of date; for I'd thought I'd be frightened of meeting a stranger, but it turned to be nothing to seeing a strangeness loom up in the dark from someone I knew. That steady, studied, unfaltering gait; that even, easy, animal run; that I could not associate with Wilfred. And after I'd reunited myself with the crowds the running stayed and haunted me. The running coupled with more concrete facts made me certain beyond a shadow of doubt it was this fellow who'd gone to the court that evening and informed my father of the accident.

A pair of mud-caked rugger boots thumped my bottom, and I knew I was amongst friends. It turned out to be only one, but he was in a sense plural as he now represented (alas) the sum total of all my friends.

"Hi, Joe."

108

"How d'you manage to look spick and span with mud on your face, and grass in your ears?"

"I scored a try. Your House lost to ours fifteen-nine."

"I should have been there."

"Got kept in?"

"Yes, I told the louse we had an important house-match on, but he said in that case I'll take more care not to be detained in future."

"What a rotten dukkur."

"You don't know half of it," I told him grimly. "He's ideas he's a great tin god. He gave me hundreds of lines, but I'll give him something one day, a good solid——" I raised my fist and found him looking disapprovingly at it. "Tell me," I said, "what's your opinion of Titmus?"

"He's a damn fine bloke, one of the best; almost good enough to be a Jew."

"But you just said he was a rotten dukkur."

"I only said that to *you*, not to myself," he explained. And I felt like punching him in the face—both of them: his and his shifty old ancestor's, Mr. High Priest Aaron.

"Baal-worshipper!" I spat.

"Yes, quite," he nodded agreeably, although he could not have had the faintest idea what I was talking about.

"What d'you think of me?" I demanded. "Am I a purblind moron?"

"What do you think of yourself?" he countered warily.

"I'm kind, diligent and ordained by God," I claimed.

"That's just what I think," he nodded. "You're kind, diligent and ordained by God."

"Have you no opinion of your own?"

"I'm always out-numbered," he shrugged.

"Even against *one*?"

"One?" he echoed dismally. "I wouldn't want to make him unhappy."

"You'd deny the facts for his sake?"

He nodded uneasily, beginning to edge away.

"I want you to come to the Reclamation now. For my sake," I added.

"I've homework to do."

"It's important—about Wilfred."

"Where'd you get to yesterday?" he asked unexpectedly. "You said you were going to see Wilfred."

"It was just as well I didn't go to his house. I met him by accident on the Reclamation between Churchgate and Marine Lines."

"Did you really?" he said, his eyes going round with astonishment.

"At about twilight. It was quite frightening," I added, as the mention of fear never failed to capture his interest. And now it did too, with a power seldom attained before.

"At about twilight?" He gulped, looked at me horror-struck and said all of a sudden, "Wilfred told me not to tell you this but I think you ought to know."

"When did you speak to him?"

"He said he did it for your own good, because little crimes going unpunished lead to greater and greater crimes."

"Is that so?" I marvelled. "What did you reply?"

"Nothing. He did all the talking. It was he who told E.E. who'd punctured his bike."

"He told——!" I sprang at him, and catching his arm by the wrist, turned it behind his back. He squalled before I'd time to twist. "Who told Wilfred I meddled with E.E.'s bike?" I hissed.

"Ow! I've promised, I can't tell you!"

"Did Wilfred tell you not to tell me you told him?"

"Yes! Ow! Yes! Ooooow!"

A crowd of chowkra boys had begun to collect and I let him go through sheer disgust. "Why were you yelling? I wasn't twisting."

"I know," he nodded quickly recovering his dignity. "I

110

always find if I start yelling before people start twisting, they're quite satisfied, and there's no harm done."

"Only to your pride," I said contemptuously, "only to your pride." I heard a distant chanting in the direction of the Causeway. It grew, as it always did, steadily louder, and well knowing what we were about to witness, I thought, by God he's right. Pride? What's that? Nothing but a bloody vain word we imagine isn't gibberish.

"Beram."

"Sitam."

"Beram."

"Sitam."

"Berama."

"Sitama."

They came into sight, curling around Waterloo Mansions, a slowly moving Hindu procession. One group cried, "Beram," the other answered, "Sitam." And it struck me then that such was the tone of the whole procedure that never once during all these years did it occur to me to ask what the words meant.

"Beram." "Sitam." "Beram." "Sitam." There were four pall-bearers carrying the bamboo and rope-work stretcher on their shoulders. The corpse lay face up to the sky, his body covered in an intricate mantle of flowers. At walking pace he hardly stirred, but now as they broke into a trot his body bounded on the taut net like a living thing, and his head shook and nodded as in animated conversation. "Beram." "Sitam." "Beram." "Sitam." They passed on.

"Not as musical as the Mohammedan tamashas, but there it is. What difference does it make? This one's going to be burned to ash, his head'll explode. The Moslems, the Jews, the Christians are buried; the Egyptians are mummified, the Parsees are eaten by vultures and crows, the Vikings by fishes, the cannibals take on the job themselves. What's the difference? Why should a chap punish himself getting to the

111

top of the political ladder? writing symphonies? spreading knowledge? helping the poor? saving folk from dying? or sending criminals to the gallows for murder, when they're going to die anyhow?"

The effect of my musings upon him was really quite extraordinary, although I had spoken more to myself. His face, which for some time had been steeped in gloom, slowly lightened to an expression denoting ecstasy, and speaking with considerable jubilation he said, "That's true. It never occurred to me before. Nothing matters. We're all going to die. Nickie Sutherland would have died anyway, whether you killed him or not. All night I was fretting after I'd left Wilfred, wondering how——"

"Who said I killed Nickie?"

"——wondering how I was going to face a murderer, when the fact is——"

"Who said I'm a murderer?"

"——the fact is that Nickie would have died anyway. Just like you said, Joe," he concluded approvingly.

"Who said——?"

"Forget it, forget it," he said, waving his hand airily. "I imagined the whole business anyway."

"Imagined what whole business?"

"You'll laugh," he chuckled. "Yesterday after you called I changed my mind about going to see Wilfred an hour or so later, and went. I was really quite worried about him, on account of the accident you see. I whistled for him, but he wasn't home. The old chap below said he saw him going towards Arthur Bunder with a fishing-line. So I went along and saw him sitting on the jetty fishing. I mean, I imagined I saw him because it was just after sunset, the same time when you saw him on the Rec."

"You saw someone dressed like him in khaki from the back and went away."

"Oh, no, we talked about you for an hour at least."

"You swine!" I burst out. "Are you accusing me of lying?" I made a grab for him, but forewarned he danced away, his rugger boots clicking like castanets. He didn't go far however, but hung around just out of reach. I turned right and made for the Bandstand. He followed.

"I'm not accusing you of anything, Joe. Why don't you listen?"

"I deny it," I flung back. "I too can deny the facts."

"These are not facts. It was a dream I had."

"Some fantasy, hah?" I stopped. He stopped.

"Yes, we had a long talk till it grew dark." I sat down on the pavement with my feet in the gutter. "Are you sick, Joe?"

"Go away!" I shouted. "I don't want to hear your dream!"

"O.K., Joe, O.K." He'd shied off when I raised my voice, but came back hovering over me as I had not moved. "We went up to his room then. He has a very tidy room, d'you hear?" he whispered. "A tidy room, just as I would have imagined it. Ha! ha!" he tittered. "Imagined it." His laughter was not convincing, and I vaguely became aware he was frightened too. He was looking to me, tormenting me, through fear. Fear: the strangeness within us. Again the definition dated. A dream could not be denied. I seized him by the throat.

"What did he tell you?"

He did not struggle. "All this stuff about you causing Sutherland's death by first knocking his topee off. That's why he was reaching out of the bus. Wilfred saw him——"

"He saw him! Why didn't he warn him?"

"I told him that, Joe, my very words. He said, 'I'm short-sighted, I couldn't make out what was happening——' "

"Short-sighted, damn! He saw poor Nickie well enough to——" I got up still holding on to him.

"Let me go. Where are you pulling me off to?"

"I'm going to see Wilfred," I said frog-marching him down

Mayo Road, "and tomorrow I'm damned if I'm having you saying you saw him on the Rec or anywhere else."

"But I told you it was all my imagination, Joe."

"Or mine. So this evening your imagination and mine are going to join forces."

"Yes, but at what point?" he wailed hopelessly. "Suppose tomorrow we should find that when you were shoving me along Mayo Road I was actually at home doing homework?"

"That," I said fervently twisting his arm, "is a risk we'll have to take."

"Ow, you dog!" He swung out and landed me such a crack on the shins with his boots that I felt as confident he was with me as I had ever been. In all my life I never knew a better way of making sure I existed than by fighting. I let him free as I no longer needed him. The truth about Wilfred had come to me then. Fighting. That's what he was up to. He hated to touch, so this was his fighting. The idol had cracked and emptiness issued. It drained the worshipper. He felt his existence slipping out of him, and thrashed the air for some other. The Golden Calf. Anything would do. Revenge. Yes, why not? Revenge was the greatest idol of them all. As a replacement it had no peer. "The character of Judas is mysterious too. That he did not betray the Saviour merely for silver——" To hurt, betray, accuse—it was a way of filling emptiness. I had done it all my life, and could grumble when it was done to me.

Passing by the Cooperage which was erupting every few seconds with the internecine cheers of Hindu and Moslem football fans, I thought I'd better warn him of the possibility of violence in the coming encounter with Wilfred. I listed his crimes, both against me and others, to which he listened unmoved; and when I suggested he could turn off at the corner and go home, he shrugged and said, "Oh, it's all the same

114

whatever happens. Bangalore Moslems or Calcutta United, we're all going to die."

"What about your homework?"

"Who cares about homework? We're all going to die." He happened to look down at his feet then, and, stopping, uttered a gasp of concern. "Look!" he pointed. "I've put this sock on inside-out!"

"Heaven preserve us!" I cried. "Whatever can you do now?"

"I can change it around, can't I?"

"Change it around then," I urged. "Quick, before it is too late."

He seemed about to do so, then said with a devil-may-care flip of his hand, "Huh, why bother? We're all going to die. Nothing's worth worrying about."

At the bottom of Wodehouse Bridge a boy on a bicycle breasted us silently. It was E. E. Braithwaite. He ignored me, but he turned to nod deferentially at the mugger. "That was a fine try. Congrats."

"Thanks, E.E.," he blushed.

Two other boys on bicycles, also from higher classes, followed. "Great run through," said one.

"You should make the Second Fifteen next year," commented the other.

"Thanks," blushed the mugger.

He stopped a few seconds later, and I sat on the railing by Wellington Mews to watch him take off his shoe and sock, and readjust it the correct way around.

"What d'you intend to do in life, my dear fellow?"

"My mother wants me to be a rabbi."

"What do *you* want to be?"

"My father wants me to be a merchant."

"What do *you* want to be?"

"Aunt Rachael wants me to be a doctor."

"And *I* think you should be a manufacturer of Golden

115

Calves, but just for the hell of it, brother, tell me what you want to be yourself."

He stood up, having now made the necessary adjustment to his appearance. "Myself?" he echoed, as though he'd never considered such a thing before. "Why should I want to be anything myself?"

I opened my mouth to tell him, and realized there was no answer. So I shut it in case a fly got in. Of course, no one became anything if not for someone else. We began to walk uphill. "For whom *do* you intend to be something then?"

"For God."

There were lots of flies by lots of horses in Wellington Mews, but the best bet in the stables was God. If only one knew what colours he was running under tonight.

"Who would you say is God?"

"God," he answered swinging his boots in abandon, "is the All-knowing."

"You mean Jesus?"

Bang! He carried the next swing to its ultimate and hit a lamp-post with no little fervour.

"Krishna?"

Bang!

"Allah?"

Bang bang!

We carried on up the bridge. "It seems to me the joy of knowing who God is, isn't half as great as knowing who he is not."

"What?"

"Nothing." I felt I had grown in the past few hours. I had suffered and in suffering learned not to speak. What next? Could I learn not to think? That would be the best lesson of all: to look, to smell, taste, feel—without the blemish of thought, the alloy of relations.

At the crest of the bridge came the sight of the sea, and the two familiar arms curving towards one another in the vain

116

effort to clasp hands in mid-ocean. A reclamation scheme, some dreamer's vision of glory, had long ago come to nought. Dates escaped me, but as far back as I could go, as a toddler on the sands, I could recall the sight of that defiant gap through which the tides rose and fell, and sail-boats passed unimpeded by the walls of cement and rock. They were in their unfinished state a godsend for anglers and the general public to promenade upon, at least, and helped create a setting that was quite ideal for the watchers on the shore to rest their eyes on. Life, as all life in the twilight should, went along in slow motion, majestically. People as big as needles with umbrellas like pins moved to and fro on both walls. There were no clouds but in early September one could not be too careful. In place of the clouds, and quite as high were the hawks. This was the sacred hour, the time when they soared highest, still catching the sun after we humdrum humans had lost it.

Jing jing jing jing. The temple bells started up. Hawk-time in the sky was temple-bell-time in the city. There were always connections, always relations. Heaven, Hell—the farther apart they were the closer were they linked together. Nothing could exist alone; alone no one laughed, no one talked; the Parsee boy shrieked at the sight of his mother. We crossed the desolate waste ground between the seaface and the Causeway. Jing jing jing jing. The bells increased in urgency as we approached. Our instinct was to quicken our pace, and I felt him go, but resisted it myself, dragging my feet when by signs he urged me on.

In spite of the rapidly falling darkness several pairs of Indians began mock dandu fights, as they habitually did at this time in open spaces all over Bombay. The failing light did not worry them as their movements were set beforehand, and once the rhythm of battle, the steady metronomic thud thud of the opposing cudgels was started there was no fear of striking their opponents. To fight without hurting: it seemed

117

the ideal way, but the snag in this case was the ritual, the lack of freedom: choice.

"Come on, Joe, let's get this cursed thing done with." He was over twenty yards ahead now, his voice shrill with impatience. The sense of urgency I accepted, but compulsion, how I jibbed against it. This evening above all, I felt, having to was hating to.

"What have you stopped for, damn your eyes?"

"Why don't you go home, do your homework?" I advised, fighting back the rage that rose against his—false rage, machinery, my mother's. It was hard, yes, no lesson was more difficult to learn than unlearning.

"You said we had to see Wilfred."

"I can change my mind, can't I?"

"Well then are you or aren't you?"

"In my own sweet time," I answered. He waited in silence, and seemed calmer when I reached him. I was relieved. I did not want to send him away, nor force him to come. I felt my own sense of freedom began in him. Going or staying, he would infect me in a way I could never infect myself. Masters were the more enslaved. For a split second Mr. Titmus's problem, the dilemma of teachers, expanded before me. The fight not to cane, the need for a central authority—I saw it vivid as a dream, then it slipped away. I felt my youth, the frustration that arose from the need to know, the emptiness. I stumbled, and he caught me.

A great deal of half-finished building was going on in the fringes of the waste ground, and the dirt path to the Causeway should have been lit. The Causeway itself was bright enough though, and looked like fairyland, until one came near enough, was part and parcel of the thing. A cow bearing a load of hay bumped into us. It was being led on a rope by a kind of sadhu figure in saffron, who went from shop to shop offering the hay for sale. It was bought an armful at a time, and the purchaser, who paid according to his spiritual means, then fed the sacred animal himself. It was on the face of it an ideal system. The quicker the beast worked, the more it was fed, the lighter became its burden, the more uplifted the clientele, and the richer its master. And had he thought it up himself I would have kissed the hem of his garment, called him Father, and followed him infinitely more willingly than the cow. But he hadn't. There were a thousand others doing the same thing. It was ritual; dirty, corrupt, dehumanizing ritual.

Jing! Jing! Jing! Jing! The temple bells which had not meanwhile ceased for a second had in fact through sheer monotony become unnoticed, a solid homogeneous background of sound, suddenly driven like a spearhead into our consciousness by skilful fluctuations of volume and rhythm. Jing! Jing! Jing! Jing! It pulled, I resisted. Automatically, I realized. And I thought, to hell with it, I'll come—but in my own sweet time.

I turned left into the Causeway, where the way to Wilfred was towards Arthur Bunder straight ahead. Like moths to flame the stream of people moved faster, and I let myself be sucked along. "Where are you going, Joe?" I did not answer.

Jing! Jing! Jing! Jing! He could be seen standing, his fat-quivering brown torso glistening with perspiration, as I had first seen him when my father had lifted me as a child, through an arched aperture in the temple wall. On the broad flat sill were the same two earthenware bowls; nor was there any reason why they should be changed in another hundred years. One contained a quantity of red powder; the other was an alms bowl. The idol was also visible, though thanks to its monstrous proportions, only in part. Every now and then a passer-by would stop to move his lips in a bell-drowned prayer, plant one finger in the powder and depart to make way for another. They seemed twice the men for having done this, their steps jauntier.

Jing! Jing! Jing! Jing! The climax was coming. The mugger

made distressed signs indicating he was going—he didn't care which way as long as it was away from this ungodly spot—in truth he would obtain more joy from his repulsion than he would care to admit—though no more perhaps than Mr. True God would care to admit how pleased he was with Messrs. False Gods—certainly not a word about him suckling them on his great accommodating bosom. It was a thought-provoking vision which would have to be dwelt upon at a more tranquil time. Jing! Jing! Jing! Jing! The very substance of the thickening, brain-compressing noise made thought impossible. I had wondered if I could learn how not to think, and here was the answer in one word: noise. Noise when it reached this volume paralysed thought. I'd felt it in in the synagogue too, when the voice of the whole congregation thundered out in concert, numbing, killing reason, bringing us down to our knees to a kind of bestial prostration.

A man could never pray alone. He couldn't create sufficient noise. Jing! Jing! Jing! Jing! I was being jostled by cattle it seemed; humanity transformed, degraded. They jostled one another obliviously, their very sense of contact, their differentness, lost. Similarity was madness. Jing! Jing! Jing! Jing! I had an over-powering impulse to still this noise, to rush into the temple, tear down the pillars, bring back reason, the loved one logic, kick open the void in the great belly of the idol. But was it from choice? Was it not a ritual too? Moslems rushed out like cattle from their mosques and sundered temples; and Hindus sundered mosques. Revenge: just another little tin god. Noise for noise. Jing! Jing! Jing! Jing! I felt his hand desperately pulling at my shoulder. I was not stopping him from going, but of course he would not flee alone. Fleeing alone, no one fled. He needed a herd, a congregation. Jing! Jing! Jing! Jing! I snapped back his hand and pushed my way through the dense knot of people at the aperture. Jing! Jing! Jing! Jing! These shuddering spasmodic movements, where had I seen them before? In dogs in the last stage of copulation. Jing! Jing! Jing! Jing! If I did it at all I had to do it now, and I had to be quick. I mumbled the only prayers I knew, dabbed my forehead with a red spot, and dropped in a coin.

When I rejoined the mugger I felt very much quieter of mind, though of course this blessed relief may have been due to the fact the bells had stopped. The bells that had started had created noise, and in stopping created silence, a state just as concrete as the noise, though not a whit more concrete, more wall-like than that thrown up by the friend at my side. It was a large wall this; stones several feet thick and a hundred high; he'd seen it once on a trip to Jerusalem, now here it was miraculously transported. The Wailing Wall. And well might he have wailed on my behalf too, were it not patent that he felt he would have been casting pearls before swine. Had he not always said it? One day I'd do something beyond hope of redemption.

He stared straight ahead as we walked, only acknowledging my existence by occasional side glances that searchlighted his face with horror and contempt. Oh, yes, he saw the beam in my eye all right. He didn't say a word till we got to Wilfred's place. The one and only window of his first floor room was shut, the curtain drawn but alight. "Give him the whistle, Joshua, you do it so much better than I."

"Joe, boy, what's this on your head? What have you done?"

"Done? Such a poor little word? I've solved a problem that's been worrying me for centuries. I've dedicated myself."

"What was it you muttered when you dabbed this crap on?"

"Shemah Israel, Our Father and Allah Inshallah."

"Why did you do such a thing, why, why?"

"Well, I reckoned, why go for half-measures? With Jehovah, Jesus, Krishna and Allah in the bag I shan't go to

121

Hell alone, eh?" I cordially pressed his shoulder. "I'm with you now," I said gravely, "in the Golden Calf trade. I should have seen the Light earlier. Your way is the way, Master. It's suicide-resisting. When they shove it at you, swallow the damn thing and be done with it."

There were no street lights in this poverty-stricken corner of Bombay, but I could almost feel the look he gave me. He shrank back wiping off the touch of my embrace in a way he had never done when I'd threatened to twist his arm off. Fear—another definition. He would rather be beaten for no fault of his own than embraced for mine. He seemed about to run. "Come, come," I urged him, "we came to see Wilfred, remember? So let's have a whistle."

I did not attempt to detain him physically however, and he actually took a step back to go, to wash himself no doubt from the taint of my heinous forehead-spotted presence once and for all, when he paused suddenly to ask, "How much money did you put in the bowl?"

"Eight annas."

"That dud?"

"Yes."

I felt him relax. He seemed much relieved, more than relieved, profoundly stirred. He took out his hanky, wiped my forehead, murmuring something I could not make out, and gave the general impression that my past iniquity was not as bad as he'd imagined; the synagogue was still waiting to receive me.

Pheeeeeep! His whistle had the exultance of a shofar blast on Passover night.

Pheeeeeeeeeep! Little did I realize that my salvation on earth and life hereafter could be bought for less than a mess of pottage, a dud eight-anna bit.

Pheeeeeeeeeeeeeeeeeep!

Wilfred answered to neither whistles nor shouts. There

122

wasn't any doubt that someone was there as in addition to the light a shadow moved across it to signify the passage of a quickly moving body. This occurred with such great frequency that the mugger said what was in my own mind. "Looks like he's got a party going on up there."

"Or else it's just him scuttling to and fro."

"Who, Wilfred? Ever seen him move like this? Lazy bounder."

Discounting my ghostly experience last night, I had to admit I hadn't seen Wilfred move like this; but it was not a profound accusation and practically worthless. Wilfred's immobility never gave me the impression he was lazy. He was too removed from the rest of us to be afflicted with so earthly a failing as laziness, or greed, or vain-glory. A deep rasping voice interrupted my reverie on the subject.

"Prior's a pal of you chaps, mun?"

We recognized the face at the curtain directly below Wilfred's window. It was the short, white-haired, long, black-faced old Goanese bloke, who during the day would be sitting there at ground level, smoking six-a-pice bidis, watching life go by. We nodded blinking in the sudden light cast on us by the drawing of his curtain.

"He's doing koosti from the sound of it," the old chap informed us rather plaintively, "or Hindu dances. Damn well rocking the place."

"Shall we go up and see him?" I asked.

"Why ask permission of me, mun? I'm not his father. Wouldn't want to be anybody's father, not with my experience of life."

"Is his aunt with him?"

"What aunt?"

"He told me he lives with his aunt."

"Never seen aunts around here, mun, and I've seen everything round here. Love is commercialized, beauty prostitutionalized. He's stopped now," he added ungratefully. "Must

123

be exhausted, been going steady for an hour. Got a girl up up there? Where's he from? Never says much. Is he Catholic or C. of E.?"

"Why d'you want to know?" I inquired.

"Mind your own business," he snapped, withdrawing his head suspiciously. "Huh, I know your type. Wiseacre. Tell you this, though, people who live on the stupidity of others would thrive on dung. Huh, I ought to know, many a Jew's made a meal of me."

"Excuse me, sir," said the mugger earnestly. "May I ask you a question?"

"Certainly not. What's the question?"

"How can I ask if you won't let me?"

"You can ask, but I'm not answering."

"What's the *good* of asking then?"

"Good as living, mun," he grunted. "Life's one big question without an answer, so if you want to ask this is your last chance as incidental to the case I've diarrhoea."

"Well, sir, I don't want to keep you, I only wanted to ask what was your occupation in life."

"Forty-one years a booking clerk on the B.B. & C.I. Railway, mun." He snapped shut the curtain and I half-expected his short, white hair and long, black face to reappear with a COUNTER CLOSED sign, or some indication to show us what significance this chance encounter had for us; but a moment later his light went out and we were left wrestling with darkness.

It was in the darkness I realized that at some indeterminable point *en route* here we had become pall-bearers. There were no lights on the stairs, and as we creak-creaked our way slowly up with him leading I became conscious of a sort of deadness that had often visited me before in transits of every nature. I had a while ago made a firm decision to see someone and on the way had undergone experiences that had rendered

124

the decision null and void. Never had I turned back or questioned it however, and never till now had it occurred to me why I was compelled to carry on with the dead weight on my back, the corpse of that decision whose features I could not even remember.

It was not any sense of pride that made me persevere. Pride was too flattering an excuse, and only too easily taken. Pride kept alive, were it simply to rankle and fester. Pride created. The decision itself was born of pride. Pride was no grave-digger. Burial was the work of ritual.

Creak, creak, creak. Up went the funeral party of two. I found laughter bubbling to my lips. I was caught. All evening I'd fought off its shackles, but in the end it had trapped me. The joke was that I had in all seriousness expected to evade capture. It was ludicrous. Ritual would always win; and the more easily when we were united; for even now I could have turned back, or sat on the stairs to formulate some new life-giving resolve which would render the encounter excitingly worthwhile—if I was alone. There was no freedom in numbers; only conflict or co-operation—which was precisely how ritual was evolved: by co-operation.

Knock knock. He was at the door. There was no answer. Whatever Wilfred had been doing he had ceased. Knock knock—louder this time, but still no answer.

"Hey, Joe, let's go and assassinate the Viceroy, it should be easier."

There was a faint glow from the glass-framed vent above his door. It was shut tight, however, and we could see that the keyhole was plugged with a pencil. There was a newspaper packed all around the door-jamb, and I began to get interested. While a few moments before I felt I needed some new resolve to help me enter, the fact that I could not itself comprised a resolve. The place was almost hermetically sealed, but a peculiarly pungent odour, one that I had never smelled before, penetrated through.

"Psst," I whispered, "Wilfred's got the Holy Ghost in there, smell it?"

I saw him stiffen. He'd been quite flippant till now, cracking jokes about assassinating the Viceroy, etc. "Joe, let's come back tomorrow—in the daylight." Before I could reply however he continued in tones of firmest resolve, "No! I must see him tonight."

"Why *must* you see him tonight?"

"Well, I've been putting off seeing him and putting off seeing him the whole week, and I'm fed up. If I don't ask him tonight, I'll never get it back."

"Get what back, Mugger?"

"Have you also forgotten?" he stated, his voice rising to a height of indignation that completely overwhelmed his fears. "About ten days ago I paid for both of you at that Tarzan film. I was first in the crush, remember? Neither of you paid me back. I waited and waited day after day, what the hell, I mean to say——!"

"Sssh, ssssh."

"—it's a damned disgrace, a chap has to beg back his own——"

"Sssssssh!"

"—paltry, miserable——"

"Sssssssssssh!"

"—four annas. I mean it's a lot of money, hell! It's nothing really, it's the PRINCIPLE——!"

"My dear boy," I soothed, "I promise on my honour to pay you both his and mine directly. Just stop shouting, that's all."

He calmed down instantly, and asked, "Have you got the money on you?"

"No."

"Hah!" he snorted in triumph. "Just as I expected!" Throwing caution to the winds he went up to the door and gave it a resounding double bang with his rugger boots. "Open up, Wilfred! It's your father!"

126

It was a stroke of inspiration. After the briefest pause shuffling footsteps approached the door. The end of the pencil disappeared. The tip of a key appeared. It turned. The door was pulled in an inch, skidding over the paper on the floor, and wisps of smoke curled out. We at once took this as a signal to enter and pushed, almost falling in as there was no resistance. The door shut, at least we heard it slam, as we could not see. Our ears were just about the only organs that were not affected by the thick swirling blanket of fumes that instantly enveloped us.

The smoke seeped deep into our lungs, and we reeled about coughing till the tears poured out of our eyes. When we grew a little accustomed to the fog it became apparent the room was a shambles. All the furniture had been moved to provide a clear space in the centre. In looking around to acquaint myself with the place, for I had never been invited up here before, I began to feel light-headed, almost headless, and at the same time experienced a sense of freedom too intense to question the matter, whether it was good or bad, right or wrong.

"For God's sake, Wilfred," gulped the mugger, "open the window."

"Keep that closed!"

"Well, then stop smoking."

"The thicker the smoke the quicker you get used to it. Fresh air, that's the devil."

His voice had lost its customary drawl, and snapped like a whip. I could barely distinguish his thin lanky form curled in a semi-circle on his bed around what appeared to be a make-shift hookah. I stepped closer to inspect it and recognized one or two items. So this was why he'd got me to pinch stuff from the Lab.

"Wilfred," I began, "what's been——?"

"No questions!" he shot from the corner of his mouth. "Make you think. I'm through with thinking."

I looked to the mugger for a clue. I might as well have looked for the leak that caused the oceans. He was crouching fascinated by the bubbles passing through the U-shaped water-trap from the fuming retort, into the rubber tube that led the smoke around to the pipette which served as a mouthpiece. "Look at this, Joe," he signed, "how d'you suppose——?"

"No questions!"

I seized the tube leading to his mouth and pinched it. From the way he reacted it could have been his windpipe. "Let go!" he screamed like a child in a tantrum.

"Just you stop shouting at me," I hissed. "If you want to kill me, kill me quietly. I get shouted at by my family, I get shouted at in school. No one shouts at me any more. You shout at me again and I open the window, understand?"

He collapsed like a pricked balloon. I released the tube and he carried on puffing like a child permitted to suck a lolly it had stolen. "You have a father," he whined, "you chaps you have fathers, you've got to help me. Don't ever open that window."

"Just you answer one or two questions, Wilfie, and the window stays closed. Firstly——"

There was a soft thud. The mugger had rolled over on to his back, striking his head on the wooden floor. I'd have thought he'd fainted if it were not for the look of utter ecstasy on his up-turned face. "Get up!" I snarled, digging my shoe in his side. I didn't know what had come over me, and I didn't care. My brain had become as clear as a crystal. I felt for the first time in my life I knew exactly what I wanted. I didn't know what this was but it did not come in the way of the feeling I had—not a whit. It was a thing apart. Everything was a thing apart. There were no relations. The blanket had nothing to do with the bed, the bed had nothing to do with the floor. The whole room seemed to be floating about in the clouds.

I could however see one or two flies in the ointment, and these irritated me with the same burning intensity I regarded everything. "Come on, get up!" I literally lifted him, while he offered only the most blissful of protestations, on to a chair.

"And there I sat all through this wonderfully exciting film wondering when are they going to pay me back? when are they going to pay me back?"

"Shut up!"

He was just as happy, indeed more happy to obey than to keep on yapping, and in general I began to feel some sort of orderly conduct was being restored to this room. The incessant noise of bubbling annoyed me but I decided to ignore it. I did not want to overreach myself in my desire for perfection. Perfection? Of what?

"Now he's here, and you're here, and I'm here," murmured Wilfred. "Who's missing?"

"You'll answer for him if I say?"

"You say and you answer, because you killed him. Didn't you, Joe? Skillet and I saw you tip his hat off. He was revenging himself that's why he died."

"Let's take this point for point," I said. "How d'you know Sutherland is dead?"

"Rusi Muttonwallah told me. He lives near here, you know, in Parsee Colony."

"When did he tell you?"

"That same evening."

"But weren't you on the spot yourself? Hey, Mugger, wasn't he?"

"Yes, but——"

"You heard the witness. Answer him."

"I might have been looking in that direction, your worship, but I'm short-sighted. You're my best witness to that. I just saw a blur. When I realized someone was killed I was so panic-stricken I turned tail and bolted."

"Very good," I nodded sardonically, almost feeling for my

snuff-box. "Neat. Nice picture of short-sighted student too poor to afford glasses. Panic-stricken. What next? Thus unfolds. Comes home to be told that same evening said victim of said short-sight is Nickie Sutherland. A cousin?"

"No!"

"An old friend from Lahore, then. Great wailing and gnashing of teeth?"

No answer.

"Guilt of silence? Maybe, but neat. So Rusi Muttonwallah told you that same evening, in spite of the fact every single Parsee in school was absent on the day of the accident."

The bubbling in the water-trap had ceased—whether the tobacco, or whatever he was smoking, had given out, I could not say. He dropped the tube, and lurching more clumsily than ever got up. There were some bananas hanging on a nail and he took a whole minute to cut one off with a long pointed kitchen-knife, committing himself to elaborate ritualistic motions, which he invariably muffed, when the thing could more conveniently have been torn off by the hand. I naturally supposed he was playing for time, and I myself could already think of a dozen good ways out of his situation. Instead of which he said, "All right, you got me, Joe. I watched Nickie die because I saw and recognized it was him."

"I don't see what you could have done anyway, Wilfred." We looked at the mugger, who'd suddenly piped up. "I've thought this out, you see. You had to shout to save Nickie, and you never shout, I've never heard you shout in my life."

"Neither have I. You're dead right." He took a bite of the banana, spat it out and flung the rest at a waste-paper basket, missing it by yards. "Shit the bloody thing! I look at it, I'm hungry. I take one bite, I want to vomit." He raised the long kitchen-knife and slowly in the air made a shaking barely recognizable sign of the cross. "See? I'm just a mess. A walking brain. I've no body, but look at me. I'm awkward." He stabbed the air making bayonet passes. "I've got to change. I've got to

130

stop going to school. I've got to labour with my hands. To fill my lungs with air, and stand on a mountain-top and shout. Suppose I did want to save Nickie, suppose it was my father? I'd still have been paralysed at the sight of that head approaching the post. I can't cry. I couldn't save Jesus if he was drowning. I can't swim a stroke. And on land I'm a fish out of water. I've got to change, I've got to box, be like others, not left out. I've got to labour with iron and rock, so that my body can be fit for the sacrifice." He stopped, his head hung forward on his chest, his arms dangled loosely by his sides, the right still pathetically clutching the knife.

"Well, Wilfred," I pronounced, "grieves me though it does to say this: you were guilty of murdering Nickie, weren't you? For Christ sake admit it and be done."

"Guilty?" he gritted, taking one step towards me. "I'm not guilty of murdering Nickie. I'm guilty of not murdering him with my bare hands. I'd planned it. Now he's dead. I lost my chance."

"What did Nickie do to you, Wilfred?"

"He insulted my mother. There now, I've told you," he said holding up his free hand. "You shan't ask me to say any more about it."

"Very well, I shan't," I agreed. "Let's conclude then Nickie himself was the cause of his death. What d'you say, Mugger?"

"I say what was Wilfred's mother doing being insulted?" He seemed to find this question hilariously funny in retrospect, and tittered. "What sort of a hat was she wearing?"

"What d'you mean what was she *doing*?"

The mugger smiled up at him, then looked at the tip of the knife trembling within an inch of his nose, and still smiled. This boy with the protective coverings, I thought. He saw danger everywhere but where it really existed. He could not believe Wilfred had anything against him, and he was in fact right. His death would have been quite accidental. He just

131

happened to be the one. It was as though Wilfred had all his life been bound, frightened of moving, and had decided to cut himself free with a single, the supreme stroke: murder.

I braced my muscles to spring at Wilfred, but at the same time was overpowered by the temptation to sit there watching, saying nothing, doing nothing, mildly curious to see if Wilfred could bring it off, for, poor fellow, he could not hold the thing straight. It was pointing right into the crown of his head. He spoke, his voice barely intelligible. "Doing what? What's so funny?"

"Your mother," he explained. "Why does she go around in that ludicrous hat?"

"Hat? Hat?" He raised the knife higher, and slashed the air. One could see what he meant; he was quite fantastically awkward. "What d'you think, you dull-mettled bookworm?" he choked. "You can only insult a woman for her crude, her ugly, her vulgar, obscene, dirty, filthy, infectious, diseased old HAT?" He fell on all fours to save himself toppling backward. "Oh, Jesus," he cried into the floor, "I can't deny it any more. That's the root of the trouble. I loved Nickie until my mother let herself go to be insulted. By Nickie. By every man, every little boy in Lahore. Even I, I insulted her. In the highways and byways. And all she said was I had to be brave. Be brave. Timidi mater non flet."

He still had the knife in his hand and turned the blade this way and that to send its reflection slashing across the walls and ceiling. "Let's go and see my mother," he said.

"She should be tried," I retorted. "If it hadn't been for her Nickie would be alive today and you'd have been a hero for saving him. Your mother's the guilty one, so that's the end of that."

"Yes, let's go and see her," he repeated, getting up.

"We'll try her," I announced, also rising. "What d'you say, Mugger?"

"I've got to be home in time for dinner," he protested.

132

"All right, go home."

"But I don't want to be left out of it."

"All right, then, come."

"But my mother told me never to go to other people's houses."

"Look, are you coming or not?"

He blinked unhappily, then his face shone. "I'll come halfway," he said.

"Have we got everything?"

"Yes."

"Joe, you take the knife. You know me. If I have it we might as well not bring it."

"O.K.," I agreed, taking it, but at the same time wondering what I was supposed to do with it; for by now I had become fully aware we were acting under the influence of a drug. That smoke, of course, It was deep into Wilfred especially.

We trooped out shutting the door after us. We ran down the steps, reckless of the pace we made in the dark. "Now listen," said Wilfred as we came into the open road, "when we get there we might find someone else. We must wait till he goes. He's innocent. It's all *her* fault, understand? I want you to repeat after me; it's *her*——" He suddenly drew a long shuddering breath and looked up. "We must be quick about it," he said mechanically, not looking down again. The night was particularly clear.

"Just look at those stars!" the mugger cried, "they're jostling one another for places in Heaven!"

I dropped something, but had plenty of time to pick it up. In five yards we had slowed to a crawl. A white cat walked across our path without danger of being trodden on. Still we went, it was the direction we happened to be facing. The Causeway was not all that far. We drifted obliviously jostling the people. The smell of buggias made us aware we were famished. We stopped to buy some from a man who raised himself from his squatting position by pulling on a chain dangling from the ceiling of his shop. As he stirred the deep boiling fat with a ladle the mugger said somewhat inconsequentially, "It's rather late to pay visits anyway."

"Yes, it's late," Wilfred nodded. "She went back to Lahore a fortnight ago." He bit one of the buggias, threw it down in the gutter and without a word turned and went back. I thrust the newspaper bundle into the mugger's hands. A tram prevented me from crossing at this moment.

"You going back there?" he asked tonelessly.

"Yes."

"What shall I do meanwhile, Joe?"

"You be careful."

"One of these days," he murmured bitterly, "I'm going to kill myself."

The tram passed. "Now why would you want to do a thing like that?"

"I'm always being left out of things anyway. What's the good of living? I might as well be dead. I'm going to kill myself tomorrow. No," he continued, changing his mind, "tonight."

I crossed over.

"Hey, Joe! I've left my boots behind, will you pick them up?"

Within the same five yards I felt it go out of me again; like a puff of air, furtive as a New Year resolution. I'd smoked this time too. But it wasn't any good after one quitted the room. The fresh air nipped it in the bud, and it was only by the most concentrated effort that I could at all reconjure the stark clarity of my mind in that brief interval. Brief interval? It felt like a matter of minutes, but was it? A world of time had passed during which the whole span of my friend's life had unfolded before my eyes. Under the spell of the fumes, in seeming to become totally unrelated, the insidious ties of fear and prejudice had been cut away, and with them would those

134

of love be gone too—if there had been any but the counterfeit, the assumed. We were strangers, and always would be, until the ties of fear and prejudice rerooted, I supposed. In the meantime the union of strangers was the only true and possible one. And was it not the ideal? There was no competition between strangers because there were no emotional links, only those of fact, and the thing that stood out, towering head and shoulders above me was Wilfred's tragedy. There it was at last starkly unveiled, and I could no more be jealous of it than my little finger could be jealous of the strength of my thumb.

I walked on head down, and passing a street-lamp I noticed a figure with a sola topee on his head and a satchel across his shoulder overtaking me. I stopped. He stopped. I put my hand up. He put his hand up. I went on. It was my shadow, lengthening rapidly as I left the lamplight behind me. I walked on feeling the world I was about to re-enter closing soundlessly around me.

My tragedy. I used to laugh at Gladys fretting herself to tears about her pimples when crutchless beggars crawled the city. And weeping I cut a comic figure too. Didn't we all? Where was the mirror that answered the question: Who is the saddest of them all? Where was I now? What time was it? What month? What year? Wilfred hadn't been kidding in his decision to set off to apprehend his mother. The fact she had left for Lahore a couple of weeks ago meant nothing. Under the influence of the drug differences of place and time did not exist. The past, the present, the future, the cities of the world fused and shrank to a pinhead. It was unquestioned then, for it gave one the feeling of incredible power; but how useful was such an illusion now? I found myself getting giddy. The after effects were not so nice. Objects lost their clarity and merged. For all the brilliance of the street-lamps there was nothing to focus on. The transition back to reality, the world of relations, had to go through a kind of No Man's Land, a terrain of solid unyielding vacancy: madness. Everything

135

lacked distinction. The insanity of similarity. I stopped walking and the sickly giddiness cleared. I'd been walking in small circles around a telegraph-post for I could not say how long.

There was a large, elaborately constructed road ahead of me, which I could not at first recognize as Colaba Causeway since I was not accustomed to seeing it like this. Why was there not a soul about? No trams, no gharries, cars, bullock-carts, hand-carts, bicycles, no animals, people? Why were all the shops shuttered up? Such questions were beyond me. I saw a mongrel curled up on the pavement and wondered what fried dog would taste like. I had a hunger for meat such as I'd never experienced before. I stepped over the snoring body of a proprietor asleep outside his shop, and went on repressing the desire to look back.

A lone tram passed, going from Colaba back to the Depot. This meant I was walking in the wrong direction. Wrong direction? Where was I going? A word occurred to me. It did not have any meaning at first, it came automatically. Home. The horrible grinding of the tram's wheels had just died away when a clock began to strike. I cocked my ear hypnotized. Why did I feel guilty? Between the first and second stroke I thought nothing. Nor between the second and third. Between the third and fourth it began to dawn on me that I was late. Late for what? Had I an appointment? Between the fourth and fifth stroke I thought of my family, and this real world, the world of relations which had been soundlessly creeping upon me, finally crashed like a tidal wave about my ears.

Physically as yet unable to respond, it was my mind that went spinning, caught in the cataracts racing me to where I did not need to ask now: retribution. Between the fifth and sixth stroke I thought, God! it's late, dinner is ready, the table is laid, my father is looking at his watch, my mother is saying, "I hope nothing has happened to him." Glad is saying, "Calm yourself, Mother," and Dorothy is saying, "Let's eat."

Between the sixth and seventh stroke I thought, by God! it's late, dinner is ready, the table laid, my father's frowning at his watch, my mother is crying, "God! I hope nothing's happened to him!" Gladys is crying, "Calm down, Mother!" and Dorothy's saying, "Let's eat." Between the seventh and eighth stroke dinner is ready, the table laid, Father's glowering at his watch, Mother's shrieking, "God! I hope nothing's happened to him!" Gladys is shrieking, "Calm down, Mother!" Dot is saying, "Let's eat." Between the eighth and ninth dinner is cold, they're sitting at table, St. Paul is serving, Father's fuming, Mother's phoning the hospitals, Glad is wishing me dead and Dot is eating. Between the ninth and tenth dinner is over, the dishes are cleared, Father's reaching for his strap, Mother's prostrate, Glad's applying her pimple lotion and Dot is in bed. Between the tenth and eleventh all is saved. I am in the nick of time bursting in and all past grievances are forgotten in the general hullabaloo of rejoicing.

Indeed, so long was I permitted to dwell on this heart-warming scene I naturally presumed it was the last. The fatted calf was just about to be slaughtered, and I was literally salivating when the twelfth stroke fell. My mind went blank. The fatted calf went trotting back to pasture. The Chinese lanterns were whipped out of sight. Twelve o'clock. All I could think then was: No! There must be some mistake! I teetered on the edge of the pavement waiting for the thirteenth stroke, the kindest stroke of all, the stroke which would prove it was all part of some nasty nightmare. A beggar cleared his throat and spat. And it could not have brought me to reality better had it hit me straight in the face.

I began to run. One hand holding down my satchel and the other my hat, I pounded across the waste-ground. A startled dog chased me, but soon gave up. I was moving. Up the bridge I tore, cursing it, this futile elevation of the road to provide for a useless train tunnel. I made up for lost time on the down grade past the Mews, and nearly killed myself in

137

the bargain. During the last hundred yards I got to thinking about what was ahead of me, and slowed down to a jog. What I had to do at this stage was to plan the kind of entrance that would prove most effective in these straits. I could not think at all in my condition and started walking, as I fought to regain my breath.

Feverishly I groped for the perfect excuse, but soon gave it up. I had made this mistake before. Long experience made me realize that no excuse worked out in advance was worth a tinker's curse. How often had I come rushing in with this carefully concocted excuse blurting out of my mouth, only to realize in that instant, when it was too late, the MOOD of the family was all wrong for it; that some other excuse would have worked a thousand times better. It was obviously a great advantage to be forewarned of their MOOD before deciding on my line of excuses, so my preliminary course of action was clear. I would watch them for a minute from outside. Another minute later at this stage? A drop in the ocean, I thought.

I avoided the gravel by walking in the flower-beds, and stood on the hydrant by the front window. There was a chink in the curtains and I could see two of the gang. The window was open and I could also hear, but for some time all that came through was the panting of the punkah as no one spoke. My mother was lying full length on the sofa with her face turned up, her great swollen eyes in a state I recognized as being past weeping. She was always a trifle pale like her refugee friends, but tonight she was a sheet.

Gladys was looking at her with clasped hands, saying nothing. She was in her dressing-gown but hadn't got her lotion on yet. I couldn't see either my father or Dot, but heard papers rustling just under me by the window. Bracing myself I stood on tiptoe and saw the top edges of the *Evening News*. So I presumed it was Dad, as neither of my sisters read the papers. Glad mostly read *True Romance* and Dot went in for

138

ancient classics. But this time it turned out to be her in fact, as the phone rang and I heard my father's deep resonant voice answering it.

The papers rustled on, and as my father talked I found I could not listen as I was strained to the limit taking in the significance of the visual side of the situation. These three points were really alarming: Mother stunned speechless, Dot reading the papers, Glad not having her pimple-lotion on. Then my father's voice came booming its way through.

"There's absolutely nothing to be done at this stage, Reuben. It's too late. He's been playing up before but this time he's committed himself. Gestures of conciliation are out of the question, they've been tried too often in the past. He's gone wild, he'll tear through one end of the country to the other without a stop."

So they thought I'd run away. That was the thing to play on. I'd make out my love for them proved too strong however, and I came back.

"Indeed, I'll be very much surprised if he stops at the border. You mark my words, I don't want to sound pessimistic, Reuben, but by the autumn of next year he'll be in bloody Vostock."

Bloody Vostock? Where was that, near the Black Hole of Calcutta? I wondered. And in my wondering I must have shifted my foot an inch. I had temporarily forgotten where I was standing and let rest the full weight of my body on to the wheel of the hydrant. I fell, turning it full on. I bashed the crown of my topee on the ledge, and if my involuntary cry did not wake them, the spluttering of the hydrant gushing into the earth did.

The curtains slashed open and the light from the room fell on me lying prone on the sod. Dorothy peered out. "Is that you, Joe? Stop messing about. Shut that thing off and come in. Where have you been anyway?" The curtains closed again without a pause for my answer.

I did as I was told, and slunk in through the door, feeling thoroughly hang-dog in my damp pants and sola topee. The latter I kept on for further protection, and my satchel I held before me like a shield.

For some time my father said nothing. The punkah panted above my head like a bloodhound straining at the leash. I bit my nails into my palms and waited for it. He never ever forgot he was Bombay's most feared attorney and always allowed plenty of time for his pregnant pauses to ripple through the court. It never seemed to come. And when I saw that my mother looked at me unmoved and shut her eyes again, and that both my sisters barely noticed me, I began to realize something odd was going on here.

"I suppose this means," said Gladys instinctively patting her curls, "I had better cancel my appointment with the hairdresser."

No one replied, though Dorothy did look at her. My father opened his snuff-box for the third time since I was at the window and at last addressed me. "Where have you been, Joe? It's late. Everything's been cleared. Go and get yourself something to eat from the kitchen. Don't disturb the servants."

I sidled up to Dot. "What's been going on, Dottie?"

"Hitler's invaded Poland, Joe."

"They were coming here in December. They had tickets," I heard my mother say. "They'll be butchered." She closed her already closed eyes tighter as though she could avoid the sight. "My mother and father, and Esther and Isaac and their families—they'll be butchered in cold blood."

I went to the fridge in the pantry and got myself a breast of chicken. I sank my teeth into it. In spite of the steady grinding of my jaws in my ear I could hear my father in his most telling courtroom voice from within. "Well, it has happened. Today is September 3rd, the year 1939, and the Second World War had begun."

Golly, I thought, what a stroke of luck.

140

PART TWO

The Sutherland affair was finished and done with. Everything that happened recently pointed to the fact it would be so. The younger Sutherland had not returned to school as he had been his brother's charge. My father had not mentioned the matter again, and even Mum had stopped saying we should forget about it. The morning after the hookah party Wilfred had returned to school with the mugger's rugger boots and a letter of explanation regarding his absence. As he told Mr. Titmus it was from his mother I presumed she had returned overnight from Lahore. On the Punjab Mail? I did not ask. I did not wish to know. Nor did I notice the mugger puzzled to death about it, and as far as I could make out he'd even forgotten all about his "miserable paltry four annas".

As a group the three of us became neither more nor less united following the events of that peculiar evening. It had led to nothing further. I had no desire to smoke that muck any more, and was not curious as to whether Wilfred did. For myself at least the only lingering vestige of the entire affair appeared in the form of a nightmare—not for its content, but merely for its sequence in time. It occurred on the same night.

It was, to be precise, not a true nightmare, but a kind of corollary of one. Whereas in the latter one dreamed under the impression it was real, this particular occurrence in all its gruesomeness affected me not in the least, as I was fully convinced it was a nightmare. I dared say I was even smiling as I lay quietly there watching the scene unfold through a white obscuring mist. No question occurred to me. In the first place I did not ask what had awakened me, as I did not concede I was awake. And, secondly, what was this mist? I did not ask. The shuffling, sniffing noises I could hear made me suppose it was an animal; something large, perhaps a bloodhound. But as it approached stealthily closer I noticed it stood upright; so I thought it could be a gorilla. Its eyes, on the other hand, were glassy and owlish. Yet it could hardly be a bird as it did not have the characteristic jerky motion of winged creatures on the ground. On the contrary, its deliberate precision then gave rise to the idea it must be an invader from another world. It seemed surely too grotesque to be human. The head was over-sized, the garments ritualistic—a sort of uniform, vertically striped, rather like a convict's. Its broad dome, hairless save for two horned tufts above the ears, moved into a shaft of moonlight, bringing into stark relief the ukth mark, the strange scar that struck in childhood, to thenceafter bear witness to a man's Iraqian origin better than any legal document. It was him in pyjamas.

I saw him approach my bed. He touched the chair by it, and out of the corner of my eye I saw him run his fingers over my shirt and shorts, which I had discarded in a heap on the seat. He picked them up one by one, and pressed each to his face, inhaling deeply. He then grunted in a manner that only an intimate could have identified as satisfaction, put the clothes down, and tiptoed out.

I must have gone back to sleep at once. I did not recall this incident, as was usually the case with dreams, until much later. And the abruptness with which the recollection came, in the middle of Mr. de Lima's algebra period, at once filled me with puzzlement, revulsion and horror. There seemed no sense, in it, though if there was I felt I could not have picked a more appropriate time to sort out the riddle.

"$13dx^2 + 65md^3$. What is common to these two expressions? You, Levy, pick out the common factor."

Smelling my clothes? Smelling was common, and my clothes was common. But what was common to smelling and my clothes?

"You, Hosea!"

"I—I don't know, sir. Honest to God, I'm stumped."

"I'm grieved to hear that. But pleased I must say, surprised and delighted that you show such tragic concern about your ignorance. Cheer up! It won't kill you—alas."

There was laughter I barely heard. That scene haunted my mind like no mere nightmare. During the Physics, Latin, and the last, the Scripture period, there was one factor common: the picture of my father with his face pressed to my clothes.

That night the same thing happened. He didn't come in from work till midnight, and on entering this was the first act he committed. Concealed behind my mosquito-net, the white obscuring mist of my supposed nightmare, I was able to watch him without fear of discovery; though my fear of the event itself was now greatly increased in my readiness for it. It was as though I'd been all my life living blissfully unaware in the presence of a bogeyman, and was now made conscious of the fact. What I found particularly upsetting was that while in my previous encounters with my father I could open my heart to all and sundry, this grim, ludicrous and recurrent (for it happened the next night too) incident, was something I found myself unable to divulge.

"My father on coming home each night secretly smells my clothes." It was curious how in trying to see who was best suited to receive this information, my friends and relations fell into distinct categories. Factorizing, simplifying, and cancelling out assiduously in a way that would have thrilled Mr. de Lima I came to the conclusion after a week—during which time the nocturnal visit was faithfully repeated—that the only person I could speak to was Mr. Titmus. Yet even there some distaste rankled, and more and more did I feel bound to wrestle with the problem alone. If only I had a single clue to work on. He'd even stopped grunting now, and uttered not a single sound. On the eighth night, out of sheer desperation, I sprayed my shirt with Gladys's lavender. I had the satisfaction of hearing his grunt again, but all in all I was bound to admit I was no nearer the riddle.

I was indeed profoundly distressed, having by then grown so accustomed to the ritual of his nightly visitations that I could not sleep until he'd come and gone. Some nights I got no sleep at all, and the black circles under my eyes grew blacker. The whole day I found I was involuntarily keying myself up for the event to come. On the eleventh morning my father asked Gladys in front of me the reason for my piqued appearance.

"I expect he's worried about Mum like we all are," she replied.

"Am I?" I inquired.

"Naturally, as she's in hospital."

"Is she?"

"Joe," he said, "do you mean to tell me you are unaware your mother has been in hospital the past three days?"

"I didn't know," I admitted. "Should I have?"

"Young man," he said, "it's high time we had a little heart to heart talk."

"You're telling me?" I echoed. "You're telling me!"

He would take me out to dinner, give me a rare treat. We had arranged that he should pick me up in the car at school after the final bell. "Unless, of course," he'd added, "some urgent matter turns up at the courts."

"Or that I get kept in," I'd countered.

"You'll see to it that you don't, won't you?"

"*Deo volente*," I shrugged, reluctant to yield the only card I held. And now I had begun to play it consciously, as Mr. Titmus had so generously drawn my attention to it.

144

"You're not a bad fellow, Hosea, you're not fooling me. You're empty and transparent into the bargain. You just don't know what to do with yourself. You simply get people to expect evil deeds from you, and then they more or less happen. In the Middle Ages they called it Devil Worship, and have we a better term for it?" I'd told him that although I'd tried my best I could never see any difference between God and the Devil; but apart from our religious disagreements things were going very nicely between Mr. Titmus and me. I was making a vast improvement in my lessons and my position in class had moved up to third last. The masters in general were so pleased at my placid state of attentiveness that I did not think I could have been kept in that afternoon with the Devil's assistance.

After the last bell I looked over the balcony and found my father's car parked by the telegraph-post. He himself was looking at it, for stains no doubt, but by now the tell tale patch scrubbed clean on the pavement had been dirtied over by heavy showers of rain. There was nothing to be seen. It was as though the boy named Nickie Sutherland had never existed.

"So I was lucky I wasn't kept in, Dad."

"Lucky? or more diligent? or careful?"

"Lucky."

We got in. Bang! Bang! Bang! Bang!

"When are we getting a new car, Dad?"

"When the war ends."

"Even if we lose?" We were heading for Charni Road. "Why don't you answer?"

"Because I know that my reply will not affect you in the least."

"Mr. Titmus says although he knows what he has to say will not affect me he still says it."

"Mr. Titmus has not had you for fourteen years. Nor has he the prospect of another. You know, Joe, a parent has a peculiarly difficult——"

"Do you mean he's LEAVING?"

145

My father shot me an astonished look, for I had to admit I had half-shouted this out. He gave the slow-down signal at a crossroads, and then went through. "I don't know anything about Mr. Titmus's private affairs, Joe, but conscription into the Armed Forces is in full swing in England. I should hardly imagine that an able-bodied man like your Mr. Titmus will be exempted from military service."

We turned right at Charni Road. "Where are we going?" I demanded.

He didn't answer. "I said where are we going?"

"What does it matter? You're with me."

As we were approaching the sands of Chowpatty I said, "Would you have minded if I'd brought my friend Wilfred with me?"

"Who's Wilfred?"

"What does it matter? He's my friend."

"Your best friend?"

"Yes."

"Your only friend?"

"Yes."

"Does he smoke gunja too?"

He threw a casual glance at me in the driving mirror. We had begun to ascend Malabar Hill in second. He repeated the question even less accusingly than before.

"What's gunja?" I inquired, completely baffled.

"It's that stuff you were smoking on the night war was declared. Do you remember you came in at about midnight? You were reeking of it. The girls smelled it, but didn't know what it was. I myself did not smell it till later, as I'd been taking snuff. Your room was full of it. It's a dangerous drug, Joe."

I didn't say anything, and neither could he for a while, as the old Ford always made conversation impossible in first. I even found it hard to think with that racket and like hell I knew I needed to be smart and quick. Did he believe I was still taking that stuff? I'd clean forgotten about it until he'd mentioned it just this minute. Every night. This gunja, I marvelled, must really be lethal. It would be interesting to try it again.

I heard him clear this throat and realized we were in second once more. "How many times have you had it?"

"Oh, about half a dozen. *You* know how it is with that stuff. One forgets."

"Yes, I ought to know," he nodded. "Are you aware of the sort of case I've got on my hands at present?"

"No."

"Where d'you get that dope from?"

"I'd honestly like to tell you, Dad, but I don't want to get others into trouble."

"Do you know what you just uttered, Joe? In the criminal courts the most common expression is, 'I'm innocent.' The second is, 'I didn't know it was all *that* wrong.' The third is, 'I'd like to say, but I don't want to get others into trouble.' "

I said nothing.

"Do you know what the fourth expression is?"

I kept silent.

"Silence," he said.

The Ford roared again at the last grind up to the top. When we finally got there my father said, "I doubt we'll do this climb again. So let's make the most of it, son."

The Hanging Gardens were situated on Malabar Hill, the highest part of Bombay. There was an Observatory there, and the public grounds were tastefully decorated with flower-beds and neatly divided by hedgerows, some of which were trimmed into bird and animal shapes with great care and skill. Towards the end of the monsoon it was particularly pleasant to be up here, on one side overlooking the city and the other the Towers of Silence.

The last rains, the Elephants, were expected any time now, but today there was only one cloud to be seen, lazily circling itself, like some weary whirlwind on vacation. From time to time a shrill hawk or vulture cry erupted from its depths, to be answered before it cut off by a chorus of inestimable numbers. To those tourists who came up here looking for the Parsee Towers of Silence this pillar of cloud by day could serve as a signpost; though sometimes it was not there, and at more rare moments, if one was lucky as we were now, it could be seen swooping to disappear downwards; on its way to earth to save the worms a job, or rob them of a treat. It depended on how one looked at it; one's mood at the moment. That was of paramount importance.

"How long does it take to pick a body clean to the bone, Dad?"

"I wouldn't know. Let's move to a bench overlooking Chowpatty."

"We'll soon find out," I said, pointing to the Observatory clock, "when the cloud comes back. It shouldn't take long and it's only ten to five."

He nodded abruptly and seemed determined to please me —as far as was humanly possible.

"Naralwallah. Meeta naral, sahb?"

"Let's have onc, Dad, I'm awfully thirsty."

"Utcha paniwallah," he said to the vendor. The fellow whose skin was a shining black from walking about all his life in the sun, lowered the basket from his head and began to rap the coconuts experimentally with his knuckle. He found one that seemed to offer more juice than copra, though to my ear it sounded no different from any of the others he'd struck. I said nothing of course, as these fellows were not the ones to interrogate. He drew out the sharpest knife in the world from the sash around his waist, braced the coconut against the inside of his black fatless thigh, and began to slice off narrow segments of the husk, most of which fell neatly back into the basket. In between cuts he turned the thing gradually till after the second and third rotation the hard darker surface of the

148

shell appeared. I said, "What is it you actually want to speak to me about?"

For an instant he hesitated. Then he drew out his snuff-box and said, "In a minute I want to ask your advice."

"Fire away."

The vendor, exchanging his sharp knife for a heavy one, and holding the coconut vertically to save spilling struck the top off in three blows. He ripped off the few unsevered fibres with his hand and gave the dripping coconut to me. I waited for my father to speak before drinking. The coconut wallah waited for me to finish drinking so that he could scoop out the copra with a third knife. "Yes, Dad, you were saying?"

"Hie! Naralwallah!" A call came from a fez-capped Moslem on a bench way across our section of the gardens.

"Ahta seth! Zaroor ahta!" The coconut seller vigorously signalled with his knife-hand for his next customer to wait. He then looked at me, waiting for me to drink. I waited for my father to speak.

"You were saying, Dad?"

He seized the coconut from my hand, pitched the milk into the hedge, tossed the nut into the fellow's basket, gave him two annas, and said, "Utcha bhai, jao."

After a while two slim dainty young Hindu girls went effortlessly by, more sailing than walking, with the breeze billowing out their multi-coloured saris before them. The breeze had arisen rather suddenly.

"You satanic child," my father said. "Where did you pick that trick up from?"

"I think it was from you," I said. I made to go on and lapsed into silence.

"Well? Continue."

"You remember the last time I came to see you in court? It was when that young chap Kassem was being tried for murder. Kassem's main alibi was in the witness-box. That was the part I remember. I can't remember a word of what you were asking him or what he was replying. You were doing something with a glass of water which sticks in my mind like a leech. You kept raising it to your lips but never quite letting it get there. In the end everyone in court was more interested to see whether you would drink than in what was being said. You did drink in the end," I remarked, looking ruefully into the hedge, "But I didn't."

The breeze had brought life to a scene that had been merely pretty. There was still no sign of rain though, and it promised to be a glorious evening. The same lazily whirling cloud had taken its position again. I glanced at the clock.

"Where are you taking me out to eat, Dad?"

"I think it's time we went home," he answered.

Not a word was exchanged on the way back, till we got to Charni Road. "Do you work that one at school?" he asked.

"Yes," I nodded rather proudly. "Of course it's more effective with a new master. As soon as he addresses me I make as if I was about to sneeze. I stand up snatching the hanky from my pocket. 'Y-Yes sir?' I say, struggling desperately to suppress the sneeze. It's quite an exhibition and by the time he's asked his question it sounds less important than it might be. 'The B-Battle of Huh-Huh-Hastings?' I sniff, 'Er-er-er——' And he soon passes on to some other boy or drops the matter altogether. The question of the moment is not the result of some battle in 1066, but will Hosea sneeze?"

Near the Oval I heard him utter a kind of animal sound. I looked in the driving-mirror and noticed him grinning broadly to himself, about what I could not say.

"Spontaneous retribution," I heard him murmur, and didn't feel inclined to ask him what he meant. We were not more than a minute away from home then.

"Did you notice how I dealt with Kassem's second alibi though?" he asked, still faintly smiling.

"The prostitute he greeted in the street?"

150

"Uhuh," he nodded.

"You kept her in the stand for hours," I complained. "You just went on and on asking her about what he was wearing, and what she was wearing, and comparing it with what he said he was wearing and what she was wearing, and how was it he was wearing a Hindu type of turban when he was a Moslem, and how he could have been smoking on Ramazan when Moslems are forbidden and so on and so on, till I nearly fell asleep."

"Did it feel as if Kassem had spent hours with the prostitute?"

"Half his life, Dad."

"When in actual fact," he chuckled, "they passed one another without stopping."

"You sure cooked Kassem's goose, Dad."

We were in such good humour I hadn't noticed where we were. The engine was idling. We'd stopped outside the house. He switched off. Then slightly lowering his tone he said, "You'll cut out the gunja, won't you, Joe?"

"*Deo volente*, Dad," I shrugged. I opened the door and got out on to the pavement, leaving the door open for him.

"Shut it," he said. I slammed it shut first go. "Tell them I've some business to attend to and won't be in for dinner." He switched the engine on again.

"Is it about me, Dad? You're not going to see Mr. Titmus, are you? You're not spoiling it between us, are you?"

"Joe, one day the world will teach you a lesson you failed this evening to learn from me. The sun does not shine out of your bottom."

I could tell before I entered our visitors were new. Gladys never laughed quite so titillatingly on the second meeting. She was at her bosomiest best in the first flush of acquaintance. Dorothy was the opposite. It took months to draw her out. She wasn't in the sitting-room at all and had probably

151

gone out or locked herself in her room as she detested Gladys's friends. I hardly blamed her.

There were three girls all new; but something about their faces, a look of thoughtless and predatory greed, made one aware one had met them a hundred times before: in Glad's other friends.

They all stopped talking when I entered, and from the suppressed giggling I could guess that Gladys had been regaling them with stories of her notorious little brother. I slid into the piano stool.

"Well, Joe, aren't you going to say hello to my friends?"

I played two bars of "Chopsticks". Then I got up and softly lowered the top. They looked at me, their eyes glittering in anticipation.

"Well, Joe, tell us: are you any the wiser for your little outing with Father?"

"Yes," I lisped rather shyly. "It takes nine minutes for a flock of vultures to strip a man to the bone."

During the few days before my outing with Dad my admiration for Mr. Titmus had grown by leaps and bounds. My work didn't get any better, but I wrote less. So whereas before I used to get no marks for rubbish I now began to get none for nothing. Mr. Titmus thought this was a vast improvement, and the way I felt towards him made me disinclined to contradict. I found when with the help of my earlier experiments with Theorem 1 I checked myself from making an automatic refutation to the things he said, I began to experience a kind of freedom. It was something I could not at first identify as I had not felt it before; but by and by I came to see it was the freedom from ritual.

When I'd felt bound to contradict, my own answer in turn bound me, and then there was no retreat from the advance of the Juggernaut. Propitiation, revenge, the automatic response, machinery—it was how millions of Hindus had senselessly

152

crushed themselves under its wheels; it was how Nickie had died—though never once did Mr. Titmus make any open reference to the accident.

"Now, Joe," he said to me one evening after class, "you're beginning to plant the seed of self-control. When you stop blurting out or doing the first thing that comes into your head you make a decisive step to ending the stupidity and violence in yourself, and ultimately the world. Out of the ashes of the present the Phoenix shall presently arise; but what use will it be if it is not the Dove of Peace, and just another vulture?"

He spoke frequently now of the war and of Mahatma Gandhi, though not to the class, only to Wilfred and me. The mugger was getting to be a thorn in our side. Mr. Titmus did not address him in such terms, as he invariably got hold of the wrong end of the stick, and often he would confide to me that I should be wary of Mr. Titmus as he was not a Jew. He was not a bad chap, the mugger; he was not spiteful, not greedy, not unreliable, not silly, not unlikeable; one did not miss him so horribly.

The day after my outing with Dad we had Boxing the second last period, and Scripture the last; two periods I could both physically and spiritually survive without. Wilfred could never be persuaded to do a bunk, but when I mentioned the matter to the mugger he led as if it was his own idea. Scripture he didn't mind, but funked boxing so frantically he would have run into a burning house to escape it.

We left our hats and macs behind in our lockers to avoid suspicion, stuffed our homework books into our shirts, and sneaked out as soon as Mr. Titmus gave us our Latin prep and left. Our route in the circumstance lay through the Esplanade Maidan, as in the more direct one through Hornby Road and the Causeway we were likely to be spotted by a well-wisher or two.

All went smoothly as far as hostile action from the teeming world around us was concerned. In the relative security of the

153

broad serene green maidan we extracted our books and tied them with two pieces of string he had the forethought to bring along. As he so satisfactorily put it: "One for you, Joe, and one for me, Joe."

For a few suspicious and unwarrantable moments I thought this was a prelude to his asking the return of his four annas, as I always got the feeling when he did me a small favour that he was about to demand something twice as large. But on this occasion he seemed so carried away by the success of our evasive manœuvre that he in fact divulged a confidence of much personal value which he would never have granted otherwise.

"You know, Joe, I don't mind admitting—you won't tell this to anyone, will you?"

"No, no, never."

"I'm scared of boxing," he said—then added by way of some devilishly subtle rearguard action, "also."

"I'm not scared of boxing," I said.

"Oh, you aren't, eh? You aren't? Why did you suggest bunking then? I only did it to keep you company. Doesn't worry me one way or another."

"Well, it does me," I stated, "I'm against violence on principle. Violence breeds violence."

"Oh, yes, quite so," he nodded, not to be outdone, "I rather enjoy boxing myself, but it's the principle. All this violence, ugh."

We scrupulously skirted roped-in cricket pitches which we usually hurdled our way through; and I didn't know about *him*, but I personally looked around all the time to see if there was a Hindu-Moslem riot I could mercifully put an end to. But at that drowsy period in the sunny afternoon there were just a few people who were all either sleeping or steeped in tranquil delights. I was, indeed, quite without resentment stowing away my pacific resolutions for use another day, when in the centre of the maidan we heard behind us a

154

voice raised in song. And such a song it was that though the words were completely foreign to us it could not possibly have been expressing anything but the purest jubilation.

We looked back and saw approaching at an easy, flowing pace, rapidly overtaking us, a tall white-turbaned, black-bearded Sikh with a large bag of puffed rice, which he scattered about in handfuls as he went. A flock of pigeons flecked with doves attended him; messengers of peace. They clustered fearlessly around us as he passed, and we felt a part of them during those moments; rising and falling, wheeling, cooing and brushing us as they brushed one another with their wings. My heart swelled; the sense of mission repossessed me.

"Look at this man," I said. "He is a saint. He should be sent to wherever people are fighting and put an end to it all. The War for instance. It's a rotten disgrace, grown-up men going around—all Europeans too, *white* people! fighting and shooting one another with bows and arrows. If people would only get together and stop doing the first thing that come into their heads, then, and ONLY then, would the Phoenix be the Dove and not——"

"What bows and arrows?" he asked.

I knew exactly what he meant. I could easily there and then have admitted it was just a sort of metaphor, the kind that Mr. Titmus explained often enough; it had flashed into my mind accidentally, was of no consequence, certainly not to be taken literally; but the scoffing way he said it: "*What* bows and arrows?" as though to add, "Huh!"—it riled me horribly, and I felt bound to prove my point—in as nice a way as I could, of course.

"Don't you see the papers? The *Times of India*? The *Evening News*?"

"Yes, I see the papers," he retorted, "I look at POP every-day."

"POP! Huh!" I exploded—good-humouredly though, very

155

good-humouredly. "Sir, I am refering to those maps of the War in Europe. Those arrows, you know?"

"Oh, those *arrows*!" he exclaimed, his face clearing.

"Yes, you know one arrow stands for a thousand bowmen," I said, "or is it a million?"

We diligently skirted another cricket pitch in silence.

"You know, Joe," he said, a trifle uncertainly, "those arrows are not really arrows; they're symbols like in Geography maps."

"Yeah?"

"Yeah."

I remembered my resolution and let him proceed unimperilled. "Those arrows signify the strength of winds in the fighting areas. Climate is a very important factor in warfare. E.g. Napoleon."

"In all humility," I shrugged, "I suppose you're right. If there's a high wind for instance it would deflect the arrows."

"Yes," he nodded. Then gradually he stopped nodding, and screwed up his lips. "You know, Joe, I don't think bows and arrows are *actually* being used."

"Why not?" I challenged him, quietly enough, very quietly. And just *because* I was so nice about it he began to taunt me. He didn't even consent to answer but raised one eyebrow in that supercilious sneer of his.

"Why NOT!" I repeated in a shout—not a loud shout, not *very* loud. And that was just the trouble. The ignorant fool, he took meekness for weakness, and still deigned to reply nothing. By now we had come to our rugger pitch, and I stopped him against one of the H uprights. "Quit smirking and answer, boy! Why not?"

"What an ignorant fool!" he yelled. "They've got guns and tanks and bombs, why in blazing hell should they use bows and arrows?"

"Look here!" I yelled back, though much less angrily than he did, "I could kick your teeth in with my boot, but I'm not

156

going to, see? I'm going to use my *fist*! Why? Because we've got a CONVENTION! We've got a convention not to use guns, tanks, boots and poison-gas, see?" I was crushing his throat now as our convention permitted that, and he dropped his books to take a blind swipe at me. He missed by a yard and I helped him on his way with a left hook to the ear. On the second spin he grabbed his bundle of books up and hurled them into my chest. The string burst and I staggered and fell in a cascading shrapnel of books. I was up however, and in the next second we were pitching them at one another at point-blank range.

We gradually got driven apart in our search for those that had missed, when into our line of fire stepped Wilfred. He was half a head taller than the mugger and a whole taller than myself, so we couldn't help but notice him.

"What's the row about?"

"This wise judge of Judah says the arrows on the war maps are the prevailing winds!"

"And Goofy says they're *real* arrows, like at the Battle of Hastings 1066!"

"What do the papers say?" he asked.

"What?" we inquired together.

"Don't you *read*?" he snapped. "The newspapers aren't picture-books." He jerked his head nervously, hitched his satchel and made off in a manner which did not invite us to accompany him. In any case we had a great deal of sorting out to do before we could continue our way to our respective homes.

"Something wrong with Wilfred lately, Joe?"

"Yes, must be."

"What d'you suppose?"

"Search me."

"Must be because he's not a Jew."

"Yes, that's it."

"Always tells in the long run."

157

"Yes, too true."

"Good chap, though."

"Yes, too bad."

When I left him I could only think of one thing: is it possible to fight ignorance without warfare?

It was a question I was still brooding sombrely upon when I got home, otherwise I might have realized how very early it was. In spite of our scuffle in the maidan I was on the door-step before four, which was before school had finished. From past experience I knew there'd be awkward questions—if anyone was in. To kill time I thought I could go and steal mangoes from the back gardens, or sit in the Catholic Church. There didn't seem much to choose from. I was tired of detours anyway, so I decided to creep into my room, which had a garden entrance and lie doggo till 4.30.

I stole around the house and on entering the room what added greatly to the stealth of my movements was the sound of my father's voice.

I laid aside my books, and tiptoeing to my bed sat down inch by inch. In my heightened condition I could tell at once what was happening in the front room, having nothing to go on save two or three disconnected words. He was firstly speaking into the telephone as he was never at his best there. He was strictly a visual talker and knew it. Hence on the phone his voice carried a note of frustration, especially if he was addressing someone he wished to impress; in which case he could not be speaking to Uncle Reuben, nor any of our close friends and relatives, but someone comparatively new, since both he and Gladys were always at their most impressive during the early stages of acquaintance. The proverb about familiarity breeding contempt was, to my way of thinking, a futile mumbling half-truth, until it entered our home. Then it really found its voice.

"Well, thank you, Arnold, it's very kind of you to say so.

I never knew you were in the gallery yesterday or I might have exerted myself a little further and got him ten years more. Ha! ha! yes, why not? A killing under the influence of dope isn't manslaughter, it's murder. But the trouble, no matter how long a sentence I got him, is that the power of criminal appeal in India is excessive. . . . Ah, yes, I've heard that argument put before, it's begging the question, isn't it? . . . Precisely! The trouble is that to extend the powers of criminal appeal does nothing to provide a safeguard against the inefficiency of the judges in this country. More appeals demand more, not better, judges. The only law that's well served here is that of diminishing returns. No, what this country needs is a small hand-picked number of English trained legislators and the introduction of the French inquisitorial system. Then the wheels of Justice will have something to GRIP on to. . . . Strong measures, I admit, but the effect of these appeals is particularly galling to us on this side of the fence. I go to all the trouble of getting a felon, as say yesterday, a ten-year sentence, to find him ten months later thumbing his nose at me in the street. . . . Of course I agree there's a great deal more to be thrashed out in a matter of this nature and look forward to a *tête à tête*, though not on Friday since it seems I am not permitted to be present. . . . No, there's no need to consult him, *he'll* be here. I'll see to that, and don't worry about me either, I'll see to it I'm not here. . . . Very well, then, my daughters will effect the introduction skilfully enough. But— just a minute—I want to impress on you that this present trouble, the narcotic taking, has nothing whatsoever to do with the home situation. It is purely derived from suppressed feelings of guilt after the misadventure. . . . Ah, yes, but that's putting the cart before the horse, isn't it? . . . Precisely! Yes, hmm, quite, well, good-bye, Arnold, I do hope the fact of my absence will be of enormous advantage to all concerned. Good-bye."

Cling! It was an angry, buzzing, penetrating noise. I could

still hear it after he'd gone. The house was as quiet as a tomb save for this ever-diminishing but never quite silent cling. And still I could hear it. At what point precisely would I stop hearing it? I wondered. I listened harder and harder as the sound grew fainter, throwing all my resources to the attainment of this one single aim, till quite suddenly I, so to speak, overtook the rate at which the sound was receding and it actually began to get louder!

Lying comfortably in bed as I was I scarcely apprehended the danger I was running until it was too late. Indeed, like some innocent child quite carried away by the novelty of the thing I strained harder and harder, and the sound having passed the volume of its original cling began rapidly to rise to a deafening pitch. I tried desperately to check the whole machinery but it was accelerating now beyond control. I thought my ear-drums would explode and my head with them, when—"Woof! woof!" a dog barked outside.

I found I had reared stiffly up. I was pouring with sweat. Phew! I sank back. This should serve as a lesson to me. Mr. Titmus was right, dead right. If a chap didn't have self-control he didn't need a war to kill him; a little musical sound could blow him to pieces as effectively as a bomb. In all conflicts large and small there was only one way of fighting back; instead of violence: self-control. And of course one had to know exactly what one was fighting. A true knowledge of the enemy called for study, for acute and accurate observation.

I saw a letter with an Indian stamp on my bedside table. It was addressed in a strange looping hand, which in spite of its striking symmetry proved very difficult to read when it actually came to it. I was cautious. I did not want to open a letter that was not addressed to me—not by accident anyway. Joseph Hosea. There was only one of those in Bombay. Having thus ascertained it was beyond a shadow of doubt mine, property I was lawfully free to dispose of in any manner I pleased, I was seized by the impulse to tear it up unread. It galled me to think that I should *have* to read it. For the next five minutes I reconsidered the matter in the light of my past experiences, and at the same time sensed Mr. Titmus's advice on the problem. I cut it open with my penknife. It was from my mother. My mother in hospital.

Before I could read a word, tears came into my eyes. Well, well, I mused, this is an historic moment: the first time I've had a letter from Mum.

I read it through once. I reread it. Then I read it upside-down. I turned to the other side. It was blank. This I found, after some application and study, to be instructive. I saw visions, delicious visions of a particular kind. For a while I let myself be entranced. A little more down-to-earth consideration, and I thought: no, it's not a possible solution to my problems. I couldn't see Mum as Mrs. Titmus. Not when it came to it.

For one thing, Dad would be against it. There were a thousand and one insurmountable hurdles I could think of, but they weren't worth recording. Those days when I made a count just for the fun of it were over; and lately I more than once had the urge to throw the total book away. It reminded me so much of my childhood, my wasted years when the ordeals I had faced were more imaginary than real. This that I had on my hands now showed all of them up. It was concrete, it was real. The enormity of the thing appalled me. How could I forge a more binding link with this perfectly faultless and godlike man? How? How? How?

I could not know how long I lay there struggling to find a relevant, an adult solution, before certain alternatives occurred to me. If not Mum, what about Glad? Oh, she'd be keen enough to meet him. She'd positively gush at the first meeting. She'd trickle at the second. On the third, if she suffered it, she'd emit a kind of sluggish vapour, and she'd yawn, oh, boy, how she'd yawn. She'd look from left to right

161

while he was uttering pearls of wisdom, and then suddenly excuse herself to phone. A matter of life and death, very grave, to be sure. She'd laugh on the phone, boy, how she'd laugh. She'd laugh and laugh so merrily that when it became obvious to him she'd found happiness at last, he'd get up to go. She'd gallantly tear herself away from the phone then to see him to the door with sudden gushes of renewed enthusiasm. She'd be heart-broken he couldn't stay. Couldn't he stay a teeny-weeny, just a teeeeny-weeeeeeeeeeeeeeeeeeeny bit longer? He'd hesitate a second. But he'd know. Mr. Titmus would know counterfeit from true.

I knocked on Dorothy's door.

She wasn't pleased to see me. But who ever was? Or who cared who was? Not I. As long as I was there, throbbing with confidence for the success of my venture, the opinions of others could take a trip. Though of course a bit of charm was not out of place. A little oil to the wheels, those unseen, unseeable but indubitably rusted old wheels. When had they last moved? Slyly I'd asked her. She couldn't remember. I could; almost to the day. They used to bowl so effortlessly along it seemed as though there was nothing there to go wrong, like a car without an engine. Then things began to grate and shudder. A thousand little unmusical sounds rang out; noises that were horrid to listen to, but much more instructive than any sonata. It was only when one heard them one became aware how bafflingly complex the machinery was; and how perfect it had been.

It had happened about a year ago. It was all her fault I'd reckoned. The evidence was pretty clear. The gulf had parted her not only from me, but the whole family. Her adored father. It was the first time in my life, at thirteen, that I looked at him and knew what he felt deep down inside the heart of him. And now I knew how *she'd* felt. The idol. It had cracked. Her face had changed; her features tightened, moved closer together, became sharper. Cleverness turned to cunning. She was seldom now at home, always in the library, had no friends about her, but books. Nothing fancy like *True Romance*; ancient, musty-smelling books. No pictures in them; only words, just words, very closely printed words.

"What's that you're reading?"

"*Hamlet.*"

"A new book for a change?"

"Well," she said, looking up with a sigh as she realized that for better or for worse I was here to stay. "It's one of Shakespeare's latest."

"Oh, Shakespeare," I waved conversantly, "Mr. Titmus knows him, he's also English."

"Is he indeed?"

"Yes, he's always remembering how Shakespeare says this and Shakespeare says that; and what Shakespeare definitely does *not* say. So he must know him personally. Mr. Titmus is the cleverest man I've ever met, Dorothy. He says just the kind of things you say, but better, of course. He's a man."

"I'm sure," she answered, looking really interested.

"He's twice the man Dad is. He never takes snuff." I curled my nostrils in disgust. "Has Dad just been in here?"

"Yes. As a matter of fact he——"

I sniffed contemptuously. "Poor Mum, what she has to put up with. You know, Dorothy, if Mrs. Titmus asked—mind you, he's not married—not *yet*—I'm just saying *if*. If Mrs. Titmus asked Mr. Titmus, not ten thousand times, but just once, to stop taking snuff, or any other revolting habit he might have, he'd stop it. In fact he'd stop it without her saying a word, he's a kind of prophet, you see?"

She nodded wordlessly. She had put her book aside altogether and was listening so intently I knew I was making headway. But I must not rush him on to her, I cautioned myself, she was a fish who reacted violently against any sort of pressure. I'd lay the bait, and let her come.

163

"He's terribly handsome, has wavy brown hair and steel blue eyes. He's strong, and gentle, and completely fearless. His teeth are a bit crooked, but no crookeder than yours; and a lot whiter. You shouldn't eat so many chocolates, Dorothy, you started on this box only this morning, and it's not what you might call a small box." The three-layer box was almost empty. "Though, of course," I assured her, "if you *insisted* on eating them I doubt he'd say one word to stop you. In fact he'd bring you a couple of boxes every day. When he came home after work."

"Sounds like a paragon of animals," she sighed wistfully. "I'd like to meet him, but——"

"You *would*, Dorothy?"

"Yes, but I'd much rather meet his friend, Shakespeare."

"Oh, him!" I snorted. "He's not all *that* marvellous. I mean—as Mr. Titmus points out—what would Shakespeare have done without *Lamb's Tales*?"

"That's a shattering thought."

"Precisely! He's nothing but a great cribber, and I shouldn't be a bit surprised if he's in the lock-up."

"So why does Mr. Titmus hobnob with a scoundrel like that?"

"Because Mr. Titmus has a big heart, Dorothy. He'd hobnob with anyone. I mean, even you." I leaned forward confidentially. "Do you know what he told me?" My voice fell to a whisper. "He said the ultimate solution to the world's problems is mixed marriages."

She'd stopped eating chocolates, and that really meant she was at the bait now; looking at it, sniffing it, fingering it. "What d'you say, Dorothy?" I tried to conceal the excitement in my voice, but couldn't. At the same time I didn't think she noticed though, not at this stage. Her brown, deep-set father's eyes had a distant smiling look. She was hooked, nicely hooked. "Well, Dot, will you meet him?"

"All right," she said, "we'll fix a day. In the meantime though——"

"Hurray!" I cried. "Hurray!" I crouched at her feet, for we were conspirators now. "There's just one thing, Dottie," I said, "you mustn't rush him. He's a fearfully timid sort of man, and liable to shy off when directly approached. We must——"

"By indirections find directions out."

"What? Yes. A rugger match, that's it. When he's on duty with the boarders he'll be on the touchline, and I'll sort of casually introduce him to you. Dorothy?"

"Yes, dear?"

"What will you say? You won't talk to him NATURALLY, like you do the rest, will you?"

"Upon my honour, I won't."

"Then after the third or fourth meeting, you'll ask him around to tea. But you must wait for the signal. I'll sound him first, O.K.?"

"As you say, dear. But speaking of inviting people to tea, Dad was just speaking to me, and we—I'd like you to be here on Friday. Have you a match on?"

"No."

"Then you'll come home soon, won't you? I—we want you to meet a friend of ours."

"Of course, of course," I nodded. "I'd love to." Nor was I fooling. I was so thrilled at having her agree to meet Mr. Titmus I would in return have consented to meet the Gorgon. If she only knew it!

On Friday there appeared, driving a fat black Buick, a big smooth man in a sharkskin suit, to which, to what and to whom I took an instant dislike. I didn't know him and he didn't know me; but he looked at me as if he was going to, and that got my BACK up. When I answered his questions, he nodded familiarly as though to show he'd heard all these replies before, and THAT got my back up. About half-way through tea he began to talk to Dorothy about God Almighty, which was an infallible indication he'd taken a fancy to her, and that got my back UP.

Not to mince words, it was a foregone conclusion, before I had even met him, that there would be no love lost between Dr. Frumbusch and me.

He was one of a growing group of European Jews in Bombay. Germans, Austrians, Czechs, Poles; doctors, dentists and post-hole makers, all busily setting up practices far, far superior to our poor native ones. They were to be found waltzing around the Jewish Club on Saturday nights, gargling their Rs and zissing and zatting of beautiful things, namely the things they left behind. They greatly added to the local colour, being of many varieties themselves, though the mugger with his genius for essentials could only distinguish two types: (1) Those mit eyebrows; (2) those mitout eyebrows.

Dr. Frumbusch belonged to the latter class. His vast blond flat face, crying out as it did for more decoration than normal, was strikingly devoid of eyebrows. Apparently to make up for the deficiency however, he had acquired under his left eye a recurrent twitch that stabbed like lightning when he was excited. He was on the whole a very well controlled man, of large, slow, almost hypnotic gesture, but who had bouts of nervous gesticulation when he was really worked up. This occurred mainly in conversation with Dorothy, not me. Gladys was absent, which was the mystery of the century, until I heard during their conversation about God she'd already met him twice at the Jewish Club. This I instantly regretted, wincing out loud, so that they both paused in their conversation to look at me—though not for more than a moment, before turning to reimmerse themselves in their discussion.

I very soon came to realize exactly how fell a blow Gladys's absence was to the furthering of my plans. How typical of
166

her, I brooded, the Mistress of the Wrong Moment. She always arrived in state when her absence was desperately desired; and when, to be precise, once every fourteen years I needed her, she was not to be found. And then I dropped the Taj-bought cake I had in any case been nibbling without relish, and exclaimed, By God! Mum too! If Mum were here this would not be happening either. Mum would have been a more invincible ally in such a circumstance, for if Glad was the Mistress of the Wrong Moment, Mum was the Mistress of All Moment. She would without any of those exceedingly embarrassing trills, the preening, the gurgling, the cooing, unquestioning and unquestionably taken possession.

Dorothy would not have got a word in edgeways—not that she'd ever wanted to. Or had she? How could one tell from that sphinx-like expression? Now I had to ask. I'd once seen Gladys naked and she'd looked to me very like a naked woman twice her size. Dorothy looked clothed; annoyed certainly, but unembarrassed, unexposed. There was an air of reticence about her that was impenetrable, a mystery she was not going to offer up to the first-comer, and in the three days following on her vow to meet Mr. Titmus I had come to the conclusion that no couple in the world were more suited for each other than these.

As the significance of what I was planning to do became clearer, I thrilled at the prospect involved. Not only was I at a single stroke forging a new link with my master, but recoupling one broken off in the past with my sister. Prospect, indeed, was a miserable expression; a whole new world was opening up, a realm in which I would take my place as Prince —no! Creator! For, without excessive modesty on my part, what would have come about had I not instigated the affair? Nothing. And out of nothing I had seen it evolve. My world. Scores of times over the past three days I had seen it in ever increasing detail in my mind; I could see it now as they talked, crumbling in front of my eyes, aghast, helpless, open-mouthed: the astonishing spectacle of my sister Dorothy displaying an interest in a man.

Astonishing was a miserable word—as miserable was the man. Odious, smarming, guileful, conceited. A big, pink, over-stuffed prig. And she? Was she any better? Any more sincere? Or had she simply a bad memory? She with the memory of an elephant for details smaller than pinpricks? Had she abandoned Mr. Titmus after so fleeting an acquaintance? *Before* the first meeting? Dorothy out-Gladysing Gladys?

"Ha! ha! ha! ha!"

Who had laughed? Both of them, they'd laughed spontaneously and together. I felt a kind of panic arising out of my frustration, but compelled myself not to act on first impulse. This was, needless to say, to order my sister never to see this man again; but such a thing would only drive her more quickly into his arms. No, what I had to do was to make a blatant effort to stampede her into his arms, and she'd go off like a rocket in the opposite direction. It was hence with no faint-hearted sense of purpose that I determined at the moment when tea had ended to hang on whatever the cost.

They got up from the table to sit in easy chairs, and I was not slow to take note of the familiarity with which he waited for her to occupy the long upholstered cane one, and then take his place by her side. Concealing my feelings as best I could I went and sat on a hard-backed chair, dragging it as near to them as the intervening vase-topped table would allow. This was I felt an improvement on my original impulse to ram myself between them, and it augured well for the battle to come. I was sitting there wondering what I could do to break up their discussion, as Dorothy looked as if she were about to resume it, when our guest thought it fit and proper at this stage to take a little notice of me.

"Well, well, well, well," he remarked jovially, "and what are you going to do when you grow up, Josef?"

168

I rapidly scoured my brain for the answer that would involve us for as long a time as possible, and said, "I'm going around the world."

"Doing what?"

"Looking."

"Looking for what?"

"My true mother."

His left eye twitched. This was the first time for *me*. And Dorothy was no less affected. "Don't be ridiculous, Joe." She turned apologetically to our guest. "You mustn't take any notice, he's been saying this off and——"

He quietly and politely put up his ample hand. "Let Josef speak."

"It's a fact," I continued, stubbornly avoiding her eye. "There was a mistake made at the hospital. Some stupid nurse put me in the wrong cradle. The cradles looked alike, the babies looked alike, and some nurses are cross-eyed, so what can you expect?"

He nodded accommodatingly, as though he'd heard all this before. "I do see what you mean, Josef. A mistake *may* have been committed, but have you ever realized that two mistakes may have occurred? That one nurse may have put you in the wrong cradle, and a second may accidentally have put you in the right one?"

This floored me. "It may be," I had to agree, "but how can we find out?"

"I can help you," he said, glancing slyly at Dorothy.

She said, "Dr. Frumbusch is a teacher, Joe, and he——"

"Another private tutor!" I exclaimed, instinctively rising to go.

"Look, Josef. Dorothy——" he turned to her with a delicate sway of his corpulent bosom. "I hope you don't mind me calling you Dorothy?"

"Not a bit!" I roared. "She likes you! She——"

"Look, Josef," he interrupted with two twitches in a row,

"Miss Hosea, your sister, is quite wrong about me. I am not a teacher at all. I am—what shall we say?" He raised a great soft hand as though to milk an imaginary udder drifting about in space. "The opposite!" he cried, snapping shut his fist. "I am an UNteacher! I do not teach but take away and throw out all the useless things you have learnt. Do you understand?"

"Yes. Latin, that's a dead language."

"No, no, no, no, noooooooooooo," he sang. "Look here, Josefff, I want you to do me a grrrreat favour. I want you to come to my—er—classroom on Hornby Road tomorrow at eleven. Tomorrow Saturday. See, I will write it on my card. There! Come and I will show you how I can improve your lessons at school by UNteaching!"

"Oh, I'd like that, Dr. Frumbusch," I said, regarding the gilt-edged card with genuine awe, as I'd never been handed one of these before in my life, not even in dramatics.

There was a long pause as they both watched me. Then Dorothy said with a note of finality, her most favourite note, "Well, you needn't stay if you want to see Aaron." She explained to him, "That's his best friend."

"Oh, I've no friends," I interrupted, "I'd much rather stay here with you."

"You have no friends? Ah, surely you exaggerate."

"No, I don't, I hate everybody."

"What about yourself?"

"I like myself," I admitted. He nodded to show he knew he'd catch me out; he knew everything about me, he only listened to me out of sheer charity, and on his fourth or fifth nod I was impelled by a desire to get a hold of that big, bulbous artificial flower vase on the table between us and smash it over his smooth, slickly pomaded skull. But thanks to Mr. Titmus I was learning how to deal with such situations more effectively. "Yes, you're quite right," I nodded keeping time with him, "I like myself quite a bit, Dr. Frumbusch, though not half as much as I'm beginning to like *you*. Of course," I

170

added glancing slyly to one side, "I shall never ever like you as much as Dorothy does. Don't you, Dorothy?"

"Yes, I do," she nodded.

Did I hear right? For a minute I couldn't speak. I had no first impulse, no second thoughts, nothing. It was all I could do just to sit there pretending to listen. "Yes, I do," she'd said. Was that not an expression used at marriage ceremonies? I could hardly believe my ears.

"To continue with the point you raised a few minutes ago, Dr. Frumbusch, I have a bone to pick with you. Why can you not accept my statement that I am an atheist?"

"Now I am not saying you aren't—er—Miss Hosea. It's simply that you have not yet defined God in your refutation of Him. God, in most general terms, is man's relationship to what is unknowable; and since we are always bound to relate ourselves to the grrreat preponderance of unknowables about us——" he circled his arms like a windmill in a gentle breeze, "—how can we deny the existence of God? Do you see what I'm getting at, Dor—er—Miss Hosea?"

"She doesn't mind you calling her Dorothy, Doctor——"

"Yes, I *do* see what you're getting at," snapped she, half to him and half to me. "And while I admit it is true that in my refutation I did not define God, did you in your introduction of the unknowable define it? I mean, what exactly is unknowable, Doctor——?"

"You can call him Arnold," I whispered, showing her the card. "Or Wolf."

But he'd got her on her favourite subject now and she was so carried away by the argument she brushed my hand impatiently aside. "Don't think I am all that easily deluded, or side-tracked by sophisms. When I say I am an atheist, that's just what I mean."

"But I am not denying that you are an atheist!" he retorted getting all upset himself. "What I mean is," he jutted his great face nearer towards her and described nervous arcs with his

171

hands, quite ignorant of the fact that the flower vase on the table between us could be knocked over by a touch. "I mean you are being unfair! You ask a question and then fly off at a tangent before I can answer it!" Another couple of inches and he'd have sent it flying with a crash. It did seem a pity. As he went on, waving, hooking and uppercutting his way through the unknowable, I pushed the table leg with my foot. It slid on the thick pile of the carpet with thrilling ease.

"Stop! Stop!" cried Dorothy. Guiltily I stopped. But she wasn't talking to me at all. "Your definition of the unknowable is quite unacceptable to me, AND (I dare say!) to the most ancient of astronomers too. For if they'd have said the cause for the retrograde motion of Mars was unknowable we would have been no wiser today. But that cause, as you know (I hope!) is knowable. Furthermore——"

"Please! Please!" he half-shouted, flinging his mighty arms about in abandon. "That is not what I mean by my definition of the unknowable! My definition is not FIXED, in so far as the boundaries of the unknowable are NOT FIXED, but constantly in a state of movement, both inwardly," he crossed his arms on his bosom, "and outwardly!"

CRASH!

"Dumkoff! Look what's happened!" he shrieked. Then recovering with the blithe ease of a spring lamb he laughed. "Ha! ha! ha! This is my definition of the unknowable! Accident, Dorothy! Accident!" In his excitement he seized her by the shoulders.

"Oh, Arnold," she nodded, "I do begin to see what you mean."

I left the room in case she'd get me to collect the pieces.

A bloke never feels so alone as when he's trying to help someone in secret. Plotting his death is jollier. I stayed in the garden, not knowing what to do with myself apart from resisting the impulse to go back to school to inform Mr. Titmus

172

of the matter. What could I tell him? I rehearsed it aloud, since from the time I could speak I had found the actual utterance of a thought gave it sudden and altogether un-expected significance, or demolished it completely.

"Sir," I addressed the jack-fruit tree, the nearest stand-in I could find, "the woman of your heart, your soul-mate, the mother-to-be of innumerable little blue-eyed Titmuses is right here and now being stolen from under your nose. But *nil desperandum*! I am doing all I can to thwart the villain. I'll be his brother-in-law over my dead body. Back on watch now, next report sundown." I took two smart steps to the rear, saluted the jack-fruit tree—one pause two—right-turned and dismissed with no dearth of heel-clicking. I then saw our next-door neighbour without his cap looking at me through the barbed-wire.

I waved my arms stiffly about. "I'm practising semaphore, Major."

He couldn't have heard as he went in wordlessly. There goes another, I thought, lonely as the last of the dodos. When people get that broken, hollow, sequestered look they were going through it. They were helping others in secret. What were the highest dividends? Sloughed off snake-skins. The way to help was *his* way: with drum and trumpet fanfares, and signboards all along the route saying: THIS WAY FOR HELP—DR. FRUMBUSCH. I extracted his card: ARNOLD WOLF FRUMBUSCH, M.D., D.P.P.S., VIENNA. And now? Bombay. Not doing too badly either. His big, fat, shining, black-assed Buick was still outside. It was really very strange how one could look at an owner's car and tell exactly what he was up to. A car talked. It leered, sneered, spat contempt, or in reserving comment said, "You? How could you kill such an immense man?"

I got out my pocket-knife, and began to sharpen it on a stone. Rasp rasp rasp. I was not so foolish as to think of stabbing him, but if they came out here into the garden—to

173

romance, for example—rasp! rasp! rasp!—and if he stood there at that spot, and if I happened to be on the bough directly overhead, and if I happened to be cutting into the stalk of the twenty pound jack-fruit hanging there, I might as well have a keen blade I reckoned. Rasp rasp rasp rasp rasp rasp rasp rasp rasp rasp rasp rasp rasp rasp rasp rasp rasp rasp rasp rasp rasp rasp rasp rasp rasp rasp rasp rasp rasp rasp rasp rasp rasp rasp rasp rasp rasp rasp rasp rasp rasp rasp rasp rasp rasp rasp rasp rasp rasp rasp rasp rasp rasp rasp rasp rasp rasp rasp rasp rasp rasp rasp rasp rasp rasp rasp. It was getting blunter.

I then remembered my bowie knife in my drawer and stole back into my room. I could hear them talking softly as I eased open the drawer and felt for the weapon under my clothes.

"Are you sure he's gone?"

"Yes, you can't keep him in the house on weekends. It was only by a daring ruse that I managed to get him to come to tea this evening."

"Who's he usually with?"

"Fortunately he's most of the time with his friend Aaron, who's an awfully nice boy."

"Ah, that's half the battle, Dorothy; friends. When all the rough edges of our psychologies have been removed it will only be to expose the sharp cutting edge of friendship."

"And my only hope is that you will succeed with him, Arnold. For my sake. For years now I've been secretly endeavouring to assist him without forcing advice down his throat. He rejects everything that's directly administered. And I can tell you it's a wearying, a thankless, a devastatingly lonely experience to be with him for five minutes."

"My dear Dorothy, loneliness is a state I am well adjusted to."

"Well then, you shall survive the first five minutes."

"What next?"

"In the next five, till as long as he condescends to remain

with you, you will come to realize there's no one in the room but himself. For myself, I am beginning to see another person altogether in his presence: the kind of woman this boy is destined to marry."

"What does his father say?"

"Much the same. It is pointless giving the boy anything, whether he's in dire need of it or not. Dad is reduced to leaving these essentials lying around in the hope he'll pick them up. Anonymous fatherhood, he calls it."

"And his mother?"

Silence.

"Your sister?"

"Arnold, all I can say is that if he does turn up tomorrow I shan't be envying you. I——"

I left the drawer open and stole back into the garden. Taking position by guesswork, I stood under the jack-fruit tree. To verify I looked up. I moved an inch to the left, and one back. It seemed exactly right. I drew up to attention and shut my eyes.

"Hie, there, cocky, here's a manual on semaphore for you."

That wouldn't fall if I stood here for a year. A hundred years. I knew that. Christ, I knew that. But the postures of execution . . . the waiting . . . the imagining.

"What's the matter, cocky? Seen a ghost?"

The next day I arrived ten minutes before time at his office and dallied at the entrance. His sign was freshly painted, being as yet unmarked by the crimson beetlenut spit that streaked the others, and it gave the impression of a man newly arrived at his station in life. This, of course, was false, since pots of paint were readily available.

PSYCHIATRIST. It sounded good, very good. But it could hardly fool a seasoned campaigner like me. When a fellow weakened in the long search for his true station, it was all too tempting to snatch at a straw—some fictitious gobbledegook

175

that fooled everyone but himself. In the long run it didn't pay. It wasn't honest, and my opinion of Dr. Frumbusch would have sunk even lower were it not already on a bed of rock.

I pushed through the swing-doors and was received by a liveried hamal who showed me into an empty waiting-room which was very tastefully furnished, a sure threat of impending skullduggery. He offered me a name-slip and pencil, the sight of which at once made me tremble. I took a good hold of myself and wrote: Joseph Franklin Hosea. The second name was a fiction, admittedly, but then wasn't the first? Goddamnit! I had as much right to name myself as anyone else. Sooner or later a time came in a chap's life when he had to strike out for himself. I clenched my fist to box the air, and noticed a pile of *National Geographic* magazines on the table before me. The true character of these were well known to me from my many appointments with Mr. Tinbhoy, the dentist, and I at once swept the whole pile towards me.

This was an unexpected windfall, I thought, for I had long ago given up hope of ever seeing my most favourite magazine outside the dentist's waiting-room, where I invariably felt ill at ease. I had never complained to him about it, yet it was none the less true, that the pleasure I used to get looking at pictures of naked pigmy women at Mr. Tinbhoy's was alloyed by the noise of his drill. It was the pleasure of eating Turkish Delight sitting on a spike. Today without the prospect of pain to follow, I reckoned I would be in a position to extract the maximum joy out of looking at pictures of naked pigmy women, and I was dead right. I always was in calculations of that kind; though even I could not have anticipated the strength of the electric shock that went through me, when on opening the first magazine at random I saw the picture of a naked pigmy woman confronting me.

I could not say I actually swooned, but the pleasure was great, and very acute. Powerless to tear my eyes away had the ceiling caved in, I stared at it, bringing the picture closer, and closer still, straining at the leash in my eagerness to experience a renewal of that initial delight. But what happened in actual fact was that the pleasure got steadily less and less, till in a matter of seconds I could get no more out of this naked pigmy woman than the duck-billed platypus on the facing page.

A question struck me. A question sizzling like a red-hot poker in my brain. Why? Why did the pleasure diminish? Why did it not INCREASE? The answer to such a question was not beyond my scope, and now I felt was the time for research, now, if I'd the courage, now in the pangs of it. Resolutely I shut the magazine. Then I shut my eyes. Working from top to bottom, I turned the pages slowly one by one, palpating the surface of each carefully with my finger-tips.

By and by I came to it. I was absolutely certain it was her. If I felt anything I felt that shock, the spirit of that primordial woman surging through my finger-tips. Her form unhindered entered mine; and here lay the proof following hard upon. It couldn't have been more simple. I had merely to look. To look. Yes, and suppose I did? Suppose I opened my eyes and saw that the woman I was allegedly caressing was in fact an aerial view of New York? God! I almost cried out loud. That *would* be proof! Proof of quite another thing. Could I bear it? No—to be honest, *never*! I slammed shut the magazine and threw it aside. I heard it fall to the floor with a thump, but didn't dare look for some time yet. I felt I'd had a narrow shave and wasn't quite sure I was now in the clear; though of this I was, and very sure too: I had a whole lifetime looking at pictures of naked pigmy women ahead of me, and I was damned if I was just going to sit there letting it be proved that this pleasure was false.

I always dreaded being left alone with a problem once I'd solved it, as from bitter experience I had come to learn that in a very short while I would realize a better solution was possible. And one better than that. And so on, *ad infinitum*. Naturally I had no wish to spend my life as a missionary, as it were, penetrating deeper and deeper into the effects of naked pigmy women offering themselves up to be photographed; and it was with some show of welcome I noticed a silk-sari-draped, distinctly unnaked Parsee lady coming out of the inner office. She did not see the look of profound gratitude I gave her and wafted by. Sight and smell combined she seemed to be floating on scented diamonds, and I couldn't help wondering what Dr. Frumbusch had to unteach *her*.

I smartly reminded myself of the matter at hand, and got up tucking my total book in business-like fashion under my arm. I had thought all night of beating his brains out with, for example, a paper-weight on his desk; so I wanted very much to impress him with my intelligence, initiative and prompt attendance—and anything else that would get him to lower his guard. At the same time I was quite prepared to climb down a rung, as far as beating his brains was concerned, in shifting my ground from the literal to the metaphorical, since although I was aware the metaphorical could at its most dazzling best never surpass the literal, it had its peculiar advantages. I could, for example, beat out Dr. Frumbusch's brains just once in the literal manner—and moreover suffer to be brought to court—but metaphorically speaking I could slay him twice, thrice, three hundred times, to a number beyond limit—which was partly the reason why I had brought my total book with me. It had a hard, horny, crocodile-hide cover. I like the shield-like feel of it. In moments of danger it had its uses. Yes, by Jove, in the literal sense. I knocked on his door.

There was no answer. I knocked again. Still no answer. I pushed through and saw another door. I knocked. There was no answer. I pushed and came to a third door. Having done my share of knocking for the day, I pushed through that as well and saw a crimson cave gaping in front of me. It had a

178

crimson stalactite too. Or was it stalagmite? My knowledge of Geography being what it was, I could not say. All I could with any degree of certainty state was that I had caught Dr. Frumbusch in the biggest, most hippo-sized yawn I had ever beheld. It was uncorkable. I could have stepped in and taken residence. Jonah and the Whale, Joe and the Hippo.

I was with no little interest wondering whether life would be any different, or if (as was so disconcertingly often the case) I would merely come up against the same old problems in Dr. Frumbusch's belly, when half-way through his yawn he caught sight of me, and cut it short. I immediately felt guilty. So much so that for a moment I could not help but marvel. Here was a man, an obnoxious grasping villain, I was prepared to murder without remorse; yet I could feel so deeply penitent for interrupting a pleasurable act.

"Ah, Joseff, come in, come in." His air of forced conviviality didn't fool me. He was annoyed I hadn't knocked, and I saw my first task would be to restore myself as a polite boy in his eyes. I came timidly in, put down my total book on his desk, and sat down chewing my pencil, the very picture of youthful diligence, I hoped.

"And what is this you have brought?"

"Oh, that's nothing, only my total book. I always take it with me when I'm going to some place strange and new. It saves me from getting frightened."

"Frrrightened? Ah, but that is just one of the things I am going to UNteach you, Joseff. Never, never, never be frrrrightened of me."

"Sorry, Dr. Frumbusch."

"And never! never! never! be sorry to me!"

"Thank you, Dr. Frumbusch."

"And never! never! never! thank me!"

I racked my brains to say something that did not smack of fear, apology or gratitude, and in fidgeting with my hands must unconsciously have opened my total book.

179

"And what is in it?"

"Only totals, scores, and stuff," I said, struggling to keep the note of apology out of my voice, "I just count things when I'm alone. I enjoy counting as there's nothing to argue about."

"Rrreally? And what have we here? What are these figures?"

"This one is the total number of steps I took from home to school: 4,003. These are the number of lamp-posts, the number of steps I took to each, beggars, hydrants——" I stopped. Out of the corner of my eye I saw him put his hand to his mouth. His pink nostrils blanched and swelled like bellows in the vain effort to conceal the second of his yawns—or to complete the second half of his first—Hell! what did I care which? There was no kind of rage that erupted in me with the same lightning speed as when someone was bored with me—not a stab in the back, not a blow on the nose.

The man had asked me a question, and while I was in all politeness answering he'd started yawning. On his desk I saw he had something more handy to crack a skull with than a paper-weight: a cast-iron inkwell; but I could not afford the luxury of idle speculation at this critical stage, and making an inspired effort managed to get square with the facts before he'd finished yawning. I had come here to kill him for one reason: to keep his filthy paws off my sister—did I have any right to do so for another? I had first to dispose of my reason to get rid of him on Dorothy's and Mr. Titmus's account, otherwise I would surely be guilty of being incomplete; or what my master had called amoral. Once I'd got this point clear the storm of conflicting emotions instantly and like magic, subsided in my mind.

"I have a message from Dorothy," I said.

His eye twitched. He had ceased to be bored with me. I had killed two birds with one stone. It was a nice feeling. He waited. I waited. If he was interested in the message, well then, he would continue to be interested until he got it. It was like looking for pictures of naked pigmy women; the sooner he found one, the sooner he'd get bored.

"What is the message, Josef?"

"I've forgotten. I'll ask her before I come again. Am I to come again, Dr. Frumbusch?"

Looking down from my innocent, earnest little stare, he slowly turned forward a page. "What are these?"

"Stoppers."

"What stoppers?"

"That's another sort of list, more complicated. When we're having an argument which I'm winning my father puts in a stopper. That's one of these, it doesn't matter which, not a tinker's curse."

He read: "1) Aren't you putting the cart before the horse?
2) Aren't you making a mountain out of a mole-hill?
3) Aren't you splitting hairs?
4) Aren't you burning your candle at both ends?
5) Aren't you throwing out the baby with the bath-water?
6) That's begging the question, isn't it?
7) Isn't that just typical?
8) *I* used to say that when I was a child.
9) Now what kind of future has a remark like that?
10) PRECISELY!"

"What could you reply, honestly, Dr. Frumbusch? Or am I begging the question?" He said nothing, but gently stroked his chin. "I'm remembering them like poetry," I continued rather fiercely, "so that I can use them on HIM."

"Your father?"

"No, I can't win against him, nor Dorothy. They're too clever for me. And I can't win against Mum and Glad, because they don't like me."

181

"Oh?" He raised what could have been his eyebrows. "You can't win against people who don't like you?"

"No, they never listen. They never fight. It's HIM I've got to watch. The one that's coming."

"Do you mean the new baby?"

"Naturally."

"Are you sure it will be a boy?"

"I'm sure."

He shut the book and put it aside. "Yesterday you told me you hated everyone except yourself. Now is this true?"

"Well there are some people I don't hate," I admitted. "But that's because I haven't talked to them long enough."

"Yet there must be one single person you like. The exception, Josef, that proves the rule."

I didn't answer for a minute. It took so long because I was not searching for the truth, but something more vital: that which would rise up to his expectations. The true answer which had come to my lips instantly upon his query, I had as instantly dismissed. The idea of even mentioning Mr. Titmus to this eyebrowless ogre was utterly repugnant. Yet I had at the same time to say something that would interest him, move him, shake him up, rattle him, outrage and slay him—yes, slay him, before he with his dead weight, that visibly expanding colossus of boredom would descend upon and slay *me*— once, twice, three hundred times. He'd raised his hand to his mouth again, his nostrils blanched, his eyes shut, his chins multiplied, and I desperate to forestall the catastrophe blurted out, "The exception! It is Betty Forsythe." Then because his eye twitched I fervently added, "Till I die."

His face cleared, his expression freshened like a bed of roses after a monsoon shower. "Who is Betty?"

"She lived in the flat above us when we were in Churchgate. But she went away. Her father was on the B.B. & C.I. Railway. We used to exchange things."

"What sort of things?" He picked up a pencil.

182

I blushed in spite of myself. "Nothing really. Sometimes I'd give her an empty matchbox, and she'd give me a water-melon seed. I still have some of the things Betty gave me. Four water-melon seeds, a cigarette packet, a button, seven beads, three marbles and a broken shoelace with a knot. I had a stocking elastic once but lost that. I found another on the road and substituted it, but not for long, I threw it away as it wasn't Betty's. It was dishonest."

"Dishonest. And what age were you when you knew Betty? About ten?"

"Five."

"Are you sure?"

"God's honour," I vowed. "I know for definite because at six I started wearing a belt, and when I knew Betty she had to undo my pants by the buttons."

"Rreally? And how old was Betty?"

"She must have been the same age."

"Why, must?"

I squirmed uncomfortably and did not reply. He feigned disinterest, but had "naked pigmy woman" written all over him. "Why, must, Josef?"

"Because I could lie just as easily in her little bed."

He took out a green-spotted handkerchief and wiped his face, but not before I'd seen him twitch three in a row. This had never happened with Dorothy. Not in my presence at least, so I wasn't jumping to conclusions just because they were in my favour. I cleared my throat and asked very cautiously, "You aren't angry like the ayah, are you? I've never told this to anyone before."

"No, I'm not in the least bit angry," he assured me. "What is ayah?"

"Her nanny. She caught us on the terrace. She screamed. She told Mrs. Forsythe, who told Mr. Forsythe, and he told my father." I paused here and said, "If *you* were my father would you have beaten me?"

183

"I would not have beaten you," he said in a low voice. In the silence we heard a faint tinkling outside, and the significance of the three doors became apparent. They were there so that no one else should hear us. What went on between us was entirely secret. "Josef," he murmured, writing something I could not see, "I want you to come again on Monday first thing after school."

"I'll come," I nodded. "Unless of course," I continued, "I get kept in." He looked at me without answering. "Don't worry," I said, "I won't get kept in."

He smiled and nodded. I arose slowly and said, "Dr. Frumbusch, will you not be angry, as you promised, if I say something?"

"I can never be angry with you, Josef."

"You know when you knocked that vase over at home? Well, it was all my fault. I pushed it." Then just in case he *would* get angry I snatched up my book and ran out. I went down the three flights of stairs, bounding for joy. On the last step I sat down panting, opened to a fresh page and wrote: SATURDAY . . . 7+2doubles+1waltz=14. Underneath I wrote: MONDAY, and left a blank.

Although I usually awoke earlier on Sundays than school-days, the next day I woke up late. The fact was I did awake early, but went back to sleep. I couldn't think of anything I could do. I remembered something about a vague arrangement to whistle for the mugger. We were perhaps to go on to pick up Wilfred. There was some talk about hiring bikes from a chawl near Grant's Building and riding round town. The only actual business we had on hand was to go to Apollo Bunder to find out if the sightseeing ferry had started running to Elephanta Caves, as it was suspended during the monsoon. I remembered I had thoughtfully suggested this to Mr. Titmus myself, since he was so keen on local colour. He'd seemed very excited about the idea. I went back to sleep.

184

I was awoken by St. Paul, who told me it was 8.30 and that breakfusht was ready.

At about nine Dorothy poked her head in to ask if I'd like to come and see Mum; they were driving out to Breach Candie. I told her I had an important engagement at Apollo Bunder. She waited about, as she had last night, hoping I'd tell her about my interview with Dr. Frumbusch.

"What good are eyebrows anyway?" I said.

"They keep the sweat out of one's eyes," she replied.

"Only servants sweat," I told her. "Noble folk have no need for such things, they're perfectly ridiculous."

She looked as if she was about to go, and I said, "I have a message."

"From whom?"

"Dr. Frumbusch."

"What is it?"

I screwed up my eyes in a puzzled frown.

"Can't you remember it, Joe?"

"Yes, I can remember the message distinctly, and I can remember from whom it is; but I can't remember *for* whom it is, you or Gladys."

"Try hard, Joe, try hard."

"I'm trying."

She waited.

I waited.

She waited, did my sister Dot, like she'd never waited for anything from me before.

"She sure is a wow, she's coming in uncannily handy."

"Who?"

"That naked pigmy woman."

She left with a backward glance.

St. Paul came and told me it was 9.30 and that breakfusht was ready.

At about ten I heard them leave in the car.

At 10.30 St. Paul came in striking his own head to ask me

185

in the name of Khuddah above if I was going to have breakfusht or not. "Kaisa ahdmee ap hota, Joe baba? Sub deen
bechana me sota? Ubi Ahm janikoomanta mera doskoo.
Shunday aj nai hai? Utteri bholo! Oota aur nai? Saitan ka
batcha, kia gotala marta? Breakfusht koo ahta aur nai?"

I replied in the affirmative.

In the middle of breakfast, when, being alone, I was con-
gratulating myself on my most peaceful meal of the year, the
garden gate slammed like a cannon shot, and the mugger
turned up. He was fuming, to put it mildly. He sat in the
opposite chair, if one could call it sitting.

"You low, mean——"

"Don't breathe fire and thunder on my eggs, they're over-
done already."

"You low, mean, dirty——"

"Your sleeve's in the butter."

"Low, mean, dirty, unreliable——"

"I heard Gladys calling your name in her sleep. 'Aaron!
Aaron!'" He was madly infatuated with her. But I'd either
handed him that particular sop too often, or else no kind of
sop could have tempted him in his present state.

"Dirty, low, mean, unreliable——"

"Excuse me, please," I begged. "Just let me take one
teeny-weeny sip of coffee first, will you?"

Green and dragon-eyed he watched me with his small very
undragon mouth. I raised the cup and let it hover for a while.
Then I lowered it untasted, with an air of self-deprivation.
"Well, well? Go on," I sighed tolerantly, "what's the gossip?"

"Gossip? You crapulous vermin! We're supposed to be
making inquiries for Mr. Titmus about that boat to Elephanta, remember?"

"Remember?" I echoed, as well as one could echo through
four inches of bread, butter, hard-boiled egg, tomato, and
parsley. "It was I who proposed the trip."

186

"Yes, at 9.30 you were to whistle for me at my home."

"Yah, your home," I nodded. "I've been thinking about Beliaker Mansions all night, otherwise I'd have come in the blushing dawn. What about all those Anglo-Indian blokes next door who stab one another on Christmas night? It's dangerous out there."

"But it's not Christmas night now, is it?"

"Maybe not, but what about those thirty-five Chinamen who live in one room? And their thirty-five Chinese women? And their two hundred and thirty-five indubitably Chinese children who pitch water-melon peel, banana skins and pee all over the stairs? A chap could slip and fall. It's not right to lure me up there."

"But you were not SUPPOSED to come up, you were to WHISTLE! You——"

"PRECISELY! And what about all those other Chinamen downstairs who hang filthy lumps of fish and meat in the sun all day? It's nauseating."

"Look here!" he raged getting up and brandishing his fists. "For the last——"

"Steady," I cautioned him. "Don't burn your candle at both ends."

"Candle? What candle? Yes, and there's Wilfred, he's waiting too, and waiting and waiting——"

"Aren't you making a mountain out of a molehill?" I inquired.

"Joe, what the hell are you talking about?"

"Ah, that's begging the question, isn't it?"

"No!" He stamped his foot. "That's *not* begging the question!"

"That's what *I* used to say when I was a child."

"O.K., Joe, right then, fine." He'd decided to wash his hands off me, though not without displeasure. He was trembling all over with unexpressed and possibly inexpressible ire. "I'm going, I don't care. Do you know what my dad says

187

about you?" he pronounced. "He says you're going to end up in jail!"

"Now what sort of future has a remark like that?"

When I heard him fumbling for the catch at the front door I sang out, "Careful now, don't throw out the baby with the bath-water."

He couldn't wait to close the door behind him. I saw him bolt down the path through the window. He couldn't wait to open the gate and vaulted over. Usually he was adept at this, but as today he was putting the cart before the horse, he caught his toe on the top edge and fell headlong in a heap on the other side.

"Isn't that just typical!"

YOUR WORK IS GREATLY IMPROVING, BUT YOU STILL HAVE A TENDENCY TO DASH DOWN WHAT FIRST COMES IN-TO YOUR MIND.

O.J.T.

"Don't hesitate, Joseff. Don't be afraid. Just tell me whatever is in your mind."

Despite the fact that he sternly refrained from mentioning a single word about our, in any case vague and tentative arrangements for an excursion to the island, all that week at school Mr. Titmus got on my nerves. If he wanted to go to Elephanta Caves I wasn't stopping him. But what annoyed me most about his reproachful looks was that I'd never worked better. My marks were up. I was prompt, attentive and always did my homework. The only activity on the curriculum I defaulted in was Games. But this was not *his* province, as Mr. de Lima was Games' master. Not once did I give him or any other master occasion to cane me, give me lines or keep me in after school. I never put up my hand to ask him silly questions; and while I did commit the sin of not putting up my hand when I knew the answer of a question he asked, how was he to know I knew it?

I was utterly and completely blameless. At tiffin break I ate more quickly, quietly and mechanically than any of the Shalom robots and went on to the maidan with my fruit until it was time to return. I even avoided Wilfred whose company I usually sought at this interval. I got into scrapes. It was strange. For years I'd been under the impression that I was a bad boy; that I got myself into trouble by wilful acts of aggression. People, grown up, wise people, had told me, and I'd believed them, that if only I would desist, life would hold the promise of love and laughter for me. They were wrong. In that week I stirred up more rancour and resentment avoiding people than before when I used to go rampaging around creating mayhem and chaos.

My peevishness aroused by this discovery did little to aid me in my newly formed resolutions, and I felt more and more in need of good, solid, strong advice. I could in fact think of the ideal person who would be only too glad to discuss the matter with me; but the trouble was every evening when I went to see him after school, it suddenly became too trivial to mention. And yet, in point of fact, it was not trivial. At school the memory of Nickie Sutherland had begun to come back to me. He'd never known me like this: inoffensive, retiring, evasive. Suppose I had not tipped his topee off? Would he have been alive today? Somehow I could not be certain. What would have become of him? What in general became of acts one felt impelled to commit, but did not commit?

I racked my brains over this question and made several small experiments on myself, as I felt this problem was the ultimate one which underlay all the problems that had foxed me in the past. It was nice to know it, very nice. But the clarity with which I saw the inestimable richness of such a solution did not help me to attain it. On the contrary, the very desire to lay hold of it led me into an eerie morass of probabilities such as I had never known; and it was still no nearer. The consequence of an act not committed.

It was him asking me about my dreams that started it. He had not mentioned the accident once; but I knew he wanted me to. It was uncanny the way I could tell what was in his mind. The night after he questioned me about my dreams—especially about recurrent dreams, I had one. I was awoken by the hollow snapping sound of the trap. I got out from under my net and went to look. It was lashing the bait like a boxing-ball against the metal grill. I checked to see if it was the princess, then had a drink and went back to bed.

I lay there comparing the two dreams for some time. They were exactly identical. The car, the same heavenly roller-coaster motion, the music, the landscape, the face, and finally of course the waking sound—*that* could not by any stretch of imagination vary in tone—unless it fell on the tail. I went back to sleep very disturbed. How did I in my dream know that a rat was about to be caught in the pantry so as to dream the incidents ahead of it?

"This is what baffles me, and it's happened twice. How did I in my dream know that a rat was about to be caught in the pantry so as to dream the incidents ahead of it?"

"Well, Josef, one reason could be that the trap fell first. You didn't awake to full consciousness; then you dreamed the incidents and were awoken by the *memory* of the noise."

"That can't be," I replied. "Both times I went immediately to the trap and saw that it had just been caught."

"How could you see that?"

"Its bait was not touched. A trapped rat always eats its bait."

"You say you went immediately, but what is immediately? Perhaps you dreamed the whole thing in just one second after the trap fell."

I regretfully shook my head. "I wish I could believe that with all my heart; but it's not true. There's only one possible answer. My dreams know more than I do. They have the secret of acts that are committed; and they have the secret of

190

acts that are not committed. My dream knew a rat was going to be caught. In the same way as it knew while I was driving the truck I would run into Sutherland. In the same way as it actually happened, in a day dream——" I hesitated, though not from any sense of uncertainty or apprehension. I had too much faith in him now to be afraid. That pause was one of command, my father's pause, a sacred pause, the pause of his synagogue: the court house.

In that pause, his pause, I felt everything I knew about my father surge powerfully into me. I, almost toyingly, glanced at Dr. Frumbusch, and found him staring at me, pen poised. "In the same way as what actually happened, Josef?"

"In the same way I knew when I was walking alongside the bus that Nickie was reaching out to tip my hat off, and he would be killed if I didn't warn him. I didn't. I let him die. I killed him."

He stuck the pen back into the cast-iron inkwell, but it tumbled off. He let it lie there. "Are you making me a confession of murder, Josef?"

"Yes. I am the murderer of Nickie Sutherland, and tomorrow I'm going to Bandra to lay flowers at his grave. The police, you understand——" I hesitated. "This is of course between you and me. Between you and me. Between you and me. After all," I went on, permitting a fresh note, a note of gratitude to creep into my voice, "it is all thanks to you that I realized this, Dr. Frumbusch; otherwise I would have continued believing I was innocent to the end of my life." I heard a sudden ripping and crackling as he tore and crumpled into a ball the paper he'd been writing on. He tossed it under his desk and I heard it rattle into the waste-paper basket between my feet.

"Yes, Josef, go on. Don't mind me."

"I mind you a lot, Dr. Frumbusch, I owe you so much. The way you let me say the first thing that comes into my head without fear of punishment has made me remember all kinds

191

of things I'd completely forgotten; things which I would not in a hundred years have remembered had it not been for you. And not only that; remembering the strange little thoughts and dreams I've had in the past has made me realize that I can foretell the future. I can foretell the future. I can—oh! you need not tell me you want me to go now. I know. I know. Thursday then, Dr. Frumbusch?"

"Thursday, Josef."

I put the crumpled ball of paper from his waste-paper basket into my pocket and walked out.

When I got home it had expanded of its own accord. Afraid that its many pieces which had been so intricately compounded together, would fall apart in the course of time if handled disrespectfully, I bound it firmly around with string so as to maintain the original creases—though not so tight as to create any fresh ones of my own. Then I put it in an envelope and stowed it in the drawer reserved for other articles of value I'd acquired in the past.

I went to Dorothy's room and was about to knock when I heard her voice. It was coming from Gladys's room, which struck me as being unusual. While Glad often went in to see her, Dorothy rarely visited Gladys. I moved to Glad's door not quite knowing why, since what I had to say to my older sister was strictly confidential.

I thus made no move to knock, but stood there, not so much listening as *having* to hear. They were quarrelling. So ambiguous was my position in fact, that at least five minutes had elapsed before it occurred to me I might possibly be eavesdropping. I crept away then, and it was a lucky move too. No sooner had I regained my room than the telephone rang.

She reacted to it, even when she was sick, like a tigress in defence of her cub. No one else had a chance to answer it when Glad was home. I heard the usual scurrying of feet, the usual cutting off of the ring as the ear-piece was lifted, and the answering voice giving our number. I thought then there must be something wrong with my ears. Was it Dorothy's voice? I peered out, and saw them both in dressing-gowns. Dot had the receiver, and Glad, looking very evidently pipped at the post, stood waiting by.

"Sorry, wrong number." Cling.

They went back without another word to their own rooms. Cling. What sort of sound was that? A highly puzzled sound. What on earth was happening to Dorothy? She never ran for the phone. No one ever phoned her. Or didn't *he*? In view of the squabble I'd accidentally overheard there was no question about it. I should have stuck my thumbs in my armpits, cheered, been mightily delighted. Things were going just the way I wanted; but it was a little worrying that they should be going on behind my back. A *little* worrying? I began to tremble and went and laid down on my bed. To think: my presence, this dear devoted body of me, was unrequired. People could be happy without me. The Hell of it. People happy without me.

I opened the drawer. I took out the ball, pulled off the string, and spread out the pieces before me.

I woke up in the middle of the night to make, in faithful accordance with his instructions, a fresh entry. This was a new list he'd requested me to compile. The number of ayahs I'd had as a child. This dream brought the total to eight. I was astounded at the way a new face suddenly appeared when I thought the total was complete. The fact was that when he'd first asked me the question I could only remember two, both named Mary. But he had urged me to keep thinking about them, although he did warn me I might find it distressing.

He was, as always, right. The memory of each new face was invariably accompanied by feelings of indescribable and inexplicable desolation. He'd asked me to try and say something about these feelings, and I could only tell him, "Finding feels like losing." He did not press me further. Over and over again he showed me how profoundly considerate he was.

I crawled out from under the mosquito-net and went for a drink. I switched on the light in the pantry. The trap was vacant. I was not surprised, as I had not been awoken by the familiar snap. I stared at it now, wondering why I had apparently without thinking come to look, when I suddenly became aware of the dream I'd had previous to the one about the ayah—otherwise I'd most probably never have recalled it. I went back to my room and as per instruction made notes of both dreams at once.

The first had started in precisely the same manner as the recurrent one, which I'd now had four times. The same truck, the same roller-coaster action, the same music. But when the time came for the victim of the accident to appear, it was not Nickie Sutherland, but my father. I stamped down the brake, and waited for the hollow snapping noise. It did not come. Instead the music continued uninterrupted, and the truck accelerated faster. The scene through the windscreen was obliterated however by my father's face pressed hard against it. He was glaring accusingly at me, and I said, "Aren't you putting the court before the house?" It was a slip of the tongue, of course.

The scratching of his pen went on uninterrupted, and as he'd told me not to take any notice of what he did I continued, "The dream then took a sudden turn to the ayah. She was singing or trying to sing, or hum."

"What was she singing?"

"It was all mixed up like two tunes going on at the same time."

"Is that beggar still playing his flute under the tree?"

"What, that one-legged kid? Not a hope. He was right near Glad's window, and after the third or fourth night she had him packed off to a boarding-school in England." He smiled, but did not stop writing. "I know what you were writing: that maybe the music brought on the dream."

"Maybe. And I'm still thinking that a passing cycle, or motor-horn—you have mosquito-nets I noticed. Can you hear the insects humming outside?"

"Loudly," I admitted. "And it does sound like a flute in the distance. A clever guess, but what about the rats? More have been caught in two weeks than in two months. Do the mosquitoes bring on the rats like the Pied Piper of Hamelin?"

"What brings on the rats, Josef?"

"My dream. I do."

He stopped writing. "So you can not only predict the future, but you can cause it to happen the way you want?"

"That's right, Dr. Frumbusch."

"And," he continued writing, "how much success have you had so far—apart from the rats?"

"None."

"Why not?"

"Because I'm not sure of what I want—not yet."

"Why not?"

Because I'm not sure of what *you* want, I should have told him. I didn't. I was beginning to get worried about what he was writing. In a way I was sorry I'd opened the crushed up sheet of paper he'd thrown into the basket yesterday. I'd been happy enough till then.

One of the things that gave me no end of pleasure about my talks with Dr. Frumbusch was that he made incessant notes on everything I said. It gave me much comfort, a sense of station, a permanent place in the life about me to know that everything I uttered was going on record. It was like my total book multiplied a hundred times. My gratitude for his service had never been so profound as when I had picked out the ball of paper he had thrown away. The last thing I'd intended to do was to spy on him. No, it was just that for a

195

long time I'd wanted to ask him for something, some trifling possession of his, and had been too shy to do so. Thus when he'd yesterday so obviously scrapped and discarded that piece of paper I thought, he doesn't want this thing any more, so why let it go to waste, like all the food that pours into the trash-bin when starving mouths could have it?

His writing was rather like an iron fence; tall, even and javelin-tipped. I'd had some difficulty completing the jigsaw, as the text was no help to me. It was Viennese, I guessed. There was a boy, whom Wilfred had got friendly with, in Std. 7. He was a new refugee addition, named Klein. But he was from Berlin and spoke German. Maybe he spoke Viennese too, I thought, like I spoke Latin. But in the end my feelings of gratitude to Dr. Frumbusch checked me from approaching Klein. I convinced myself there was no occasion. I had something of his, and that was enough. The fact that I did not understand it even added to its charm. Had I not *already* put him to the severest of tests? I'd tried to find a flaw in him and couldn't. He had proved himself unshakable, and during my worst, most guilt-ridden moments, a veritable rock.

On parting from him that evening I'd openly confessed that it was only his friendship that was stopping me from going to the police and blurting out the truth of Sutherland's murder. "I only hope, Dr. Frumbusch, that one day I may have the chance of doing the same for you if you should ever kill anyone yourself."

"Joe!"

I looked up.

"You've been stirring that tea for the past five minutes," Glad accused.

"What's worse," added Dorothy—she was the great worse-maker now, "you haven't put any sugar in it."

"After all I'm doing for you," I said softly, "you speak to me like this."

196

"I don't know what you're talking about, nor do you either. Now listen to your father, he's addressed you three times."

"Yes, Dad?" I said raising the cup to my lips, but not drinking.

"Put that cup down, my lad. And don't try the sneezing stunt either."

"How d'you mean, Dad?"

"I don't mean anything that I haven't told you already a dozen times. Your mother's in hospital."

"Yes, I know, things have been much quieter here."

"Your mother is in a bad way."

"I didn't do anything."

"Joe, we're not accusing you of injuring your mother. We (and she) are merely a little hurt that not once in these two weeks have you asked to see her, or expressed a word of concern about her condition."

"Two weeks, golly." I was amazed. "Gone like a flash. Be a dear and pass the jam, Gladys." She uttered a strangled sound and went out. Dad took a pinch of snuff. Dorothy passed the jam. I hovered my knife over the open top and noticed them watching me like judges in a spring-board diving tournament. On my mettle now, as I responded notoriously badly to competition, I steadied myself; plunged in the blade and with a simultaneous half twist scooped up such an exact quantity of jam for the specified size of bread and butter that I did not need to lose a drop, nor return to the pot for more. Pleased with myself, I took my first rewarding bite, and found it to be marmalade, which I normally detested.

"Never mind," I shrugged. "Such is life. After you eat it, it's all the same."

I was still eating it when I discovered the house was empty. I wondered where they'd gone, as it was too early for the cinema.

I was speaking to my mother with my eyes closed. We had an arrangement to keep them closed. But I played unfair and

197

opened them. The room was pitch-black. I could still hear her, though. She was chiding me for opening my eyes—something worse than chiding: mocking; and I ran about like in a game of Blindman's Bluff with my arms outstretched, trying to catch her. It was a matter of life and death to catch her, and I tripped then and in falling caught her. The light went on, blinding me. I saw I was holding a telephone and awoke. The street-lamp was in my eyes. The phone was ringing in the front room.

"Who answered it?"

"Gladys."

"Does she get a lot of phone calls?"

"Yes, the most in the house, because Mum gets a lot of hers at the Gymkhana. Of course I mean usually. She's still in hospital—I suppose.

"What's the baby's name?"

"I don't know if they've named it yet. They don't consult me about these things."

"When you were a child did your mother often speak to you on the phone?"

"Yes, she was very regular and never failed me once. She always phoned just before ayah put me to bed."

"From the Gymkhana?"

"I suppose."

"All right, Josef, come again on Monday."

"But we've only just begun. And what about tomorrow? It's Saturday, so I can come earlier and stay longer."

"I'm going to Matheran for the week-end," he explained, putting down his pen and blotting the ink. "I need a change, just a little change, Josef."

"I know Matheran exceedingly well," I told him. "It's dangerous up there. Many people have died from snake-bite and from falling off the Points. Echo Point, Monkey Point, Panorama Point; you could slip and fall hundreds of feet if you haven't a guide. I'm not doing anything on——"

"I'll be with friends, Josef."

"Oh?" I was completely taken aback. "Friends? What friends?"

"Just friends."

I slouched out slowly.

"Monday then, Josef!" he sang out cheerfully. I nodded without looking back. I shut the door after me.

About half a minute later I opened it again, and he looked up, surprised. "Do you mean with Dorothy?" I asked.

"No."

I shut the door again. There was no one in his waiting room. I sat down and opened my satchel. I saw my composition book and vaguely recalled I had to write an essay over the week-end. The subject was STRAY DOGS. I wrote down the title, but could not think of an opening sentence. YOUR WORK IS IMPROVING BUT——

The door swung outward and Dr. Frumbusch seemed surprised to see me. "I was just thinking I could save you a wasted journey," I explained, starting up. "There's no road up the mountain except the rail, and that's closed during the monsoon."

"The trains are starting to run this week-end."

"Who told you that?"

"My friends."

"Oh." I got up and walked deliberately out.

"Monday, then, don't forget, Josef." I didn't answer.

On the landing I saw the notice, DO NOT SPIT ON THE WALLS. Not only were the walls crimson slashed with the familiar betel-nut juice but the notice itself used as a kind of target. As for his newly painted sign, it had quite a while ago suffered the fate of the rest. The filthy, dirty, inconsiderate pigs, I thought; there was only one way to make these people obey a simple, decent, law-abiding little request, and that was brute force. One had to stand by with a Lewis machine-gun and make an example of someone, riddle him full of lead, and hang him by the notice; then they'd understand we meant business.

He had on a hat of soft grey felt, and was surprised to see me sitting on the stairs with my satchel on my lap. "I was just thinking," I explained immediately getting up, "about your friends. You haven't been long in Bombay, have you? I mean you might be all right in Vienna and places with friends, but people are different out here. You have to be armed."

"Rreally?"

"Yes, against Jews and Indians, everyone. Even the English, they change when they get here, they go native and drink toddy, and smoke gunja and chew betel-nut. You think you've got a friend and he suddenly knifes you in the back. D'you know what?"

"What, Josef?"

"People kill their own mothers out here."

"But they kill their own mothers in Europe too."

"Oh?" I said. "Then I suppose it's all right. If you say so. If you say so." I began to descend the stairs.

"You're not thinking I said it's all right to go and kill people, are you, Josef?" He'd never shown any trace of anxiety before, and this at once intrigued me. I gave him the naked pigmy woman to find and just waited. "Why don't you answer?"

"I feel funny talking on the stairs," I said.

"Well, that at least is a problem that's easily solved," he said beaming good-naturedly. "Come back into the office. With pleasure!"

"Instead of Monday?" I inquired suspiciously.

"Good gracious, no! Monday too, and Tuesday, and Wednesday, every day!" he cried, throwing up his big, beautifully manicured hands. And I didn't know why, but I was slightly worried by his exuberance.

We sat down. "Now, I remember," he resumed just as freshly as when we'd started, *more* freshly in fact, "I was going to ask you: what is the total of ayahs so far?"

I opened to the page and said, "Twelve."

"And this was all before you were ten."

"Yes, at ten I began bathing myself."

"Why did you have so many ayahs?"

I couldn't say whether it was the question itself that worried me, or the manner in which he rasped it out. I picked up the composition book and began to twist and roll it round and round in my hands till it was as hard as a dandu.

"Don't be afraid to tell me what's in your mind."

"Mr. Titmus says I shouldn't blurt out just whatever comes into my mind. I could get into serious trouble."

"Who is Mr. Titmus?"

"My teacher. And he's a very good teacher too!"

"Ah, teacher, that's quite different. I'm not speaking to you as a teacher. Didn't I tell you? I am the opposite of a teacher."

I didn't answer although something sprang quick enough to my mind. "Why did you have so many ayahs?"

"I don't know, I don't know, I did not harm them." The book slipped from my hands to the table where it unfurled, hissing like a living thing. "Just when I was getting to like her, she disappeared and a new one came." I remembered Wilfred now, crouching like a cornered animal through the smoke. "They left me; they hated looking after me."

"You're telling the truth now, aren't you?"

I stared up at him. This was the first time he'd mentioned the word truth. All the time he'd been urging me to say whatever came into my mind, and now he'd started talking about truth. Again he asked me the same question. I nodded dumbly. "And have you been telling me the truth all the time?" I gaped at him. He picked up the total book and thumbed through it. "What is this graph?"

"That's to do with your twitch total."

"My what total?"

"There it goes!" I exclaimed. "When you're interested in what I'm saying your eye goes like this, and I count them.

One is a single, two a double and three a waltz. There! A double. That's nine singles plus two doubles plus two waltzes total: nineteen."

I looked at him and found he had gone a deep pink. He was so obviously annoyed, I instinctively shrank back in my chair. Had I said something wrong? How could I? Didn't he repeatedly encourage me to speak my mind? What *right* had he to be angry with me? It was only for a moment however, and he went on in his former cool and collected manner. "Some of the things you have been telling me are not true."

I nodded, watching him warily.

"There's no such person as Betty Forsythe, for instance."

I nodded.

"Have you been telling me these stories simply because they would make, as you might say, my eye twitch?"

I nodded. He stood up to his full height and slammed down the open book. Several crows who must have been squabbling over some titbit filled the room with their cawing. He turned and with something savage in his moves banged the window to cut out the street noises altogether: the vendors' cries, the trams, the horse-drawn gharries, the haht gharries, the beggars' cries, the drr-dtt of a mattress renovator, the gay lilting chorus of a Moslem funeral procession. He worked his fist into the cup made of his left hand and two white blotches stood out on his cheeks.

"Do you hate being in Bombay, Dr. Frumbusch?"

"It's not just that, it's the Eastern mentality——" He stopped to look down at me, as though for the moment he had not realized who he was addressing.

"Then is it me you hate?"

He sat down and at once began to beam again. "Don't be absurd, Josef. I can never, never be angry with you."

"Naturally," I nodded, my spirits instantly rising. "You did promise, didn't you?"

"Yes, yes, of course. Now what about this ingenious little graph of yours, eh?"

"Oh," I was only too eager to explain, "that's rather complicated the way I've managed to figure it out. But to put it simply, the left side is the number of days, the right is your twitches. See we've fifty-nine days to go. If the line reaches the top before running off the page, then you'll marry Dorothy, and we'll be relatives; it's all mathematically worked out."

I heard him grunt and looked to see he had covered his eyes. The bottom row of his teeth showed though. "Are you angry with me again, Dr. Frumbusch?"

"Look, Josef." He lowered his hands to disclose a gritty kind of smile, not a sincere smile. "I am not angry with you when you lie, how can I be angry when you speak the truth?"

"Why d'you keep talking about lies and truth?" I demanded. "I'm fed up. What the hell does it matter what I say if in the end I get you two married?"

"Firstly what gives you the idea that Dorothy would like to marry me?"

"They were quarrelling about you. I distinctly heard Dot tell Gladys—a waltz!"

"Yes, yes, what did she say?"

"She said, 'You dirty slut, you minx, haven't you enough men? You show no interest in any worthwhile person until I —something something—then you kill yourself snatching him away.' "

"What was the reply?"

"Why aren't you taking notes?"

"What was Gladys's reply?"

"She said, 'You should talk, you've ruined my life. The minute you see someone *I've* brought in, you sit sneering and tearing him to pieces in front of my eyes till I can't bear the sight of the poor contemptible wretch. You hate men, you're just a man dressed up yourself! You vile, jealous——' "

"All right, Josef, thank you."

"There's a bit more."

"That's enough."

"And then there's another dream that——"

"Never mind now."

"Later then?"

"Yes, yes, later," he sighed, passing back my book in half a dozen weary little moves.

"Have all those other people who came to see you today fagged you out, Dr. Frumbusch?"

"Yes, that is so," he nodded. His eyes were half shut—kept open only by the fire that kindled them: that vast dormant compassion that was ready to leap when the need arose. Why, I thought, if a man like this were not properly cared for he could perish in the flames of his own goodness. "Josef," he said, "suppose I were to tell you that you need not——? How shall we say? That I cannot——? That I do not feel well and that if I should fall ill it will not be possible for you to see me again."

"Ill? Not see you again?" I stared at him aghast. Then, recovering I continued more calmly, "I understand, Dr. Frumbusch. It's perfectly all right by me. I understand."

"You do, Josef?" he said slowly beginning to beam once again.

"Yes. I shall come and look after you. You needn't worry. I'll take phone messages and see the servants don't cheat you on the hassab. You can bank on me to the hilt, Dr. Frumbusch, I'll never let you down."

"I'm very happy to hear that," he murmured brokenly. "I really mean it."

I flushed crimson with pleasure. But not wanting to take up too much of his time, I collected my things as quickly as I could and hurried to the door.

"Monday, Dr. Frumbusch?"

"Monday, Josef."

12 singles+3 doubles+3 waltzes=27.

I was pleased enough. God knew it was the record score so far. The graph was rocketing. Yet it was this same meeting that gave me the most cause for concern.

Why?

Suddenly I stopped. Was it possible? Was it possible that Dr. Frumbusch wanted to marry Gladys? Only if he was an idiot. Was he an idiot? No. Therefore he must want to marry Dorothy. I walked on, relieved to have got rid of so repugnant a notion. Her breasts for instance, they were like watermelons. Absurd, ludicrously absurd. Dot and Dr. Frumbusch were deeply and desperately in love. Glad was causing trouble, but the real villain was Dad. Dad was opposing the match.

The melancholic fox tried to catch me offguard in the fuzzy period just after waking on Monday morning. I was fumbling for the top of the toothpaste tube in the bathroom. "Did you intercept a letter Mr. Titmus wrote me?"

"Who, me, Dad? Never. What's intercept?"

He disarmed himself by removing his glasses. He took the toothpaste tube from my hands and said, "Your beloved Mr. Titmus disappeared into thin air over the weekend. The police are searching for him."

I gaped at him stunned, as the full meaning of this sank in; the consequence of his disappearance to me personally. Then, "Whoopee!" I cried. "Mr. Titmus set us a composition to write on STRAY DOGS over the weekend, and I haven't done it, and now I needn't! Whoopee! What a stroke of luck!"

"I was under the impression you'd be sorry," he said.

"Sorry? Why, what could a fellow write about STRAY DOGS? Good riddance, not sorry."

"Well, you certainly seemed upset when I mentioned he might be conscripted into the Armed Forces."

"What's Mr. Titmus got to do with me, Dad?"

"Son, I don't know. My nose is a foot too short to keep it

both at the grindstone and on the track of your whirlwind career." He gave me back the tube. "Regarding your professed indifference I am vastly relieved. If anyone speaks to you of him today, don't try and protect him. Tell the truth, the whole truth. Understand?"

"I never lie, Dad."

"Good." He began to brush his teeth, and in between rubs mumbled a compliment. It was a performance. My father was for the paying of compliments the most unsuited man in the world—like an ape in clothes. He had to pick moments when he was shifting furniture, or about to bring his flyswatter down with crushing force, or had his head deep in the bonnet of his car, or law tome. His toothbrush was something new.

"I want to rub rub congratulate you on the rub rub effort you've been making at your rub rub rub lessons lately. The masters' rub rerubports on your homerubwork are rub rub rub rub encourubraging."

"It's all rub rub thanks to Dr. Frumrubusch, Dad."

He spat toothpaste with unnecessary vigour. It was reddened, and I didn't know if it was the sight of blood that spurred me to the kill, but I shot my brush into its slot, saying, "Is it true they're engaged?"

"Who?"

"Dorothy and Dr. Frumbusch."

As I anticipated, he was more annoyed than surprised. "Where did you hear this?"

"Everyone's talking about it in the Jewish Club, Dad, they all say what a splendid match it'll be."

"Wash your face and don't forget your ears. Have your breakfast and take your mac to school. It looks like the Elephants will come today. Your brother thanks you for your incessant inquiries on his behalf. His name, in case you're interested, is Michael."

206

A new pedagogue named Mr. Silvester de Cruz took the roll call. This was sooner than expected, but expected well enough. One by one the younger English masters were leaving. Latto and Pierce had taken commissions in the Indian Army, but were still at school awaiting their replacements, who would either be Goanese or Anglo-Indian. With regard to Mr. Titmus the whole school before the first bell had been buzzing with rumours. One boy had apparently seen him the previous weekend in Kamatipura, a red-light district; so he'd obviously been murdered by goondas. Others thought he'd been drowned swimming off an island; still others had a hunch he'd got lost in the trackless wilds of the Ghats.

I myself had been given a much shrewder clue by my father, which however I did not care to discuss. My life, I reckoned, was cluttered up enough. I was fully resolved on continuing to live according to my recent policy of non-intervention, but, as I had already begun to find out, a chap had to do a great deal more to keep out of trouble than to shut his mouth and mind his own business. It was something worth knowing; but looking back, wasn't I a little slow on the uptake? It was a simple corollary. I had for donkey's years now been aware that the safest way of keeping out of trouble was to cause it; then one was satisfactorily informed of the situation. Danger lay in the desire to avoid it. Added to that, my father's cryptic warning should have prepared me for any kind of surprise that day: my due reward for the most blameless week of my school career.

It came scarlet-sashed and scarlet-hatted, silently and bare-footed, round about mid-morning: the Principal's peon with his inevitable chitty. Mr. de Lima, pausing in his hop, step and jump through Apollonius's Theorem, read it, still panting and quivering from his exertions. He was a rather over-demonstrative instructor, who with his natural talent for bringing the breezy airs of the sports ground into the class-room, was happiest teaching Geometry. He constructed mountainous triangles, for the apices of which he had to make prodigious leaps; and if constructions upon them proved necessary they invariably ran off the blackboard on to the walls. Like a number of small men I knew, he always demanded more space than was available to him.

He looked up at me. I looked at the board. "The Principal wants you," he said. I continued looking attentively at the board. "Hoseà!"

"Yes, sir?"

"Did you hear what I said?"

"Yes, sir, the angles ACB and BAC——"

"You're wanted in the Principal's office."

"Yes, sir."

"Well, aren't you going to get up?"

"Rightaway, sir?"

"Move, boy, move!" To indicate what he meant he bounced perpendicularly up and down three times. His vivacity was not infectious. I dragged myself out of my seat.

"What are you taking your rough-work book for?"

"For—er—rough work, sir."

I went slowly. I had to use the banister to help me up, and it was slippery to my touch. The delaying tactics I'd employed on Mr. de Lima and now on the way along were a desperate, perhaps fairy-tale measure. I imagined that somewhere in the misted distance a friendly fate was galloping to rescue me. Hence every second I could defer the engagement was to my advantage. The peon who usually made up the tail end of these funeral processions had to wait at the top of the stairs for me.

"Kia hogia, bhai?" I asked him in confidence. I was after all his best customer.

"Dao poleesh inshpectur hai," he replied, shaking his head commiseratingly. "Ake juggra ahdmee, pukka harami-wallah."

I was well forewarned now, but how forearmed? I knew,

barring unprecedented aid from those friendly fates, some gloomy retort was awaiting me just around the corner. "Ake minute, bhai," I requested. I put my book against the framed photograph of our 1923 Hockey XI, and began to write. He waited quite willingly by, as I knew he would. I had examined the matter thoroughly before. The process of writing was infinitely more arresting than speech. I'd once stopped a man in the street and asked him politely to wait while I wrote something. I had the mugger watch the scene from the other side of the street. I gave him the prearranged signal and then proceeded to write gibberish Latin phrases at top speed determinedly ignoring any kind of interruption whatsoever. The mugger had to pull the pen out of my hand to stop me. By then six clear minutes had elapsed and the bloke had only just gone, apparently with the utmost reluctance.

Naturally I could not hope to get so long a respite out of the peon, but a minute was long enough as a delaying tactic, and long enough in my highly febrile condition to fulfil the second of my aims. Thus blithely unaware he had been witness to the creation of the most passionate love epistle in English Literature, he deposited me at the entrance of Miss Gilbert's office, and left to attend to some other matter.

I tore it out of the rough-work book and poked my head around the door. "Oh!" At first sight I thought it was the friendly fate, then I took a grip of myself. "Where's Miss Gilbert?" I inquired.

"She's returned to England, mun. Helping the war effort."

I supposed I'd have died the death of a broken-hearted lover—were it a man that answered. After a brief agony, I began to rally. "And what's your name?"

"Fernandez."

"Miss?"

"Miss."

I looked at my letter.

"You're Hosea, aren't you?"

I nodded unenthusiastically.

"Just wait on a minute. The Principal's got a long-distance call from Delhi."

"My God, the Government of India," I muttered. "Is it that serious?"

Miss Fernandez did not hear; or if she did she did not believe. She inserted three sheets interspersed with carbons into her typewriter, then poised her long delicate brown fingers over the keys.

"Oh, Miss Fernandez, Miss Fernandez," I sighed, "this is the moment I always dread."

"Don't worry, mun, they won't put you in jail. Those policemen are damn nice chaps, defenders of our liberty."

"It's not them, miss," I said leaning closer and putting my hand between hers and the keyboard. "It's this typewriter, the crash of the keys, that's what I dread."

"What's the matter with you, mun? Are you in some travail?"

"The piano—do you know the piano?" I asked desperately trying to make my position clear. She nodded. "The music blots you out, and the musician sings, 'I'm happy without you, I'm happy without you, so go or stay, unnecessary ape.' D'you go or stay, Miss Fernandez?"

"I stay."

"And I stay too, and the music consoles us. But the music of the typewriter, Miss Fernandez, you know that? It doesn't console. It drives me mad."

She looked with intense concern into my pleading eyes, and her purple lips moved. "What is your distress in precise reference to, mun? I cannot refuse, I'm pledged."

"Please, miss," I said, "how d'you spell your name?"

"Fernandez. F.e.r.n.a.n.d.e.z."

I scratched out Gilbert and wrote Fernandez. I then shyly gave her the note. I was not really shy, but made as if I was in order to have the excuse to yield her the note inch by inch.

When she got it then, she really knew she had it. And she made certain she read it. She took long enough.

"Is that all, mun? Nothing more?"

I looked at her searchingly for a clue. A clue for what? What was the problem? Miss Gilbert had never intimated that the matter could go any further. Miss Fernandez evidently thought otherwise. Treading somewhat cautiously on unfamiliar ground, I said, "What more can you do, miss?"

"What exactly do you want, mun?"

She was completely acquiescent, pledged as she said, prepared to give whatever she had; and I to take what I wanted. But what did she have? And what did I want? Here I realized was dawning a problem infinitely more disturbing than any other I'd encountered, when two robust bangs of the Principal's bell relieved me of it.

Instantly she went in. A few grunts and growls from the holy of holies and she was holding open the swing-door for me to enter.

Two dazzling white-clad police inspectors sat in state on either side of the Principal. Their twin white helmets glimmered side by side like miniature Taj Mahals on his desk. The obvious superior, the peon's dreaded haramiwallah, was a florid, thick-set Englishman, even broader than the Principal. The other was an Anglo-Indian with a quiet manner, rather like Wilfred's.

"Sit down, Hosea, these two gentlemen have your father's consent to ask you a few questions."

I sat down and instinctively turned left to face the mild Anglo-Indian. I felt light-headed and must have gone pale. "There's nothin' to get frightened about, son," rumbled the broad one far to my right. "Just tell us whatcha know."

"I don't know anything about Mr. Titmus," I blurted to the Anglo-Indian. "He just disappeared."

"How didja know we was going to ask about Mr. Timus?" I heard the broad one say.

211

"I don't know, sir," I replied to the mild one.

"Did Mr. Timus say anything of an innermit nature to you?"

"No, sir."

"Was he innermit with any other boy?"

"No, sir."

"Did he ever mention a gennerman named Mahatmahama Gandhi?"

"No, sir."

"Was Mr. Timus your classmaster?"

"No, sir."

"Diddy teach you Latin?"

"No, sir."

"Diddy——"

"No, sir."

"Hosea! Listen to the question, boy!"

"Diddy write you letters?"

"No, sir."

"Then what's this?"

"No, sir."

I heard a paper being thrust across the desk towards me, but took no notice of it until the mild Anglo-Indian, on whose face my eyes were rooted, took it up and gently spread it in front of me.

It appeared to be the last page, numbered ten, of a letter in his familiar round handwriting.

". . . to your father in form. Hoping that some day I shall come to learn what became of that counterfeit thing, I close.

May the love of the Man, Jesus, enter your noble soul.

Yours affectionately,
Oliver John Titmus."

"Ever 'eard of Oliver John Timus, son?"

"No, sir."

"Never gives nothin' away, does he?"

"All right, Hosea." The Principal's voice was slow and

stretched taut. Between words it hummed the familiar old refrain. 'You have let the school down, you have let the school down.' "You may go back to your class."

"Thank you, sir," I said to the Anglo-Indian.

"You're welcome," he smiled, speaking for the first time. "Did you like Mr. Titmus?"

"He was a wonderful man, sir," I said, and left.

As I passed by her desk, Miss Fernandez whispered something to me, which I did not catch. I asked her to repeat it. But when she did so I still could not hear. I nodded vaguely, and went out. She was a kind of a scrawny woman, even more dried up than Miss Gilbert.

"What happened at the Principal's, Joe?"

"There were cops, weren't there?"

"Where's this chap Hosea?"

"There he is!"

"Hold him, hold him!"

"What did the police want, Hosea?"

"Oh, nothing much. They'd only found out I was selling raffle tickets for my mother who's ill in hospital, and they wanted to buy some. It's a worthy cause, fellows; only a rupee a ticket for the Ganges and Brahmaputra Flood Relief. The first prize is a 1939 Chev, the second is an H.M.V. Radiogram, the third——" I was talking to myself now, and put the tickets back into my pocket to await the next bona fide inquirer. I'd found the original batch of them at the bottom of my locker, and they saved my life that day. There was only one person I was going to talk to on the matter, and that was first thing after the last bell.

Time crawled—I was almost willing to believe, backwards. What particularly annoyed me was Wilfred's persistence. The attempts of the mugger at tiffin, and L. S. D. Levy at practical Physics, to wrest my secret from me were customary, and only aroused my usual wrath. But Wilfred, who never asked ques-

213

tions of any kind, or of anyone, kept dogging me when all else had given up in disgust.

After the last bell, although I packed my homework books with the greatest haste, and ran down the stairs, I found him outside the school waiting for me. He was standing on the pavement at a point beyond the telegraph-post, watching me come. The school bus was there too. It did not start when I reached it. At the telegraph-post I caught his eye and looked back. There was not a soul in the bus; no driver either. We were the first two boys out of school.

He turned as I came up and we fell into step. I was looking down at the ground and began to wonder whose shoes I was watching. These were not Wilfred's. Or if they were, the feet weren't. There was nothing awkward about these firm, regular and purposeful strides. These steps were going somewhere. I heard a clock strike and slowed down.

"Why were you running? Are you late for something?"

"No," I said. "I was running to get away from school, that's all. I don't want anything unusual to happen. And I don't want to hear anything unusual either."

"Were you avoiding me because you think I have something unusual to say to you?"

"Yes, everything's just right as it is."

"That's what I wanted to tell you. At last everything's just right." We parted to avoid a beggar lumbering towards us with huge swollen legs—elephantiasis from the looks of them. We closed together again. "You and I, Joe, we know it. But no one else does. People are stupid and vicious without knowing it. Do you know what they think, Joe?"

"What?"

"That you know where Mr. Titmus is hiding. But you know and I know that everything's all right as it is."

Again I wondered to whom I was listening, for only once had I heard him speak as crisply as this; under the influence of gunja. "One day I'll come and see you, Joe, at your house in

214

Wodehouse Road." He'd never consented to come there before; wild horses couldn't drag him. The reason was my sisters, he'd said. "In the meantime you'll wait." I didn't know what he was driving at, but from the way he spoke it did not matter. Questions were not invited. "You'll never come and see me again at my house, Joe. Not until I come to yours. And when you see me in the street say Hello, but don't stop to chat. About me say nothing unusual."

We walked through the crowds in silence. "Good-bye, Joe."

"Good-bye, Wilfred."

"Just one more thing," he said. "I didn't want to be seen giving you a message in the street, so I've slipped Klein's translation of that torn-up thing into your satchel."

When I located it I saw he'd disappeared.

About five minutes later I was running as fast as the crowds would permit towards Flora Fountain. I knew if I did not catch him up before the vast and congested junction of so many roads I'd lose him. In front of the bank two files of coolies, going and coming, were transporting silver bricks from a van. A guard with a rifle tried to stop me from breaking the lines, but I went through too fast. Waddling pigeons hastening their steps rapidly before my approach, burst into flight in spreading fan shapes. The sun was shining uninterrupted by cloud. The monsoons were over. The Elephants hadn't come.

Till Flora Fountain I caught no sign of him. I was in a quandary now. Unlike the mugger, Wilfred had no fixed habits. His ways were unpredictable, truly so, as he never seemed to know what he was going to do himself. Often the three of us would be walking along, chattering our way back home, to find ourselves suddenly reduced to two. No one was waiting for him at home, not even a servant. He was completely without ties of any kind. There were a dozen routes he could take from Bori Bunder and six from Flora Fountain. But in the main there were two.

Sometimes he went straight along the tram route down the Causeway. It was the noisiest, and the shortest. Sometimes he took the quiet way, turning right at the Fountain and left along the Oval under the overhanging banyan and coconut trees. I did not choose the former although it seemed the more likely, as he was evidently in a hurry to get home. I simply did not want to meet him in a crowd. I had to see him, but not at any cost. I turned right and was lucky.

When I caught sight of him he was a solitary, easily identifiable, khaki-clad figure in the middle of the Oval. There'd not been a drop of rain for a week and the green was already yellowing, save of course for the roped-in cricket pitches. I took a shortcut into the maidan by mounting the railing that ran alongside the surrounding hedge, and leaping over.

He was about a quarter of a mile away. I'd never seen him walk so quickly. I called his name. He turned and saw me, then waved and walked on as fast as ever. I ran after him. He looked around and seeing me approach, waved again, more wildly, with clumsy pushing movements. I took no notice of the fact he seemed to be signing me to be off, and continued to approach him. He waited. At a distance of about ten yards he picked up a bulky segment of coconut husk, and pitched it at me. I dodged automatically and came on to within a yard of him, at which point he struck me a swinging blow between the eyes.

I would have avoided it as I had the coconut, if the blow had come suddenly. But the deliberate drawing back of his fist to a point absurdly far behind his head made it obvious seconds before he intended to hit me; so I made no attempt to duck. I was momentarily blinded, and stopped.

When I looked for him again he was walking straight on to be swallowed up by football fans converging to the Cooperage in their thousands. I turned right towards the open sea. Out-

216

side one of the new buildings that had gone up for the wealthy a dog barked at me, following me close to the edge of the road. I did not have to look back to see if it had a collar. A stray never barked like that. A stray had no possessions; no master; nothing to guard; nothing to bark about. How silent were those with nothing.

The tide was out. I sat on the sands. The edge of the sea was almost as far out as the gap between the reclamation walls. Needles walked about without pins today. It was fine. The sun setting earlier at this part of the year, was in my eyes. I tipped my topee forward to shield them from the rays, and in the tranquillity of my surroundings examined both letters this time. Could not Klein's translation be wrong? Or could I not have misinterpreted his clumsy, ill-worded English? Or finally, in Dr. Frumbusch's manner of speaking, could I not have misinterpreted what Klein had misinterpreted and thus quite by accident come to interpret the perfidious nature of this thing 100 per cent correctly?

The sun was in my eyes again, and I tipped my topee a little farther forward. Careful now to make certain other alterations in my position, such as the pressure of my upper body on my organs, so that I could not possibly attribute the smallest part of my total distress to anything but this letter, I reread it slowly word by word, quite prepared to forgive every one that libelled or defamed me.

"My dear Norma,

I have your eczited letters safely received. You give me time for reply of the first? Your angst about Indian Post Servis is not dezerved because servis is very good. You speak with contempt of 'Eastern Mentality' but this is a miz. To take eczample, I am sure an Indian woman would understand the lojik of a sitwaychin you do not. I am nacherlally happy that you write so often, but why write about sings which are full of pain and also tiring. I also know everysing from Arne who is in London? There is not to add. Should I spekulate? Spekulachins from her sister are not less enspired than from her huspand. Ruth was still in Vienna on 15th September. There will be no news from her till end of the war. Before it is ended I will not be pessimistic, but give thanks to God—because you at least believe in one—we have had no shildren.

Greetings and kisses,

Arnold."

Just a couple would have been sufficient. I could have milked the life out of them. I was a man of tremendous resource. But with nothing what could I do? Nothing.

I tipped my topee a little farther forward. These were the sort of notes he'd been taking while I had with such pleasure been addressing him. That was the rub: the pleasure. It wouldn't have mattered a lump of turd if I'd been compelled to speak with the lash of a whip on my back. The pain did not matter; the harsher it was, the more true; and true pain was heaven to the caress of false pleasure. The counterfeit. I could not think of Mr. Titmus without committing sacrilege in the presence of such profanity. I looked at the letter, and then at the translation, wondering which I should spit on, rip, revile, revenge myself on. The translation I hated because I understood it; but it was only a result of the original writing. Then again the writing was not original, it came from the pen; and the pen came from the hand, and the hand came from the man, and the man——?

The man came from his mother. Where was his mother, that I might be revenged on her? Where Wilfred's mother and my mother were; concealed from the searching feet of vengeance. Revenge. It was rather unsatisfactory. One could never without a shadow of doubt be sure where the evil originated. In the end one gave up the chase, through laziness, or cowardice, amorality; and spat on something handy; or burnt it, hanged it, or pissed on it—according to the instructions overleaf, the ritual, the creed.

Revenge was out. What about repentance? Self-revenge, merely a ritual too? Had I wronged Mr. Titmus, or imagined I had the power to? Were tears true? Truth had the power to cause illusions. The number of needles on the wall had doubled. I fumbled for the clasp of my satchel. My hands were shaking. I didn't know if it was the sun but I felt feverish. It wasn't at all hot, just blinding. I tipped my topee a little farther forward, and it fell crown-under upon the sand.

Shapujee Poonajee & Sons
99 Kalbadevi Road
Bombay.

The label damp from perspiration was peeling away. I tore it off. Why did they fix labels on everything? Couldn't they let well alone? When a chap examined himself thoroughly he discovered why his progress through life was so insupportably onerous. He was just a walking pack-mule for labels. There was another I could see by pulling it around, on the inside of my collar.

Solomon D. Levy & Sons
Crawford Market
Bombay.

I tore that out too. There was one inside the waistband of my shorts.

Mahareshlal Gotalal & Sons
Musjid Bunder
Bombay.

I tore that out too. My underpants had one in the same region.

Rattan Singh & Gopal Singh & Sons
Dhobhi Talao
Bombay.

I tore that out too. The examination of my shoes and socks disclosed nothing more to be concealed in my clothing, and I thought I'd completed the task when I saw the brown birth-mark on my calf. A mote struck me in the eye, but luckily did

219

not remain inside. I looked up and saw that although my topee was still on the sand the sun was not bothering me any more. It had not set, but thick, purple-black clouds were obscuring it. The needles without pins had disappeared from the wall. A sudden, fresh gust of motes freckled my face. The letters and labels had been swept away. The direction of the wind was directly onshore, and as it increased in strength, I replaced my hat and drew up my knees to protect my eyes. I felt weak and helpless, though not altogether without resource. I opened my composition book on my slanted thighs, and kept my face close to it so that it should at the same time offer protection from the sand, which had now begun to pepper my shins with stinging force. I set the brim of my topee on my knees, and circled my left arm around my legs to hold up the book on the right side. There was just enough light to write in, and I felt as safe from distraction as I had ever been. The occasional flash of lightning did not worry me, though the thunder boomed so pompously it made me chuckle. I scarcely felt the rain at all. The harder it blew, the closer together I pulled myself. At its hardest I found I'd still something left. There seemed no limit to the extent I could pull myself together. There was no last straw. I could bear anything. Nothing could break me.

I returned home in brilliant sunshine crowned by rainbow lights. I was in a gay mood, which was not the least bit damped to find I had not been consulted. Naturally, there was no need when you looked at it with unprejudiced eyes. When my mother had been brought back in an ambulance that morning it had become obvious to anyone with a grain of sense that my room would be much more suitable to put the cradle in than any other. The servants had moved the boxes and trunks out of the spare room and stacked them in the garage. They had cleaned out this little room, displacing a nest of mice in the process. I was sorry for them when I was told about it and only hoped they were taking as unprejudiced an attitude toward their plight as I was. Christ, I thought, no cloud no lining. Everything I possessed in the world had been moved in here, and when I paused to look at them in this different light they reflected qualities I had not dreamed they possessed.

There was very little light, admittedly. The only window, an exceptionally small, barred one, faced the blank wall of the opposite house. But I had a lamp, my word, I had TWO lamps. I had indeed nothing to grumble about, except now in retrospect my own peculiar attitude in the past. For months I'd idly thought it would go in *their* room. Since they'd created it, I presumed, they'd want it to be there, they'd fight tooth and nail, my mother especially, prompted by her maternal instincts. But I was wrong. And a good thing too, another silver lining that: me being wrong. I'd been wrong all my life; the whole equilibrium of the family was based on this fact: my wrongness. If I suddenly started being right my presence in this tranquil house could prove no less upsetting than if the mice themselves turned up with a Charter for the Restitution of Rights signed and sealed by H.M. George VI. I would have to be put away altogether; perhaps sent to a SUITABLE boarding-school—there'd once been talk of it, a military boarding-school in the Himalayas.

There was a key in the lock and I turned it. It let out a rusty squeak, a familiar sound at the end of the monsoon, and there was no doubt it had ended—on me. I laid down on the bed and felt the damp of my clothes gently seep through. And if in my strange shivering condition I perceived I could no longer trust my feelings I had Uncle Reuben's word for it. He'd passed me in his Rolls Royce on Wodehouse Bridge and stopped to tell me how wet I was. He'd added he'd been invited around to look at the baby and had half a mind to give me a lift as I should get home immediately to change my clothes because they were wet. Oh, yes, they were wet all right, he'd said, too wet for him to let me enter the car as I'd

221

ruin the covers. He didn't want any more trouble from me he'd said as I'd once sat in the car with tar on my trousers and he literally winced to recall the occasion when I'd the gall to start the vehicle myself having been left alone in it for a minute. He could never look at his Rolls without recalling the injury I'd caused it, so he regretted he couldn't give me a lift very much indeed as I was in a piteous state and would catch my death of cold if he didn't, so he would, yes, he was prepared to make an exception just this once and take me in and to be so extravagantly lenient as to recall my youthful impulsiveness with a twinkle and commend me for my sense of adventure for this was the stuff life was made of, the courage the leaping to clasp it, the accommodation oh yes he'd take me in to accommodate was all that the nobility of man was comprised of the rest was a scummy spineless compromise forgiveness loathsome lack of remembrance strength was accommodation was humour was gratitude this gratitude he bore me for all that secret bottled up laughter I'd released in him oh he spoke with tears in his eyes he was repenting he had not seen it before so sorry he kept passing five and ten rupee notes into my pocket and rapt though I was with the wondrous change I had wrought in this vile and virulent Scrooge I began to perceive I was delirious.

I couldn't say exactly when I became conscious I was in hospital. I was quite pleased about it. The only snag was that it turned out to be one of those Europeans ONLY Hospitals, which rather out-weighed the pleasure of not being at home. It brought back troubled memories. During the summer holidays before the monsoon I'd been to Breach Candi Swimming Pool, and that was ALSO Europeans ONLY. A black chap, absolutely pitch-black, was at the pay-box and that greatly eased my conscience at the start. When I got my ticket and went in, though, a white chap in white shorts, white shirt, and white shoes hooked his finger at me. He made

222

me sit in his office and fill in a form. He studied it carefully and then told me I could hand over my ticket and get my money back from the black chap. He wasn't very annoyed, but the black chap was. All in all it was a very humiliating experience which I did not want repeated in the few years left to me.

One day towards the end of my stay the doctor asked me why I always wriggled over to the far edge of the bed when he came into the room. He was awfully kind although he was white, and I confessed that I was worried about occupying a bed here as I was not 100 per cent European. He seemed very keen to pursue the matter, and I finally told him that as I was only half European I always felt much easier balanced on the edge of the bed. He soon convinced me this was unnecessary. At that time I was very weak, and easily convinced by anyone who cared to concern himself with this rather uninteresting subject.

Dr. Frumbusch came to visit me with two presents. One was a box of coloured pencils with drawing book, and the second a box containing all the pieces of a model aeroplane, which had to be assembled neatly together in order to provide satisfaction. I thanked him very much; I could not, admittedly, thank him very loudly on account of my weak state, but I thanked him twice as long. I asked him to put the unassembled aeroplane on the unopened presents piled up in the corner. I would have the pencils, though, they were fine pencils. He was in a jolly mood and asked me how I was in such a way that discouraged me from telling him the truth. I said I was fine thanks. He asked me if I would come and see him again when I was fully recovered. I said I would be delighted, and picked out the red pencil from the box. He said he had plenty of time so he would stay if of course I didn't mind. I said I would be delighted. In that case, he said, he would come again. I said I would be delighted and slowly wrote four on the top left-hand corner of the page so as to leave plenty of space. I looked at him attentively waiting for his next question, and he seemed to remember he'd left his bath-water running. I scratched out four and wrote five. He got up then and excused himself saying he had to run.

"One moment, please!"

I was embarrassed by the sudden way I'd shouted, and to make up for my bad manners, continued in a whisper, "Please, have you any bread-crumbs?"

"What d'you want bread-crumbs for, Josef?"

"Tiny little birds come hopping into the veranda looking for crumbs," I explained.

"Why don't you ask one of the nurses to give you some?"

"I don't know," I shrugged helplessly, "I've never thought of asking anyone for bread-crumbs save you, Dr. Frumbusch."

He looked at me very interestedly. I scratched out five and wrote six, remarking that it didn't look as if we were going to have a waltz today. He excused himself properly then and said he was sorry but he really had to rush now. I nodded understandingly and said if there was anything I could do for him and Dorothy to give me a ring, just any time. He should never, never, never be frightened of calling on me. He should also never, never—— He put on his hat and left. I scratched out six and wrote seven. Then I scratched out seven and pitched the book and pencils into the corner.

The next day I felt much better. I began to yawn and stretched my limbs this way and that so hard I thought it a wonder they did not snap. After breakfast I itched to get up. I felt prodigiously strong. I gripped the rails at the head of my bed and pulled like Samson at the pillars of the taunting Philistines. I could feel them bend like rubber, so I let up as I'd got into enough trouble with Nurse Winters. She came bustling in as I was rolling up my sleeve to flex my biceps.

224

She whipped the thermometer up and down, at the same time inquiring how I felt.

"Muscles," I commanded, "speak for me."

"Open your mouth. Shut your mouth. And don't bite on the thermometer, please."

I'd broken only one in this fashion, and that about a week ago; yet since then she never failed three times a day to repeat like grace before meals, "And don't bite on the thermometer, please." She looked up from her watch and asked, "Aren't you going to open your presents? *Don't* answer! Just nod or shake your head. And don't bite on the thermometer, please."

I shook my head.

"Show me your thumbs." I showed them. "Look at this one. Shame on you, it's beginning to look like a soggy sponge. When are you going to grow up and stop that nasty habit?" I shrugged. She pulled out the thermometer, and looked at it. "You're feeling better, aren't you?" she asked.

Not realizing the full implications of such a question I nodded. She put a mark on my temperature chart at the foot of the bed with a blue pencil and beamed at it approvingly. "Oh, yes," she remarked, "you'll be going home soon, Joe."

After she left I rolled down my sleeve, crept under the covers and lay still. I tried to recall that sick feeling but it was no good. At school Cranmer had told me he could work up a fine fever by putting sliced onions in his arm-pits and crutch, and standing with his arms and legs crossed naked in the sunshine. He was dead right, Cranmer. It was no good talking. A chap had to strike out. I watched the glass panel in the door like a hawk, and got out of bed. Pins and needles stabbed my feet, and I felt as if I was walking on pads of cotton wool. Staggering somewhat I collected the blue pencil from the box and went over to the temperature chart.

It was a simple graph, all familiar stuff to me. A time-temperature curve. Up was feverish, down was normal. I neatly scored a dot as high as I could get it without arousing suspicion and joined it to the zigzagging line. Then I returned to bed, lay back and groaned. It was encouraging to find how, once I'd done this, I actually felt piqued. I was in luck. The doctor came in a minute later, unaccompanied by the nurse.

"And how is Master Hosea today?"

"Quite well, Doctor, quite—ah, oh, er—quite well," I winced. "Steadily improving."

He looked at me, and I smiled back gallantly. Then he looked at the chart, frowned, and immediately went off. I lay in as tortured a position as I could muster for some time, but as no one seemed to be coming, I relaxed. By and by I got so bored I could have yelled. I had some school books I had asked for so as to keep abreast of my studies. I had, indeed, made excellent progress, and it was becoming more and more obvious that school was unnecessary when a chap was prepared to put his shoulder to the wheel and slog on his own. Wondering what subject I should concentrate on today my eye fell on my total book, and on opening it at random I immediately had an idea to pass the time without attracting attention.

TONG TONG TING TUNG TONG TING. It should be easy, I reckoned. The bed for instance was all metal. There were four rails at the head, and four shorter ones at the foot. I tested them all with a ruler. They sounded all right, quite harp-like in fact—until I struck the water-jug. TONG! It was a note so perfect in every respect that I almost raised a cheer, not then realizing what a deuce of a problem this very clarity, this perfection, could cause me. The thing, I quite rightly thought, could take its place with church bells, but it did not take long for the darker side of my discovery to loom large upon me. The bed-rails with which I had hitherto been satisfied, had to be scrapped. In my search for quality I had to make the ultimate sacrifice. I had to get something with a TING to go with that TONG, and that meant a TING, not a TICK or a TINK. In short, no compromise.

226

It was here that I made my next major discovery. The tumbler that stood by the jug let out the exact TING when half filled with water. I could thus play TONG TONG TING without even moving my head. With mounting enthusiasm I now began to search for my TUNG. I tried everything within reach. After several forays during which I hung perilously out of bed, I caught sight of the chamber-pot on the floor. My response was immediate, nor was I disillusioned. I somehow knew it would not fail me. I hit it square on the bowl. TUNG! Eureka! I had my first line!

I lay back for a while panting on account of the unaccustomed exercise. As I rested however I was not idle. I was forging ahead, looking about for a likely object that would ring the first note of the next line, TANG. By now I was able from my past failures to eliminate articles that were worthless, sight untried. And eventually my eyes fell on a cartwheel of six glass lampshades above and to the right of my bed. Everything I knew about this business informed me that I would find all the TANGS I needed up there—not to mention those awfully high tones for SEND HIM VICTORIOUS.

The problem was to get up there. If I stood on the bed I could perhaps reach it. There was a risk involved, but I couldn't turn back now. I slowly got up, keeping one eye on the glass panel. I tried to strike the lampshade nearest me, but found I was just missing it. There was a stuffed bedside chair near the head of the bed and I hauled it along to position it between the bed and the lamp, with the high upright of its back nearest me. I then put my foot firmly on the platform provided, and leaned forward to test the extent of my reach. In my excitement I took abundant precautions to see the chair did not tilt, but completely forgot the bed was on castors— until I felt it begin to roll away from under me.

With remarkable presence of mind I dropped the ruler, and kicked off to balance for a precarious moment on the chair top. My head began to swim, I felt myself falling; but in flaying the air I quite by chance caught the frame of the cart-wheel. It was well screwed into a beam by three chains, and by the grace of God I was saved. I was hanging thus quite securely with one foot on the chair-back when the doctor strode in accompanied by Nurse Winters.

"And what in the blazes are you playing at?"

"God Save the King, Doctor."

"Young man, it's about time you returned home."

When I got back home I was told I had to stay in bed a while longer before returning to school. I was quite agreeable to this. Once ensconced there I found I much preferred my new room. It was smaller and more cosy. After I'd been there a day or so, my mother complained that the cries of the baby were waking her at night, and it would be better to put it in the small room as it was farther away. So the move was made.

Once back in my former room I found how much nicer it was here. It was larger, more light and airy. The only thing about it that worried me was that my crying at night might disturb my mother. I managed to see reason on the issue however and it soon ceased to worry me. If the sole purpose of my crying was not to attract attention, then I would achieve it well enough by not crying. And I dared say it was this simple act of self-restraint, rather than the doctors' medicines, that improved my general condition.

The next day I left my bed to walk about the house, and took my meals at the table. I couldn't eat much in their company although they urged me to do so for my own sake, not merely with words but actions too. They tempted me with the choicest morsels, which they put upon my plate, and I could see they had all decided to behave charitably towards me. I was very touched and only regretted the fact I had no appetite at meal times. Indeed, this once voracious capacity of mine was so conspicuously absent that after a few days they began to accuse me of raiding the fridge and the larder in between meals. They offered ample evidence in support of their suspicions, which I could neither endorse nor deny; not because they failed to move me, but because I simply could not accept anything without offering the thanks due to them in return. This I found it was beyond my capacity to do; and on one never-to-be-repeated occasion I proved it so.

"Thank you, Gladys, thank you for your chicken liver. I am moved by your kindness, admittedly not as much moved as you—moved by comparison so little in fact that I humbly offer my sincerest apologies."

When I paused to regard the matter more generally I found Thanks and Sorry to be two faces of the same coin, which turned about with the fickle ease of all things counterfeit; and to avoid its tender I would rather refuse than accept, rather steal than request.

I seemed to cause them a great deal of annoyance by tip-toeing about the house, and still more by answering in a whisper when they addressed me. When they asked me why I was so uncannily quiet I told them I didn't want to disturb the baby; that was also the reason why I had not shown it my face, I didn't want to frighten it. They did not understand, perhaps because I explained all this in gestures and mime. My confidence in sign language had round about this time begun to grow, a confidence they did not seem to share. I spoke enough to the servants, they complained, why not to *them*! I went to great lengths to explain, but they were wasted, on Gladys especially. She told my mother I was with the servants all the time she was away at the Gymkhana, and that was every day including Sundays, and Mum didn't like it. She caught me one evening listening to Nancy. She was the new Goanese ayah, a girl of sixteen, who sang and played on the guitar with extraordinary skill. My mother thought this was the giddy limit.

"You'll only spoil them, Joe," she advised.

"But, Mum," I said completely abandoning my reticence on this occasion, "the girl has talent. I can hardly help *enjoying*——"

"That's just it," she interrupted, "*because* she's giving you enjoyment she'll start getting uppity and asking for rises. You mustn't spoil them. Think of *us* for a change. We have to pay, don't we?"

I had to admit she was right, dead on the mark once again, and what resentment I felt for the deprivation of Nancy's songs I dispelled by counting my blessings. Mum after all didn't object to the mugger. He was tone-deaf, admittedly, but as Mum said, "He's such a nice boy. He'll go far in the world. *His* shirt never works out of his trousers, Joe."

He used to come most evenings after school to give me the latest news. I never said much to him either and couldn't have if I'd wanted to. He used to come jabbering in like a Stop Press column, and it was just too bad if by chance something he said caught my interest.

"Jones as bin made cricket capn, Patkar's furious an refuses to accept vice, our waterpolo team's bin accused of serrepshus fouling gainst Bombay Gym, Cadet Corps swopped the Lewis gun for a Vickers tat-tat-tat-tat-tat, I saw Titmus, Wilf's living with is mum now, can't stay long, gotta lotta homework, lucky dog."

"What?" I asked.

"Gotta lotta homework."

"Oh."

We were in the garden. The windows of the unoccupied flat above the major's stared blindly down at us.

"Where did you see Mr. Titmus?"

"With a woman."

"I said Where?"

"He was in a soldier's uniform and I thought the woman was a whore till I recognized him despite his moustache and glasses."

230

"WHERE did you see him?"

"At about eight o'clock at night. The place was full of soldiers and sailors. It was a wonder I recognized him."

"WHERE did you see him?"

"On account of the way he walks, that's what gave him away."

"How did you see him?"

"On the Causeway going past the Parsee Colony."

"So he's joined the army after all, eh?"

"Oh, no, they're still madly looking for him."

"Then what's he in uniform for?"

"Don't know. Gor," he added, "I was just dying to follow him."

"Why didn't you?"

"They turned left into Ormiston Road," he explained, "and I was sent out by my mother to buy a reel of cotton."

I felt myself wanting to yell, and this time I didn't stop myself. "You dunderhead! Why the hell didn't you follow! Don't you know that this great and wonderful man is being harried and hounded like an animal? We've got to find out where he's holed up and bring him food and if need be DIE for him!"

"I know! I know!" he shouted back. "But he turned into Ormiston Road, I keep telling you, and there aren't any shops that sell cotton there, are there? Mother of Moses, think what you're saying, consider *my* position!"

The appearance of three curiously watching female heads at our windows reminded me this was the first time I'd raised my voice since my return. Too loudly for my own good too, it seemed. I felt faint and sat down on the roller. It was still warm although it was now in the shade. "Did you get it?" I asked.

"Get what?"

"That cotton your mother sent you for."

"Yes."

"If you don't think me too nosey, what colour did she want?"

"Pink."

"And was she satisfied you had the right shade?"

"Yes, very satisfied. She let me keep the two pice change."

"Thank Heaven," I murmured. "You had me on tenterhooks." I felt really giddy now, and said, "I'm going back to bed."

He followed me in, keeping close lest I should fall. He seemed very concerned about me, and I felt deeply touched. When I lay down he, without my asking, drew a blanket over me. This action, the drawing of a blanket over me, I always found to be soothing to a magical degree. It did not matter who did it, as long as it was not myself, not even an animal. In fact an animal would have been preferable, as one did not then have to say Thank you. Talking did so break the spell.

"What's actually the matter with you, Joe? Everyone at school says you're funking the exams."

"What did you tell them, Mugger?"

"I tell them you're really ill. You're so pale as though the Hand Of Death were on you."

"Thanks, Mugger," I murmured brokenly. "That Wilfred, you know, he's not a friend of mine. You're the only one I've got."

He was duly embarrassed, fidgeted and proceeded to tuck in his shirt although it was already as taut as a drum. "Are you taking Kepler's Malt?" he asked.

"Yes, also Syrup Minadex and Halibut Oil, and B and C tablets. It's a waste of good medicines," I sighed, "I'm done for, I'm sinking fast."

He regarded me with profoundest gloom, then all of a sudden sprang to action. "You know what you need, Joe boy," he exclaimed, shaking an earnest finger, "you've got to pray. You've got——"

232

"Cut it out, Mugger, don't make it worse," I implored. "You know I'm a bolshie."

"Look," he replied, snatching up three cushions from the two easy chairs in the room, "I'm not asking you to pray for yourself. Where's your prayer shawl, prayer book and phylacteries?"

"In the bottom drawer."

He knelt and pulled it open. A smell of decay commingled with camphor balls wafted out. "Mother of Moses, when was this last opened?"

"I forget," I confessed.

"This book's worm-eaten. There's mildew an inch thick on the phylacteries. May God forgive you. No wonder you're unwell."

My interest slightly aroused by now I watched him place a cane chair in the darkest corner of the room. He then added a bolster to the collection of cushions and began to shuffle them around in the chair to form the figure of a man in the bent posture of prayer. The prayer book he opened upon its lap, the shawl he arranged around the shoulders, then as best he could he noosed the phylactery around the head and topped it with my sola topee.

We studied the total effect for some time, he occasionally prodding the figure here and there into a more sacramental attitude. By and by he turned to me and asked, "How d'you feel?"

"Just the same," I shrugged.

"Weak?"

"Weak."

"Feverish?"

"Feverish."

"Near Death's Door?"

I rolled my eyes hopelessly to the ceiling.

"Well, we shall have to wait and see," he nodded, refusing to lose heart. "I'll come again tomorrow and open the book to another prayer."

233

"O.K.," I sighed. "You're a brick, boy, an absolute brick. If there's any way I can repay you, just say so."

"Yes, well, actually," he began with some show of concern, "I hadn't been meaning to bring this up, Joe, but since you mentioned it, about two months ago I paid for you at that Tarzan film, and you haven't returned the four annas yet."

There was some money lying on the bedside table and I paid him. He said, "Don't think I specially want it now because you're dying. I wouldn't mind if you did die without paying me, as it's not all that much."

I struggled out of bed and on to my feet again, then tottered into the garden.

"Glory be to God!" I heard him exclaim. "It's working!"

He was only for a moment astonished to find me the next morning stepping out of my father's car and a little palely, but quite steadily, walking in through the school gates.

"The power of prayer, Joe, the power of prayer."

I might as well have stayed at home. Or run away altogether. But I couldn't remain at home for life, and I'd run away twice before. This running away was too precious a thing, a sacred thing to be kept ready for decisive use, not rendered meaningless with repetition; like praying. Ritual. So I returned to school.

I found changes which at first worried me. Many masters and boys were new. An additional wing had been acquired. Worse still, some of the familiar faces were absent. Wilfred had been promoted to Std. 7; Now Now had returned to his native Madras; L.S.D.'s father apparently despairing of his son's academic advancement had put him to work in his hosiery store.

Why did these changes worry me? It was indeed puzzling to find, on top of all this, that I myself should seem strange to those I knew. Had they forgotten me, Joey the Jester of yesterday? They never laughed any more when I spoke. The familiar titter of anticipation when I rose to my feet in class was gone. The debts I expected to settle were gone. I asked the mugger why he had not mentioned all these changes during the course of his visits, and he replied, "I didn't think you'd be interested."

At the end of the first day I realized he was right. I was bored, so bored with this wretched institution I couldn't bring myself to do any mischief. The particular kick I once used to get out of school life was gone; and only now that it had been severed, as with limb, sight and hearing, did I realize what it was. It used to fascinate me to take a new master and by progressive stages drum it into his thick skull that I was unteachable. How painfully slow some of them were to learn; but they yielded in the end. It was a thrilling moment that last look, groan, or gesture, or whatever means the master chose to indicate defeat; when he ceased totally, and till death did us part, to expect anything from me. What a sensation of release that brought. No felon who had not escaped from life imprisonment in the first week of his term could have tasted a liberation sweeter; and I'd failed to savour it only once.

He'd gone. He'd written a letter and gone still believing without a suspicion of doubt that I would amount to something. "May the love of the Man Jesus enter your noble soul." It ate into me. It was certainly no enigma to me, that my return to school evoked feelings for someone who was no longer there. The most unsettled account of all. The idol uncracked; living, lurking, intact. Those new boys, those new masters—when I looked at them some intangible yoke of oppression settled upon my neck. There was so much newness in the world. Newness was boring.

The examinations duly took place, and there being no block-headed Levy in the way, I came last. Small wonder. Most of my evenings I spent wandering about Kamatipura, Foras Road, and other teeming, disreputable areas of the city in search of him. After a time I could not say where the greater part of my obsession lay: in the search for him, or the areas in which I chose to do my hunting. The degradation fascinated and obliterated me in much the same way as the sudden unfolding of Wilfred's tragedy engulfed my own. Humanity dragged down to the level of animals at a zoo— indeed, lower, for at least those unfortunate captives could not be procured.

There were girls in those cages, so young they were breast-less. The dancers, the gramophones wailing on the pavements, the beggars with limbs purposefully deformed from child-hood, and the holy reek of incense. The bedlam at night had a carnival air. Here was where chaos lodged contented. This was the Indian way. When Europeans found a rotten egg they threw it out. The Indians added more hot peppers and the curry was none the less appetizing. And sorrow and all the rottenness of life were similarly treated. Poor Dr. Frumbusch, M.D., D.P.P.S., Vienna. How vividly I recalled his bewilder-ment. "The Eastern mentality." He'd tried to make me happy by isolating and casting out my sorrow. Unteaching. Non-sense. It couldn't be done. I had to have the hot-curry treat-ment; the mix-it-in and gulp-it-down, and the singsong and drumming on anything that happened to be lying around, the abandonment, the orgy of wallowing that absorbed it all; the exhaustion, the letting of strange things of their own accord emerge.

One night in Kamatipura I got a whiff that came out in spite of the frying onions, the spices, and the pungent incense of a neighbouring temple. I had my friend with me, a one-legged beggar-boy named Sinha. He was a veritable mine of information. I thumbed to a form smoking a hubbly-hubbly on the pavement. This man or woman was completely en-shrouded in a blanket, its only contact with the outside world being the tube of the hookah.

"Sinha, bhai, yeh gunja marta?"

"Ha, seth," he nodded. "Idur bhot gunja marta."

That night I was late; not so late as to require the outbreak of a third World War to save me, but quite late. They were only just starting to eat, and I had no sooner taken my place than my father informed me, by way of coincidence—he paused here with nostrils flaring to repeat—by way of coincidence he was in the middle of writing to my Principal. He said since the exams were over there was no need for me to wait the few days before the school broke up for the Christmas holidays. He'd taken a bungalow in Marbleshwar.

Of course that was not all. He gave me a talking to, a long lecture in his study. "Joe," he began, "I'm a man who works hard. Sometimes fifteen and sixteen hours a day. Why? No man works for himself. I'm working for you. That's why I'm not at home to watch every little thing you do. I'm out working. Working for you."

I don't want you to work for me, Dad. I want you at home. Have you watch over me. Have you play with me.

I did not say it, but let him go on. It was too late to say it. It was no longer true. And would it always be the same? That when I grew old enough to express my needs they became untrue, they altered to needs I could not express, until I grew old enough to do so, whence they became untrue, and so on, and so forth, moving perpetually in single file: my current needs, then me, then my father far in the rear. Poor Dad, he always commenced explaining things that I'd long since proved untrue.

I couldn't say what he in his private calculations thought the countryside would do for me. The countryside was indeed superb, but it was Indian; and one night from the mali's hut, which lay contiguous to the bungalow, I caught a whiff that in the clear, unblemished mountain air proved a hundredfold more identifiable than when it was mixed with the potent odours of Kamatipura.

It couldn't have done me much harm. And a little bit of blackmail didn't hurt the mali either. He was invulnerable on the moral plane since neither he nor his family led any kind of life there. They were fanatically religious and their needs were almost exclusively spiritual. As for myself, I positively bloomed. The mali's three sons and I got on like a house on fire. I was for days on end left alone with them. The family only came up at week-ends, and every time they saw me my cheeks were plumper and redder.

What little alarm they did express, aside from Mum's usual carping about my clothes, was with regard to the number of insect bites that covered the visible parts of my body. They asked if I had khutmul in my bed, and I said, no. Nevertheless they were concerned enough to get St. Paul to take it apart, but this still disclosed no bed-bugs. Eventually, however, as these bites became a permanent feature of my appearance they were inclined to take a philosophical view of the matter. After all it was *my* body and I wasn't grumbling. Indeed I wasn't, I'd never felt so invincibly fit in my entire life. Towards the end of my stay I had a mind to show them how I could walk twenty yards over rocky ground on my hands, but somehow felt it wouldn't impress them. Or rather, now that I had perceived the need to do so, it was dead. I had no need to impress them.

I never saw the kid in my several weeks' sojourn up there. It was left behind with no little relief, I gathered, as it cried a great deal on account of its inherently grizzling nature now aggravated by the stinging effect of its urine on a belatedly performed circumcision. It was anyway in very good hands. They all spoke well of Nancy, for if they hadn't they would scarcely have taken the risk of leaving it behind.

All things considered, the renting of this bungalow for the winter season proved a much greater success than was expected. The biggest trouble they'd anticipated turned out to the contrary. I did not utter one word of complaint in all that

238

time for being left alone up there; and I even coerced my father against Mum's wishes to let me stay on to the very day before school reopened.

"You would think," my mother said the last week-end they were there, "that he didn't want to come back EVER."

My mother was always more up to date with my needs than anyone else I knew.

Returning home after my first day at school I had occasion to think wistfully back on my uncomplicated life with the mali's boys in Marbleshwar. I took the long way home through the Esplanade Maidan and the Oval, brooding upon the artificial problems of school life. With the mali's boys there had been problems too, but no one could resent them; they were real life and death matters one was only too eager to hammer out to their natural conclusions. There'd been, for example, the bother about the khutmul, the bed-bugs.

The only bed in the mali's hut was a rope-laced wooden frame, the property of the mali himself. His sons lay on the floor at night, but in the afternoon or evening they took it in turns to lie on the bed on account of the bugs, which of course could not be deprived of their natural habitat, their true station: the bed. It was not that the mali and his family feared to provoke a campaign for the restitution of the bed-bugs' rights. They were not afraid of anything. In their profound and insatiable reverence for all forms of life they abstained from eating potatoes and other root crops due to the distress they could cause the worms, and I really came to understand their point of view. Yet the bugs were undoubtedly a nuisance. They bit the old man, and very hard too when they were hungry; so his children took it upon themselves to make sure the bugs were fed. They took it in turns to lie on the infested rope-work before nightfall.

There was thus no problem—at least not until I arrived on

239

the scene. Finding, as I did after a week, the prime necessity of becoming an integral part of this family, I'd demanded my turn at feeding the bugs. My wish had been met with some considerable appreciation, but a good deal more embarrassment. They would rather I forgot it; but I insisted, and it was reluctantly pointed out to me that I was not a vegetarian. I ate meat. Was it fair to expect members of a strict Brahmin sect to have their blood sucked by bugs who'd sucked the blood of a non-vegetarian? It was a touchy problem, but it was a real one, and therefore had to admit of a satisfactory solution. It did. I turned vegetarian. To the extreme annoyance of the Hosea family at week-ends, I'd stuck grimly to my guns, for I had the moral support of the mali and his boys solidly behind me.

Now all that, I brooded glumly, was over. It was grilled sheeps' testes for lunch. It was back to the city, the killing, the artificial life, the school, to find myself Victim No. 1 of a phoney man-made division. I was declared unfit to pass. This meant all the former classmates of Nickie Sutherland were now with me. I was still in Std. 6 while the rest of the class without exception now constituted Std. 7.

Bad as my school record had been, this had never occurred before. How should I break the news to the family? Would they take it as cheerfully as I did? I had a shrewd suspicion they wouldn't. There'd be more talk, and perhaps now, action, with regard to Horace College, Dusbindi. I could just see myself extracting cube roots in the shadow of barbed-wire and bayonet. An artificial life to say the least; as was the present an artificial problem, something that would require artifice to resolve. Briefly, would it be more advantageous to break them the news myself, or wait and let them hear it from some other source?

Well that of course depended on their MOOD. Proceeding watchfully along Wodehouse Road it struck me that the best place to do it was not at home but out in the road. The open

240

sky had a nice dissipating effect. I kept a sharp look out as I occasionally met Mum sallying forth at this time. She had a full engagement book these days. Apart from her permanent position on the W.I.Z.O. and seasonal forays into Flood and Famine Relief, she was on the European Refugee Welfare Board and H.M.'s Forces Entertainment Committee. It was thus as likely she would already be out.

As it happened she wasn't. Apart from Dad they were all in, having tea. And I did not have to strain my perceptions, to prowl around peering in at windows to ascertain the quality of their mood. There was a battle royal brewing. This seemed to have become an established pattern of my existence. Whenever I came home with bad news I found some other trouble had got in ahead of me. Discarding topee and satchel, I slid into my place unnoticed, and bided my time.

"It's a dog in the manger attitude," Gladys was saying. "Don't you agree, Mum?"

"What, dear?"

"I'm saying that Dorothy is not going out anyway, so why won't she agree to look after it? Why must I stay too? I've a frightfully urgent——"

"Yes, Dorothy," Mum nodded, frowning vaguely, "if you're staying in anyway——"

"Because I happen to be staying in does not mean I'm to be put upon," Dot retorted. "I've let the thin end of the wedge get in before with Joe, and I am not under any circumstance letting it happen with Michael. You know as well as I do that the child needs more, a damned sight more than just the presence of an adult. If I have certain matters to attend to at home then you can consider me not here, not here. And that's flat."

"Shh, that's enough please, Dorothy."

"No, it's not, Mother. This child aside I've put up with too much of just the same kind of thing. When the servant's not in the house it's always I who have to answer the door. Why?

241

Because Gladys can't go in her curlers and her calamine lotion. When the fuse blows who has to mend it? I do. I have to sew on Joe's buttons, and I have to defrost the fridge, and I have to go and pay the electric bill, because I happen to be going there, or I happen to know how, or I happen to be here, or I happen to be the one who cares, who loves. It just so happens, it's only natural, it's simply a matter of course that I should be the slave in this grand hierarchy while Gladys goes gadding about with her ham-faced boy friends, and her half-witted women."

She'd never before let rip to such an extent, and not till later did I realize I'd lost my chance. Nothing I announced now would have attracted attention; but I was too caught up by her fury myself, and could only listen utterly dumbfounded by its monstrous implications. Not so Glad. Nothing penetrated her.

"Yes, yes," she nodded when Dot stopped for the sheer need to recover her breath, "you've said all that before. But you *will* be here, won't you? Just for an hour or so. I promised Samuel Geegee——"

"I'm going," said Dot, barely seeming to convince herself of the futility of another outburst. "Yes, I am going."

"Where?"

"What matter? I just happen to be going."

"To the library?"

"Yes, to the library."

"Well, in that case you can change my magazines and——"

"Confound you, Gladys! God confound you, woman!" CRASH! The cups leapt as she hit the table. That fist, it was not entirely her own fist. The inutile fist with the thumb in. My mother who had started violently at the impact, now got up; and that automatically ended the strife, for they always fought most viciously in her presence. And I arose too, thinking how unfair it was on her. She was very highly strung and always more upset by their quarrels than they were. What

242

was the rumpus about, anyway? Whoever stayed in, Nancy would look after the kid.

Its pram was as usual in the garden, so that it could cry as loud as it needed, and Mum who was well up with the latest discoveries of child warfare, said it needed to. Crying developed the lungs. Yesterday when Nancy was away on some errand I heard it gurgling with delight and found a stray cat snuggling up to it inside the pram. It was doing its usual squall now however, and as the new *Hotspur* had just arrived by post I needed what quiet I could get to enjoy it.

"Waaa!" The pram was just outside my room, and going up to it I irritably delivered it a kick. The crying stopped instantly. This interested me in a mild sort of way, and I stood by watching it quivering to and fro. Monstrous implications. The expression kept recurring, though apropos of what I couldn't quite recall. It was a well-sprung pram, no expense spared, the best English make available, and it carried on rocking for quite half a minute. When it stopped, "Waaaa!" the crying started again. I kicked it; the crying stopped.

Having thus established a workable formula to obtain this magical state called silence, I unbraked the pram and drew it near the stone seat in the front garden. Positioning it thus within comfortable kicking distance, I sat down and began to read. Monstrous implications. "Waaaaa!" Kick. Stop. Silence. "Waaa!" Kick. Stop. Silence. "Waaaa!" Monstrous implications. "Waaa! Waaa! Waaaaaaa!"

I got up and had a close look at it.

"Waaaaa!"

"Pray, sir, what are you trying to tell me?"

"Waaaaaaaa!"

"Is it better to be kicked than ignored?"

"Waaaaaaaaaaaa!"

Kick. Stop. "Holy day," I snorted, "we've had a conversation."

By and by my mother came out looking as beautiful as she ever did, with a white veil, white gloves and a white handbag.

"Can I come with you, Mum? I'll push the pram and we'll go along, the three of us. I've something to tell you."

"I'm going to the Princess Mary Gymkhana. It's for ladies only, and no children are allowed."

"We'll walk with you to the end of the road then, just to the Admiral's house."

"What for?" she asked, really puzzled. "D'you want any money?"

"No, Mum, just for a walk, that's all."

"A walk? Oh, a walk, of course. Tuck your shirt in, will you? I'm having nightmares about your shirt-ends. I do so hope your brother grows up to be a lot tidier as a person. D'you think we could get the thing to button on the inside?"

She was walking towards the gate as she spoke and I ran around her to open it. She walked through and I stood by. She turned and began to click leisurely along the pavement, swinging her handbag with the most exquisite elegance. I loved to be seen with my mother more than anyone else in the world. She did not look back till she got to the corner, meandering her way swan-like, in and out of the immensely long tendrils that dangled down from the massive 500-year-old banyan in the Admiral's garden. At this point it is true she made a full circle to face the way she'd gone, and I thought, Holy day, she's looking back, she's remembered me.

It was on account of the figs. She was in quite a tricky maze. She had not only to sway her lofty head and shoulders in and out of the tendrils, but the thick clusters of juicy, red, though inedible fruit that dropped from the tree on to the pavement she also had to avoid; and it was her weaving in and out of this dual labyrinth that had caused her to turn back. But only for a pace or two. Around she wove again in a figure of eight, till she was finally clear of it all, and continued her way on, to disappear around the corner. So I

244

could not say whether she looked back in the end, as the Admiral's house was in the way.

I shut the gate, and kicked the pram again. The front door opened. At first silent on the stone steps, then crêpe-soleing the gravel harshly, Dottie came out. Her rages had the memories of elephants; and what added fuel to them was that Glad's hadn't. In one hand this older sister of mine carried a familiar object. It was out with her in all weathers, fair or foul, having been made to order about two years ago in beloved memory of The Unknown Soldier who in the waste ground behind the Cooperage had molested her; or attempted to molest her; or something. Dottie wasn't talking. All she was saying was, "I want me an umbrella with a tempered-steel spike." She had it too. Under her other arm she bore other things, which I was beginning to realize, however, she wielded to much the same purpose. Words. Several books of them.

"Hello, Dot, going to the library?"

She did not reply.

"Want me to carry your books for you? We can put them in the pram and just sail along."

She replied. Then she swung open the gate, and wheeled right towards the Causeway, spiking the pavement rhythmically. After some moments I remembered something I'd kept forgetting to ask her, and leaning over the gate, yelled out, "Hi! What the hell became of Dr. Frumbusch?"

Two lepers who were begging on the roadside, a woman selling bananas, her three children, a Sikh fortune-teller, an Untouchable street sweeper, a gharry wallah, a gang of coolies, and a stray mongrel turned to look hopefully at me. But Dorothy, who was as yet the nearest, walked straight on, stride unfaltering, though she did lance the pavement once with undue ferocity.

The rest continued to regard me with increasing interest, and I thought: here's a marvellous thing; to evoke the spirit of hope in Bombay one had only to stand in a public place, shout, "Hi!" and a thousand hearts beat faster. How rich in hope were the poor. And we, the rich? What had we to hope for? The nearer of the two lepers began to shuffle towards me with his hand out, and I retreated hastily.

I returned to my *Hotspur*, but although the child was now asleep I couldn't continue my reading for a while. Then Glad came flouncing out, also in white and ready to go. She looked splendid on her own, but was often with Mum against whom she clearly showed up as a tinny imitation.

"You're a big boy now, aren't you!"

Mum said a thing like that without the slightest discomfort. Glad was a self-conscious mixture of unction, threat, jest and vacuity. "You're a big, fine, kind," she continued now adding a pinch of pathos, "gentle——"

"Cut it short, Glad. How much?"

"An anna."

"Make it two."

"All right, two."

"What d'you want done?"

"It's had its bottle, and I've simply got to get away. I'll leave a phone number, but in any case I should be back in a couple of hours."

"Make it one."

"All right, one." She began to fumble in her bag.

"What's wrong with Nancy, anyway?"

"Who's Nancy?"

"The ayah."

"Good gracious, was that her name?" she said.

"Yes, is she ill or something?"

"Oh, that one, Mum sacked her yesterday."

"Why?"

"Because we're getting another tomorrow."

She left the two-anna piece on the seat and went stilt-walking off on her stiletto heels. I overtook her and put my arm across the gate. "Why did Mum sack Nancy?"

"Because DEAR boy, Mama said she was too raw for one of us and too ripe for another."

I had about a minute to make what I could of this mathematical statement, then—"Waaaaaa!" I kicked and he stopped. But the novelty of this relationship was beginning to wear, and I felt I'd got to the stage when I needed a kick myself to keep *me* quiet. I flung the *Hotspur* into the air and yelled out, "St. Paul! Mistri!" But on entering the servants' quarters I found neither him nor the cook to be there.

Our evening meal was at 9.30, and the servants did not usually return till 9.00. Hence it was a good thing it so happened I was staying in. It so happened? The thin end of the wedge? Monstrous implications? So many questions, but only one answer. "Waaaaa!"

Gladys had not left a phone number. To say she may have forgotten was to bestow upon her the benefit of a doubt so vast it should by all the laws of inertia have crushed her flat. Oh, yes, she'd forgotten that number. And I could try 500 before striking the right one. I had no hope she would return in an hour and she did not fail me. Nor did any of them come back before the servants. At 9.30 St. Paul came to ask if he should serve the dinner as it was ready. I replied. He asked if he could do anything for the child in my arms, and again I had occasion to reply. He went off squirming in such a manner that gave me cause to suspect he too had a date.

When he came back at 10.00 I told him, "Khana fridge mi luggao. Jao soyo, wolok nai atha." I further informed him they'd just telephoned to say they were eating out, and in general I felt I had a right, if not duty, to make things uncomfortable for them when they did return. How long ago was it since I'd brought the pram in? He'd ages ago ceased to be assuaged by kicks, for he too reckoned the novelty of the relationship to be over. So for the sake of peace I carried him.

He was after all just like the rest of us: humanity. When he got an inch he wanted a yard. And according to my own calculations he'd got that a while ago too. I'd changed his nappies twice. But still he cried, so I heated a bottle of milk and gave it to him. When he choked I banged his back, not all that sympathetically either.

It was now 10.30. Why had no one phoned? Struck by a possibility I lifted the receiver. It was dead. The flex was loose. By now I was on the warpath. Michael, having had his milk, was sound asleep with his thumb in his mouth, and I could easily have put him to bed, but no, when they came in I was determined to show them what an ordeal I'd been through. I left wet nappies all over the place, scattered safety-pins on the floor, put the half-empty bottle on the sofa, and when they actually came in I resolved to make jolly certain they would be greeted by the loudest, "Waaaaaaa!" in creation. *Their* creation.

At 11.00, when by my conservative estimate I had been alone with the child six hours, I was startled out of my wits at the sight of a human face. There was a tap on the window-pane and having recovered from my shock recognized it to be the mugger peering uncertainly in.

"Is it an accident?" I cried aghast.

"I was just passing and saw you, Joe. Are you alone?"

"Ha! ha! ha!" I roared. "Am I alone? The joke of the century. What the hell d'you mean bursting in on people at this scandalous time of night? Have you seen any of my family? Are they dead? Is there a carnival on? Has the war ended? What? When? How?"

"I only came to tell you what happened to Mr. Titmus, that's all," he said, shying away from the window.

"Hah, yes, Mr. Titmus! What ever became of Mr. Titmus? DEAR Mr. Titmus!"

"He was found with——"

"Shut up! Go home! Can't you take a hint, boy? Send it to

the press!" I banged down the window so hard, it started him off again. "Waaaaa!"

Yes, yes, that was it, the answer. When they came in I'd let it bang and thus would the proceedings commence. I changed his nappy once again, and this time my shirt. It was all right by me, I wasn't complaining; the inconvenience was nothing to the silver lining, that fresh warm glow of human contact. It didn't last admittedly, but then what did? The joys of life were short-lived, and the only passion that had a chance to last was blinding white-hot anger. Like a caged tiger I began to pace the carpet. Then at a moment just before midnight, on the first stroke, in fact, I let them have it good and strong. I in effect threw the child into their faces.

"You! You call yourself a father! A mother! Sisters! BAH!"

"Waaaa!"

"Listen to him. D'you know what he's saying? He's saying how much he likes your game. PASSING THE BABY, he calls it. The favourite bit of party fun with the Hoseas. You, Dad, how nice to see you home so early today. You're a busy man, working fifteen, sixteen hours a day, too busy sending criminals to jail to stop your son from becoming one. And you, Mum, you're busy too; too busy saving other families to save your own. And you, Glad? What IS there of you? You hollow-headed pimple-watcher, you're not worth the spittle of a well-chosen curse. But *you* are, Dot. You're guiltiest of all. You know, you care, you love. But you're too full of hate and envy to love sufficiently. You too, like the rest of them, you'd let the responsibility of this poor helpless little infant's life fall willy-nilly on a harum-scarum murderous devil-may-caring hoodlum like me!"

"Waa! Waaa! Waaaaaaaaaa!"

"There, boy, there." I rocked him consolingly. "Save it up for when they come. We'll let them have it full blast then. This is just a sort of dress-rehearsal, you understand?" And I was pleased I did it. I learned a great deal from that preliminary outburst; how big my stride should be on the carpet, what obstacles came in the way of my gestures, how I could swing from one culprit to the next without dropping Michael. He was after all my prime witness, Exhibit A, the plaintiff, and my client in the bargain.

So far so good. What I had to exercise now was self-control. In anger especially a bloke had to keep a tight grip, for if I did not, and Glad happened to be the first to come in, I'd simply squander that marvellous outburst in the same way Dot had earlier on. I had to ignore Glad and bide my time. And the way things worked out, the precious steam I'd generated from that preliminary workout had not time to cool down, when they arrived; all of them together in Dad's Ford. The luck of the Hoseas was on my side that night. Here was the hand of Justice indeed.

Concealing myself to one side I watched them getting out. I had almost immediately quelled my initial impulse to rush out of the front door, and have it out in the open street. I'd first thought I'd increase the response by gaining a larger audience in the form of neighbours and bystanders. A second's hesitation proved me wrong. The effect would simply be to dissipate my attack and invite distraction and laughter. And laughter was my prime foe tonight. No, I would corner them in the close concentrated atmosphere of this room, this room where the majority of their crimes were committed. Indeed, so far from rushing out to upbraid them prematurely I decided to retire to Michael's room for a few moments until they settled down, whence their sense of guilt of its own natural accord would start stealing into them. Then slowly, like Caesar's ghost at Philippi, I would appear before them, with the child in my arms. I'd strike to the heart of each individual conscience with a look. They'd remember this fateful night and they'd see to it that Michael did not suffer the same end that I had come to. Poor innocently sleeping little child, I sincerely hoped I did not have to pinch him too hard to start him crying again. But for his own good in the long run I would, yes, I would pinch him hard. I would wait for the right moment and pinch him hard, and let his be my voice at the commencement.

In the darkness of his room I heard their voices before they entered. They were excited and high. Even Dad and Dot were somewhat shriller. As I'd suspected from the few words I'd overheard as they trouped along the path, they'd been celebrating, enjoying themselves with unbridled lust, while at home? Ah, that would be the first barb. They'd just come back from the Taj. They'd been with a cohort of other lawyers, and had had champagne at Uncle Reuben's expense. At Uncle Reuben's expense. I instinctively clutched Michael harder lest I should drop him when the significance of such an act fully broke upon me, like some freak tidal wave or bore. I clutched harder still and listened craning my ears, though there was scarcely any need to. Glad of course was the first to be heard on entering. It was one of her endearing little habits to insist on talking at the top of her voice a second before entering any room. She seemed to be afraid that if she was not noticed first she would not be noticed at all, and how right she was.

"And of course when Samuel "Geegee" told me the news I phoned Mum at once and we came right over to the Court House in a taxi."

"You naughty little man," came the chiding loving Polish voice, "Why did you keep all this a secret from us? Are we just members of the general public to you?"

"Ah, Nina, you'll never know how terrified I was that if I mentioned one word of this to you the whole matter would have mysteriously gone up in smoke."

There was a burst of laughter all round, when such a statement at any other time I could name, would have been more disastrous than a fire.

"But tell me," he went on, using the voice he reserved for Dorothy, "how did *you* come to hear of it? You never buy a paper."

"No, it was some Parsee gentleman whom I'd never spoken to before at the library. He must have known who I was and came over and showed it to me. Oh, Dad, I could hardly believe my eyes. LOCAL BARRISTER KNIGHTED FOR SERVICES TO CROWN."

"Sir Victor Sassoon, Sir Obadiah Benjamin and Sir Abraham Hosea!" cried Glad.

"Waaaaaaaaaa!"

"Is that Michael?" asked my mother with the utmost concern. "Where's Joe?"

There was a brief silence. Then Dorothy said, "I tried to phone here from the Taj at about eight, but couldn't get through."

"Waa! Waaa! Waaaaaaaa!"

"Ah," came his mother's voice knowingly, "all is well. That is his cry of contentment. Joe's looked after him and put him to bed. The darling, just see how much trouble he's taken. He's fed him his milk and changed his nappies three times! Oh, Abraham, I'm so happy for our boys especially. They'll grow up to be proud of you. And who knows? God willing, Joe will be moved to take a little more interest in the state of his appearance in future."

I heard her clicking towards Michael's room, and trusted she would find him as I had left him: safe and snug in his cot. I crept into bed myself without a sound, and in order to keep them from creaking and grating, I slowly let my eyelids shut.